THE MYTHOLOGY OF CHILDHOOD

The Mythology of Childhood

BETH LARRIVÉE-WOODS

Beth Larrivée-Woods

For my family, for my friends, and for Aspen.

Consequences

There are consequences for the things that happen in our lives. If you tell someone that they are your friend you need to be there for them, if you lose someone you love you need to grieve, and if you beat someone half to death you need to face the music. Strangely it was that last consequence that Andrew faced first. Despite having been off his head on crystal meth he'd been accurate in his observation, that nightmare day, as he'd snuck into the house after ditching class and spending the afternoon getting high with his loser friends. There was no doubt in his mind that he'd seen his stepmother put just a little bleach into his little sister's apple juice. His sister had been mysteriously ill on and off for four months. Enough said. Andrew reacted with his fists, which wasn't who he was. It was the drug talking, making him into a monster. It wasn't until he realized that his nine year old sister was screaming and that there was blood on his fists that he stopped punching and crashed.

Rehab was another kind of hell. Different from the hell of watching his mother die of cancer. Different from the hell of watching his father's misguided decision to remarry. Different from the hell of watching helplessly as his sister became ill. And different again from the decision to attempt, at fourteen, to silently destroy his own life with drugs, but as painful as it was, it was nothing to becoming clearheaded again and facing the consequences of what he'd done to his stepmother.

Shame? Remorse? Disgust? He knew that his stepmother wasn't a good person, she'd been slowly poisoning his little sister for God's sake, and it wasn't that Andrew didn't think that violence wasn't sometimes appropriate. If someone hit him or threatened him or someone he loved, he would hit back, and he wouldn't have a problem with that, but his stepmother had needed reconstructive surgery to put her face back together. He told himself that it was the drugs . . . but was it really? Was he a monster?

The courts decided that as a minor who had been under the influence of drugs he could not be held responsible for his actions, unlike his stepmother who had been sentenced to seven years in prison. After the courts had decided and the divorce was final, his father had made the unilateral decision to pack them up and ship them west. As far west as they could go. The islands off the coast of British Columbia.

New life. New school. New house. Andrew wasn't sure that he cared, he was still just going through the motions when they arrived in the little town on the west coast of Vancouver Island. But slowly he regained an interest.

He liked the house. The new house was old. It had a wood stove in the kitchen and his father put him in charge of chopping and loading the wood. It was on a small acreage with plenty of space to wander. There was a copse of trees where he took to spending his afternoons, weather permitting. Walking and smoking where his father couldn't give him a hard time for the vice he'd picked up during his time as a misfit, the one vice that, out of some sort of stubborn resistance, he had held onto. But he wasn't sure that he wasn't still a misfit. He had no interest in finding friends and when he started attending the local high school that spring, a few weeks after the move, he made sure that everybody knew it. He avoided eye contact and didn't speak unless spoken to. He did his homework, kept his grades up and stayed out of trouble, but otherwise, he had his dad and his sister for company.

He was a year behind owing to everything that had happened, so there he was at seventeen finishing off grade eleven, starting grade twelve. I wasn't a big deal. He'd made it obvious to everyone that he wanted space so he attended classes and then headed home as quickly as he could after school. He didn't pay attention to the other kids except to grunt acquiescence every now and again when another student needed a light at the smoke pit. That was it. So of course it came as a complete surprise when one day as he walked quickly and purposefully home from school along the country road, to see the strange girl standing at the end of the neighbour's drive watching him approach. It felt like all of a sudden he was trapped in a time warp. All of the houses along that route were old. Like, eighty to one-hundred years old, and there were blossoming fruit trees obliterating the power lines. She wore a practical but well cut dress that was nothing like what the other girls wore to school.

Light green stripes. Buttons down the front. A tie at the waist. The skirt fluttered a bit in the breeze. Her hair was a strange colour, somewhere between mousy brown and strawberry blond, parted down the side and tied over one shoulder. She was wearing practical brown leather lace up shoes and she shuffled her feet slightly as he drew near. *What the fuck is she doing there? She's just standing there staring?* Andrew tried not to stare back as he approached but he couldn't help being a bit weirded out by her and, *where the hell had she come from anyway?* Was she really his neighbour, and why did she make the road and everything else around them look like a nineteen-forties time warp? As he approached he tried to make out her face but he didn't have a clue as to whether she was plain or beautiful. He got close enough to look into her eyes. She was still staring. He came to a stop and got caught in a crazy soul-gaze. She had incredible eyes. Mixed colour. Amber around the pupils radiating out through sea green into deep indigo rings. He knew that he ought to feel awkward but staring seemed to be okay with her, so he just stood there and waited for her to make the first move. She tilted her head slightly and smiled an ambiguous smile, then extended a sheaf of papers towards him. He pulled his gaze away from her eyes and looked down at the papers. She wasn't saying anything. He reached out a hand and tentatively took the papers from her.

"Are these . . . for me?"

She smiled a little deeper then nodded. There was a strange emphasis to her nod. The movement itself wasn't exactly odd but the intent and clarity of it was.

"Um . . . Thanks?" Andrew squinted in confusion and watched as the girl turned and walked away from him back up the drive to the rambling blue and white farm house. A strange tentative walk, almost on tiptoe. She swung her arms and her fingertips fluttered.

He looked back down at the papers and then picked up the pace and hurried the few hundred metres to his own drive and up into the house. At the table, after he'd wandered the woods for twenty minutes with a cigarette or two, he sat down and looked over the papers from the girl on the road. There was a post it note stuck to the front, with pathologically neat cursive handwriting on it.

Boy next door, it read.

My locker is outside of the classroom where you attend Social Studies 11. I completed this course last year in Kamloops. I couldn't help overhear, during my spare block yesterday, that Mr. Nichols assigned year-end projects and that your subject is the same as what I did last year. You may have my paper to re-write. Please do not copy it verbatim. That would be lame. I have included my notes and bibliography and, as you can see, my grade was adequate.

Good luck

He pulled off the post it note. A+ was scrawled in messy teacher writing across the title page. The girl had given him a paper with all of the research done. This was going to save him hours of work. A rewrite would be easy. But was the old fashioned looking girl really just giving this to him with no strings attached? He looked at the name on the title page. Miranda Hopkins. He would have to watch for her at school. He didn't look around much at the people at school but surely he would have noticed *that* girl?

The New Boy

Miranda noticed the new boy right away. She listened to the whispers of the other kids, the girls gossiping in the bathroom.

"He's cute."

"No he isn't. He needs a haircut and he looks sulky. He'd be hot if he tried though."

"I don't know, I think he looks kinda bad, like he doesn't give a fuck."

Miranda had waited until the other girls left the washroom before sneaking out of her stall and carefully washing her hands. Miranda overheard more at that school than anyone would ever think or know. Even if she had been right where they could see her, the girls would have still said what they had. Now that the kids here were used to her, she was invisible.

Miranda had been the new kid only a few short months earlier, but any interest that the others may have shown in her at first had long since faded and now, weeks after the new boy had arrived, he was invisible too. He made it obvious that that was what he wanted.

At first Miranda had thought that maybe he was like her, but eventually she came to the conclusion that *his* invisibility was voluntary. He wasn't invisible to her though, and she watched him with a strange interest that she didn't fully understand.

She wasn't sure if she thought that he was cute. She tended to think, like 'girl number two' in the bathroom, that he needed a haircut. He never smelled bad exactly—Miranda would know, she had a nose like a bloodhound and would have been able to smell body odour, even over the smell of cigarettes, just from walking past him in the hall—but personal grooming didn't seem to be his priority. He was perpetually rumpled and usually a day or so past the point at which he should have shaved. He wore black. Black jacket, jeans, sneakers, and his hair was a little lank, but he had clear skin and he wasn't a skinny awkward geek. Any time he wasn't in class he kept his nose in a book, either homework reading, or fiction, but he never socialized. He never looked at anyone. Contrary to many like her, Miranda actually did alright with facial expressions. She could nail the basics, like happy, sad, hurt, and angry—actually, anger was a huge anxiety trigger for her—but some of the less frequent expressions like disgust, confusion, and boredom, were harder to peg. She had trouble telling disgust from dismay, and she wasn't sure if she could truly identify boredom as she suspected that it was always masked by the polite veneer of socially appropriate patience, but she looked at the new boy's face whenever she got the chance, and

tried to read his expression. To her his expression looked
. . . bruised? Was that it? Not broken just . . . bruised.

So Miranda watched and as she watched she wished
that she wasn't invisible to him. But she couldn't just
walk up to him in the hall and say, "Hi". Not only was
that just plain old impossible but she didn't think that,
even if she could do it, that it would have the desired
effect. He would smile without looking at her and then
wander off. He didn't want friends in the normal sense.
If he did he would already have them. Miranda was taking Civilizations Twelve that semester and as she sat in
class and listened to the lesson and made the odd note
on the sheet of notes that had been printed off for her,
she had a string of thoughts passing through her mind
that were completely unrelated to the lesson. This was
very unusual and it left her feeling unsettled. She didn't
know what to do about the boy.

His name is Andrew. Stop thinking of him as "the boy",
she told herself as she walked a hundred or so metres
behind him on the way home. He walked so fast that
she always watched his back on the walk home and he
probably didn't even realize that everyday, day after day,
she was behind him. So she watched and she walked
and she thought as his black clad back became smaller
and smaller. The next morning, standing at her locker,
a solution came along as she heard Mr. Nichols, the So-
cials teacher, address Andrew. "There is only one essay
topic left Andrew, and I see that you haven't made your

selection, so 'How the assassination of Archduke Franz Ferdinand triggered the start of WW1,' is yours."

Miranda smiled hearing the topic. If anyone noticed her smile as she stood there alone in the hall they would have put it down to some tick or random oddness of hers, not the happy topic of Archduke Franz Ferdinand. The hard part was going to be getting home before Andrew left school, but she could arrange something.

That day as she sat eating her lunch at a quiet table next to the school librarian's office she texted her mom.

_Mom, I want to leave school early today. I'm not sick and I'm not trying to do anything very bad but I feel silly telling you why I want to leave early. It's not really that important but I have a thing that I want to do and I would like to do it today. Would you please call the school so I can leave early?

Miranda couldn't lie. She *could* 'not tell the whole truth', but if she wasn't telling the truth she felt obligated to explain why she wasn't telling the truth. Her relationship with her mother was such that she felt comfortable asking for favours like this. It wasn't something that she asked for often and her mother was generally reasonable and flexible.

Miranda's phone vibrated with the returning text:

_You sure you're okay baby?

Miranda responded:

_Yes, I'm fine. I would simply like to go home an hour early today for a reason that might be silly and a little bit against the rules, but not very much against the rules. Could I?

_Tell me what it is and I'll consider it.

_I want to give the boy next door my paper from SS11 to help him with his research. You drive me to school in the morning so I can't give it to him then, and I feel too shy to walk to his house and give it to him there, but if I can get home before him, then I can wait on the road. Please? Can I?

There was a five minute wait for the next text but it came.

_Go nuts. I called the school. Let the secretary know when you leave. Have a nice afternoon.

Go nuts. Miranda's mom said that when she was happy. Miranda knew that it meant 'go ahead'; with crazy/fun implications, but the term never ceased to make Miranda wrinkle her brow in confusion. Go nuts.

Miranda left after biology which was one of the classes that she had with Andrew, who, like Miranda, was in a mix of grade eleven and twelve courses. He didn't see her but she craned her neck around a few times to look at him from her seat at the front corner of the class. He looked the same as ever. Bruised, with social walls erected around him. At the end of class the teacher asked if she had any questions and she handed him the paper on which she had written the questions to which her teacher would email detailed answers later that night, and then she headed for her locker.

Miranda left the school as fast as she could but she sometimes had trouble moving quickly. It wasn't just that her coordination was sometimes off, but that she was easily distracted, especially when there were beautiful flowers and fluffy clouds and all kinds of birds and rabbits and other things to see on the walk home, but she had a purpose that day so she made the walk in less than thirty minutes which had to be some kind of record.

"Is it that time of day already?" Miranda's grandmother asked as Miranda hurried through the kitchen on her way to her room. Miranda stopped and scrawled on the white board.

"Came home early, need to do something quick, be down soon," and ran up to her room. Normally the first thing she did when she got home was turn on very loud music and flop down on her bed, but she made a detour around her bed, opened the cupboard and took down the binder with last year's school work in it. She flipped to the back and pulled out the paper. She sat down at

her desk and wrote a quick note, then sat in the window seat in the parlour watching the road. As soon as she saw the black clad figure appear, she walked to the door, down the front steps, and to the end of the drive. He was still about a hundred yards away when she arrived and she stood on the gravel road and waited.

It was the best look she had got of him yet. He looked like a real life story book character all in black. Handsome, quite lovely actually, now that she saw him away from school, but too tall and too unshaven to look feminine. Miranda had never looked into his eyes before. She liked eyes but eyes were a tricky thing. She couldn't look into someone's eyes and keep her thoughts in order. Eyes were overwhelming. Eyes were a language all their own. He approached step by step looking at her and the minute his eyes focused in on hers the overwhelm kicked in. How could she think about anything else with his hazel long-lashed eyes fixed on hers. She felt too open looking into another's eyes like that, but he was standing in front of her now and she was caught in his gaze, like a doe caught in headlights. *What to do?* She thought, and subconsciously dug the nails of her left hand into her palm. The sensation brought regulation and she remembered the papers. That was why she was standing there. *Right. The papers.* Miranda extended the papers and felt the corners of her mouth pull up, happy that she had accomplished her objective. He looked down and away from her eyes. He took the papers from her and she had the wherewithal to let go.

The Barn

Andrew spent Saturday afternoon at the library taking notes. He didn't actually *want* to copy Miranda's paper verbatim. He agreed with her that it would be lame to just copy it so he did a bit of legwork gathering any information on the topic that she hadn't included and then walked the four km home and sat down and dissected her paper. By midnight he had written his own version and the paper was out of his hair. He supposed that it *was* cheating, but he wasn't going to worry too much about it. He could focus on studying for finals now. He spent much of Sunday studying, but mid-afternoon his sister Olivia dragged him outside to the small barn. Olivia was twelve, almost thirteen, and Andrew would move the moon for her. "C'mon c'mon c'mon. Dad went to get groceries. He says we have to work some on the barn today."

"Okay, I'm coming." Andrew followed the bobbing brown ringleted head out the back door and up the slope to the barn that needed to be cleaned out. Not that they planned on using it for animals. It just needed to be cleaned out, or at least their father seemed to think so. Andrew thought that it was just a make-work project to get him and his sister outside together, but whatever. He picked up the work gloves by the wood pile and watched as Olivia unlatched the barn door and swung it wide.

"Why does Dad want us to clean this up? Do you think that he would let me have a goat once we get it clean?" she bellowed.

"Olivia you don't need to yell, I'm right next to you," Andrew said, ignoring her questions and wincing at her shrill voice.

"Do you think that he'd let me keep goats though?" Olivia continued in a more moderate tone.

"Dad probably just wants to be able to park the car in here or use it for storage. Wouldn't hurt to ask about goats though," he added that last on just so that she wouldn't lose heart entirely. Otherwise he'd end up working alone and it would be fun to listen to his dad talk her down from goats at dinner.

"I'm going to get a wheelbarrow. You go check the back corner for shovels. I think that I saw some back there." He pointed to the back corner of the barn then headed out to the side of the house where an old rusty wheelbarrow was propped. It was heavy but functional. Andrew wheeled it back to the barn but stopped halfway to look out over the green hills to the ocean. Even from a mile away he could smell it. Ontario felt so far away. Hell, Ontario *was* far away. A world away. He turned and looked back towards the neighbour's house. He thought that he could see a face in the upstairs window, and light warm toned hair. He raised a hand and saw the returning flicker of a waving hand in the window.

Andrew shovelled old manure and mouldy hay. Olivia *sort of* helped. She would shovel for a while then grab a rake and drag more junk out of the corners, but every ten minutes or so she would flit off and start rummaging in other corners, digging odds and ends out of the piles of refuse. He looked to where he could hear her chatter. "Be careful, use your eyes, there could be sharp things in those piles," he told her.

"Come look. I found old trunks and some wood. We could build a fort in the Wild Woods," she called out. The Wild Woods was what she called the copse of trees on the property.

Andrew put down his shovel and went to look. There was a pile of two by fours, four by fours and plywood sheets. "Crap. There *is* a lot of wood here. Totally enough for a fort. I have an idea. Grab a rake and follow." Andrew lead Olivia up to the woods and followed an animal trail about twenty metres in. "Check this out." He began raking until he heard the rake scratch brick. "We can clear this off and build a fort here. It's some kind of old foundation."

Olivia grabbed her rake and set to. It took them about forty-five minutes to clear the five square metre foundation. "Will this make a big enough fort?"

Olivia nodded grinning, then headed off yelling, "C'mon! Lets go see if there's anything cool in those trunks."

Unfortunately, damp had gotten into the trunks and what would have been, to someone somewhere, an incredible find of vintage clothing, was mostly just a pile of crumbling mouldy cotton and linen. In one of the trunks however, there was a box of incredibly gaudy forties and fifties rhinestone jewellery that thrilled Olivia beyond words, and a tin box of what must have been some long gone male inhabitant's keepsakes. Cuff-links, an old watch, a medal of some sort. Andrew's dad pulled into the drive as they finished loading the garbage onto the utility trailer.

"Wow. You two are filthy," James Warren said climbing out of the family Toyota and heading for the car's trunk. Andrew and Olivia's father was average height and bald by choice with glasses.

Olivia made a b-line for the bags of groceries. "What did you get! Is there anything good?" she shrilled.

The Ocean

L ynne drove up the gravel drive, the sound and feel of the rocks under the tires signalling her body to relax, telling her that she was home. It had been a long time since coming to any particular dwelling she'd lived in had done that, and each night the car tires on the gravel reassured her that she'd done right to divorce her husband and move with her daughter to the edge of the world. They'd only been in the house for eight months and already it felt like home in a way that she hadn't felt since childhood. After the divorce had finalized her life had fallen into place as if by magic, as if life had been sitting there doing all the planning and all she had to do was say, "Yes!"

Her dream job, running a satellite branch of the oceanography research institute, had fallen into her lap the moment her colleagues discovered her plans for divorce, and her mother had finally let go of the family home in Manitoba. "I want something new Lynne. I want to live next to the sea, I want to walk in the sun and feel the rain. I don't want to sit here on this empty prairie alone getting old just because it's where I've always been. Come with me."

The final sign had been Miranda's breakdown. How many diagnoses can one child have? Lynne had her in every kind of therapy there was. That was, of course, at Jeremy's insistence. "We should do everything we can, we're her parents. If there is something that can help her we owe it to her to try," he'd always said. Lynne's mother had always said, "She just needs to be a little girl. She walks to her own drum and follows her own path and that isn't something that needs a diagnosis!"

The fights she'd had with Jeremy about her interfering mother had been the worst. But she knew that Jeremy's take on parenting Miranda had a lot to do with his own struggles and not enough to do with what Miranda actually needed. She'd been on the brink of confronting him because she couldn't break their marriage anymore—it was already broken—and compromise was something that he'd proven he didn't want to learn. Lynne knew he loved Miranda but he didn't love Lynne, his wife, anymore, and his career meant more than either of them. And then June had arrived and Miranda had come home from school, showered for an hour, thrown her clothes in the garbage, and then refused to get out of bed. It's one thing to lift a four year old out of bed but you can't do that with a fourteen year old. Miranda just said no. No. She just stopped. She wouldn't speak, other than that one word, she wouldn't get up, she wouldn't shower, she wouldn't eat, she would only drink water and grape juice.

She'd sneak to the bathroom when she was left alone, and to the fridge for yogourt in the middle of the night, and that was it for three weeks.

Lynne compiled every assessment that had ever been done on Miranda and sent it to a new psychologist, a psychologist that Jeremy had refused to consult as her area of focus was autistic females; and autistic was the one thing Jeremy refused to believe of Miranda. But Lynne knew.

She filed for divorce and began packing while Jeremy was away on business. She rented a U-Haul trailer and packed everything of meaning while Miranda lay there. The night before they drove out she called her mother to tell her that she was coming. The next morning she went into Miranda's bedroom and told her, "I'm taking you to the beach baby. Will you let me take you to the car?"

The House by the Sea

The day they arrived at the house by the sea was the best day of Miranda's life, up till that point. She was tired from the trip, and from lying there for so long, but the July sun and the ocean winds pulled her up and sent her spinning. She ran and laughed and twirled on the big grassy slope out front of the house until she started to cry then she cried till she wasn't tired anymore. That scared her mother at first but it was okay. Nanna was there and she was cooking all the best food. Miranda ate and then her nanna took her upstairs to her room. "This is *your* room," Nanna said proudly, looking around at her decorating handy-work. "Do you want me to help you unpack?" Miranda's mother was bringing in boxes and lining the hall with the boxes marked 'Miranda's Room'.

Miranda nodded, fingering the Edwardian wardrobe with the oval bevelled glass mirror in the door and matching chest of drawers, then swinging gently around on the carved post of the Victorian four poster bed and flopping down on the soft mattress, smiling as she snuggled down into the robins egg blue velvet coverlet. She wanted to say how perfect it was, like Anne of Green Gables, or Little Women. Maybe Jo March's room felt like this. Miranda wanted to tell her nanna that she loved it, but every time she tried to talk she felt as if she was going to cry more so she hugged her nanna tight and started to pull boxes into her room so she could arrange her treasures and put her clothes away.

The rest of the summer she roamed free and wild, running between the new-old house and the beach, waking each day and eating toast made from homemade bread with butter and jam from the farmers market, and then racing outside to pick wildflowers, chase rabbits, and look for birds, and every evening when her mother came home from her new job they would walk down to the beach with a picnic dinner and watch the sunset. Nanna said they were 'elephants on the beach'. A matriarchy.

On rainy days she spent her time getting to know her new house. This house had life in it somehow. It was old and beautiful with a hand carved banister leading up the stairs and wainscotting and wood floors that felt like satin under her bare feet. It had built in shelves and cupboards in every room and a giant bathtub and a sink with separate hot and cold water taps. There was an attic that felt like it might have a ghost and a room off the kitchen that Nanna called a larder. Nanna said the house was just over a century old and that the acreage had been a working farm; "back in the day," as she put it. The barn and other out buildings were long gone, but the house was still standing strong.

In August Nanna decided that Miranda needed new clothes and took her into town to shop.

"Any ideas Monkey?" Nanna asked as they stood on the main street looking at the limited selection. There were only three stores with clothes. Miranda took her nanna's hand and lead her into the Sally Ann as the other two stores were not options. They didn't find much at the thrift store but there was a big bin of old dress patterns that Miranda would flip through when her mother was at the grocery store next door, so she pulled Nanna over to the bin. Nanna used to make costumes for the Royal Winnipeg Ballet. She had six different kinds of sewing machine. "Okay . . . but now we need fabric?" Nanna had said.

"Go see Charlotte," the voice seemed to emanate from nowhere, then a plump woman who was the human embodiment of a country mouse bustled around the corner to the checkout counter and said again, "Charlotte's who you want to see, out on the reserve. Three blocks past the gas station, right on Beech Creek Road. She'll be in one of the two houses right at the end."

Miranda got back in the car with her grandmother and they drove on a winding road through the forest till they passed a gas station, then down Beech Creek Road to the end. There were two houses in the woods. One little cottage painted purple and green with some folk art on the lawn, and an old Volkswagen Beetle with no tires that had been painted to look like a real ladybug—it might also have been folk art—sitting in the driveway, and then a larger plain house that had a neatly painted sign over the front door that read,

Charlotte Henry

Professional Hoarder

Miranda's grandmother took her hand, "This is certainly an adventure."

They made their way up the front stairs and through the open front door and when the living room opened around them. Nanna gasped, "Well pinch me now Miranda. I think we've found Aladdin's cave."

"I thought of that as a shop name but if I'd gone with it I'd have lost a bet." A native woman, Nanna's age, sat knitting in a lazy-boy in the corner and smiled up at them.

"What was the wager?" Nanna asked.

"A salmon."

"Was it worth it?"

"Every bite. My kids like to joke that I'm a hoarder and that the business is just a front for my proclivities."

Miranda liked this woman.

"We're looking for fabric," Nanna told Charlotte.

Miranda looked around the room at the quilts and wedding dresses, knitted sweaters, and cloth dolls.

"Quilting and sewing supplies are in the family room just through the knitting room."

She motioned to the left and Miranda headed with her grandmother to the sewing room.

There were so many pretty fabrics Miranda had to come up with an internal algorithm to choose, otherwise it was just too overwhelming. First fabric type and texture (had to be soft, preferably cotton or rayon), then colour (green), then pattern (stripes and/or flowers), then pattern size (small flowers and stripes were better). She and Nanna headed back to the living room with a bundle of fabric.

"What are you making?" Charlotte asked, and they showed her the old McCall's and Simplicity patterns.

"Come with me." Charlotte groaned as she got up from the lazy-boy, "Oh my knees!"

"I hear you!" Nanna had bad knees too.

They followed her down to the basement which was a very organized cave of Rubbermaid bins.

"My four girls were the best dressed girls on the Rez and now I have eleven grandsons and not a single granddaughter. I kept everything I made for them. Have a look and, if there's anything you like, you can take the dresses for fifteen dollars each and the blouses and skirts for ten."

They left with an armload of clothes and fabric and a big bag of cashmere yarn for a sweater.

* * *

A week before September Miranda's mother came into her room after dinner and sat on the mist green velvet parlour chair Nanna had put in the corner. Miranda put down her book and looked at her mother waiting for her to speak.

"Do you know what's been going on this summer with me and your dad?" Lynne asked.

Miranda wobbled her hand.

"Your dad hasn't been doing great as a partner or a parent for the last couple years."

Miranda nodded agreement. "I know," she whispered.

Miranda's mother almost started to cry.

"I filed for divorce in June and he has agreed to my terms including allowing me full custody of you, on two conditions. One, that he can come visit as long as he gives us forty-eight hours warning, and two, that I keep you in public school."

Miranda nodded and exhaled. She almost felt a bit faint with relief. She had been unable to ask her mother what was happening but her Nanna had told her that this was home now, and now she knew it was for sure, for sure, real.

"Do you think you might be able to talk at school?"

"I don't know," Miranda whispered.

"That's okay baby. I've talked to the principal and she thinks we can work things out so that you aren't under pressure. We were thinking that if you took an extra semester or two to finish grade twelve, then you could do shorter days and have more time to decompress. You'll still graduate early and you'll have plenty of free time."

Miranda nodded.

The Flu

Andrew felt like shit when he came downstairs on Monday morning and as soon as he made it to the kitchen his father looked at him and said, "Andrew, you look awful."

"Thanks," Andrew mumbled sitting down at the table.

His dad smiled, "Sorry, what I meant is, are you alright? You don't look at all well."

"Puked a couple of times last night. I'll be fine. Do we have any Gravol?"

"You should go back to bed. I'll get you a Gravol and bring you some toast and tea before I head in to the clinic."

"I'll be fine," Andrew insisted. "Maybe you could just drive me to school today . . ." But then he lurched to his feet and ran back up the stairs to the toilet.

He puked again, brushed his teeth, got back into his pyjamas, and went to bed.

"You must have really wanted to go to school," Andrew's dad said, perplexed, as he came in to the room with the promised toast, tea, and Gravol. "I think the girl next door is in the same grade as you. I'll stop by and see if she can get your class notes. Would that be helpful?"

"Uh, yeah. Yeah. Sure," Andrew mumbled as he slurped down a sip of tea with the Gravol.

"Text me if you get worse, I'll come home." He rumpled Andrew's hair as he left.

Andrew ate the toast and sipped a bit more tea before the Gravol kicked in and made him sleepy but he dozed off wondering how his dad knew about the girl next door and he didn't. When he woke that afternoon the nausea had passed and he felt like he was probably over the worst. He went downstairs to lie on the couch and watch Netflix with a bowl. Olivia arrived home from school nauseous. Andrew held her hair while she puked then texted his dad.

It was Friday before he got back to school and he couldn't focus on anything because he was obsessed with finding the girl next door. Where could a girl like that have been hiding for two months? *I know I've been keeping my head down but, really?* He thought to himself. *There are only seventy kids at this school!* She had collected all his homework for him all week and his dad had picked it up on his way home from the clinic. Apparently they were in some of the same classes. Every few minutes he would sit up straighter and look around the room to see if she was there and all the kids he'd been so studiously ignoring for the last two months would look at him funny. It wasn't till after school that he found her. He'd stayed after Chemistry for a few minutes to hand in the homework from his sick days and headed home about ten minutes later than normal. The school was in an old building and once upon a time there had been more students than the building could accommodate, so a few portables had been placed at the north end of the school yard. There weren't enough students for the old building now and part of it had been turned into a senior's centre. Now the portables were used for storage, which meant nobody ever went down there unless they walked in that direction on their way home from school.

Andrew heard a cry of pain and feet in the gravel, then a taunting voice, "What? Do you want this? Say it and I'll give it to you?"

"You know she can't say it Rob. Pass it here I want it," a female voice piped up.

There were more footsteps in the gravel.

Andrew slowed down as he approached the first portable and slowly peered around the corner. It was Miranda and two other kids. A guy and a girl in jeans and hoodies. Miranda's bag was on the ground, the contents strewn around and trampled. The girl held an iPhone out of reach and Miranda grabbed for it. The other girl laughed and moved out of reach again. Miranda's knees were bloody and she was obviously distraught. She lunged for the phone again and caught the other girls face with her nails in the process.

"Robin! She scratched me!" the girl yelled, suddenly unreasonably angry. She threw the iPhone on the ground and stomped on it with her heal.

"Don't touch my sister retard!" The guy headed for Miranda fists raised as Miranda, terrified, stepped backward into the wall of the portable.

Andrew tackled the guy so fast they were tumbling across the gravel before he even understood what he'd done, then he rolled and got to his feet and grabbed the girl by the back of the hoodie and then pushed her away from Miranda yelling, "Get the fuck away from her!" and shoving both of them so hard they were stumbling as they ran away. "Stay the fuck away!" he yelled, watching them run and starting after them on impulse just to make sure they kept running.

After fifty yards or so he turned and ran back to the portables. Andrew hadn't been scared chasing away the hoodie freaks. He'd just got angry at the shittiness of what they were doing and intervened without stopping to think. In fact the first thought he'd had on the subject was relief that neither of the hoodies were going to have to go to the hospital, he'd kept his fists in, but back at the portable he didn't even have a gut instinct to follow.

Andrew had lost his shit many times over the last two years but he'd never been there to watch someone else lose their shit. Miranda was pacing frantically, looking for her phone then stopping and hitting her head with her hands, then she'd try to pick up her things and put them away. She was crying and gasping and she'd stop and crouch, make herself into a tiny ball then lurch to her feet again and start pacing. Now she was crouching and hitting her head. She couldn't seem to co-ordinate her movements to actually accomplish anything and when she stood again her feet tangled and she crashed to the ground hard. She curled up into a ball and sobbed ragged sobs.

Andrew didn't really know what to do so he gathered her things into her bag and picked up her cellphone and tried to turn it on but it was toast. There was a rock imbedded in the screen. He sat in the gravel, gingerly, next to the strange girl and pulled the hem of her skirt down over her thighs and took off his coat and carefully tucked it under her head to protect her cheek from the rocks.

Wait it out? Try to get her to stop? Try to calm her down? No . . . wait it out. Andrew sat there waiting. He figured she'd probably be less embarrassed if he waited and talked to her than if he left now. That's how he'd feel, that staying showed he wasn't embarrassed, and that she shouldn't be either. Then he realized that he should call someone and he pulled out his own phone about to call his dad but stopped that too because another stranger might be the wrong move, *that might freak her out more,* he thought. Plus his dad was probably in the middle of an appointment. But she was almost quiet now and pushing herself up to sitting. "We should call someone. Can you text your mom?" he passed her his phone and she took it but looked at it like it was alien. *Of course, it's a flip phone,* he thought, the kind with three or four letters on each number button. Her iPhone was the newest, slickest, thing on the market. "Just dial her number and I'll tell her what happened if you want."

Miranda dialed and gave the phone back.

"Hello . . .?" came the mom voice over the line.

"Hi. Uh, I'm Andrew, Andrew Warren from next door. I was walking home from school and I caught some kids giving Miranda a hard time. She's really upset, can you come get her?"

"I'm getting my keys. I'm leaving work now, as we speak. Where are you?"

Andrew told her where they were and promised to wait. This was obviously a call Miranda's mom had expected some day. Most moms didn't come running quite like that. Then he turned to Miranda. He'd been waiting to meet her properly for days and this isn't how he thought it would be. She was looking at him with wide eyes and when they made eye contact it seemed okay to not talk so he just stared back for a minute before saying, "I know you're not intellectually impaired. I read your social studies report. I didn't copy it verbatim by the way, the report. I did a complete rewrite and added to it. I spent most of Saturday on it. Thanks though, you know, for letting me use it. I know it's sort of cheating in a way, but it's going to give me a lot more time to study and, what with coming here at the end of the school year, I'm kind of behind."

Miranda nodded and looked down into her lap then at her knees.

"Do your knees hurt?"

She just nodded again.

He wanted to ask her why she didn't talk but it seemed like maybe that was too much. But sometimes when he was having a rough time, Andrew wished that people would just say what they were thinking so he asked, "Do you talk?" He asked it gently, as a genuine question, because so many people would put a sarcastic spin on it and it would come out so, so mean, so cruel, and if she really didn't talk then she would be hurt by it.

She took a few deep breaths and opened her mouth a couple of times but then sagged and shook her head. She wiped her eyes with her head hanging, staring down at the green fabric of her dress.

"It's okay, I mean I guess it might be frustrating for you sometimes, but I'm a recovering drug addict and I almost went to prison so really, you know, in the big picture, not talking is fine."

Miranda looked up at him with her eyes flicking on and off of his, and smiled.

Andrew smiled back because when Miranda smiled, it made his soul sigh.

A Disaffected Youth

Violet hadn't really expected it when her husband of forty years had keeled over from a heart attack. He'd been so stolid, so very present his whole life. Losing him had been almost as big a surprise as falling in love with him in the first place. She'd never have met him if it hadn't been for the polio. It stole everything, and then gave her a new life.

Ballet had always been her first love and it had been like a death when it was stolen. Every movement a caress, every step a step closer to her heart. And she'd been *good*. And then one day she could barely move. Her doctors were ecstatic when she came through the other side. They said she had made a ninety percent recovery and that she should be happy. Happy? That last ten percent meant everything to her. That last ten percent was the difference between dancing and not dancing. It was like a death.

She'd picked up and carried on as best she could. Tried not to think about how she would have been starting out in the back row of the corps de ballet just that week. Tried not to think about the pile of point shoes— all ready for the stage—at the back of her closet, about standing poised and ready for the music, for the magic, waiting for the lights. Tried not to think about all she'd given to her chosen art. She tried walking away but walking away was too hard and after a six month dress- makers course she ended up working in the costume department at the Royal Winnipeg Ballet. She was good at that too and her training and physique put her in a special position for designing costumes, but it was like watching the one you loved walk away with somebody else over and over again, and she cried herself to sleep every night. One evening, in a moment of weakness, she bought herself a ticket to Swan Lake. She wanted to be close to the stage but it was too hard to watch and she sat there crying in the back row of the theatre next to a shabby young farmer and his kid sister. He'd saved up all year to take the kid to the ballet. She hadn't realized how obvious her tears were and she hadn't heard him whisper to his sister, "Be right back Suze. Right back." She hadn't expected to be almost bodily lifted and whisked out to the mezzanine.

"Come on Miss, the bally is pretty for sure, but it's not *that* moving. What's wrong?"

Violet burst into tears and the young farmer put his arms around her. Two days later she left Winnipeg with

Callum and Susie on a train out to the countryside and she never looked back. Life on the farm had been tough but ballet dancers are tough people and Callum's family had made her one of their own from the first day. Her mother-in-law had been one of those women who could do or make anything. There wasn't anything she wasn't up to. Birthing a calf, making a wedding dress, and everything in between. Violet had done and learned so much living that life; loving Callum and raising their girls on that wide open prairie. And then that too had ended.

West had seemed the only way to go. Helen, her oldest was back east and she was the most capable of souls, and Adria was the independent one. The globetrotter. But Violet still worried about Lynne, her youngest. And suddenly it seemed that Lynne needed her and life had presented its next plan.

And that's where Violet found herself, living *so far west*, looking out over the Pacific ocean, which was almost like a prairie, when Lynne and Miranda came storming in the door of their old/new house on a balmy west coast May afternoon with a bewildered, unkempt, teen-aged James Dean lookalike trailing along behind. Violet lifted the tray of cookies out of the oven and looked around at the disconcerted faces.

"Cookies?" she offered.

And They All Fall
down

J ames Warren wasn't perfect. He knew that, but he
   hoped he was good enough. He hoped he was good
enough to deserve his children. He'd almost lost them
when he disappeared into the fog after his wife died.
When he stepped out of that fog for the first time,
his house was surrounded by emergency vehicles and a
social worker was explaining to him what had happened.
How could he have missed it all? How could he have
become involved with a woman who would poison his
daughter. How hadn't he noticed that his son was a sui-
cidally depressed, crystal meth addict.

After the ashes stopped coming down and the fall-
out cleared he looked around and saw that they needed
a fresh start. As a GP he could work almost anywhere
and the further away the better. When he first viewed
the listing for the practice for sale in a ghost town on
Vancouver Island he laughed, because no one in their
right mind would buy that practice. Saint Fina had once

had a population of three thousand but the combined factors of isolation, economic downturn, and a road that washed out at least once a year meant that unlike Tofino, Ucluelet, and Sooke, tourism had never really taken hold. Fishing, farming, and logging were the town's primary industries at the turn of the twentieth century, but then the little peninsula had been surrounded by a provincial park. Logging had trickled to a stop and when the industry pulled out there weren't enough people to buy what the farmers produced. Fishing held out a little longer until all that was left was a handful of die-hards— precisely four-hundred and ninety-three die-hards. The only thing the town boasted was good cell service.

James sold the townhouse and most of their possessions and packed them all up and told the kids that they were just going on vacation. Andrew was subdued and unsettlingly pliant on the trip and Olivia was a ball of lightning as they explored the west coast. When eventually they arrived in Saint Fina and he told them that he was thinking about buying the medical practice there, he'd expected some kind of push back from the kids but he didn't get it. Olivia was explosively enthusiastic, so much so that James was suddenly worried about what would happen if he didn't buy the practice. Andrew started researching the town and actually seemed interested. When he took the kids to see the the house, that was the final piece to fall into place. James wasn't imaginative but even he could feel the possibilities contained in the old house. He sat down on the back step next to Andrew and looked out at the ocean. "What do you think of the house and the idea of staying here?" he asked gently, looking at his damaged teen-aged son.

Andrew didn't answer right away and when he did his voice shook, "I could be here dad. I mean, I could *Be* here, without wanting to die."

James nodded and put his arm around Andrew's shoulders.

"How did *you* come up with such a beautifully fucked up plan?" Andrew asked.

"It's what your mother would have done," James admitted.

"I miss Mom."

Andrew started to cry just as Olivia came running around the corner eyes blazing. She ground to a halt. "What's wrong?" she asked, in dismay.

"Nothing's wrong Olivia. Everything's fine. We're staying."

"Oh thank goodness!" the words tore from her throat, then Olivia was sobbing into his side too.

James looked out over the Pacific with an arm around each of his children. Maybe he'd done it right. Maybe they'd make it after all.

Friends

Miranda sat next to Andrew in the gravel of the school yard for the short time before her mother pulled up next to them. Lynne leapt out of the car and ran to her, examining her and peppering her with questions that Miranda obviously couldn't and didn't answer, except by passing her mother the shattered phone. Lynne looked at the phone and shook her head then hugged Miranda tightly.

"Come on let's go home, get in the car. You too," she addressed Andrew. "Miranda ride in the back seat so he doesn't feel like he's in a taxi."

Miranda got in the back seat next to Andrew and she tried to hold her body still. She was incredibly agitated in the aftermath of what had happened and every nerve in her body felt like it was firing and jolting so hard that she could barely process anything. She wrapped her hands around her elbows and dug in her nails to breathe normally. The fear, and then the mortification, left her alternately shaking then sweating, and the feelings were interspersed with violently sensual flashes of Andrew's hazel eyes in her mind.

The moment the car pulled up to the house Miranda bolted. She barrelled through the front door and ran to the living room. Hands shaking, she grabbed frantically at the pile of CD cases, spilling them to the floor in a distressing, disorganized, clatter but she saw an option in the chaos on the floor. She grabbed the MGMT disk and shoved it impatiently into the machine, spun ahead to track five, *Kids*, cranked the volume, and let the wall of sound wash over her giving thanks that her mother was nostalgic about outdated modes of audio technology. Miranda pressed the heels of her hands into the table top and leaned into the music, gripping the table's edge so hard her fingers hurt, but the feelings eased as the music pushed them out of the way, taking up all the space.

"Miranda, you've listened to the song three times," her mother put her hand gently on her shoulder and turned the volume down to a reasonable decibel. "Come have a cookie and some grape juice and tell me what happened."

Miranda turned and tried to reintegrate herself into the moment. She was tired now so she followed her mother pliantly to the kitchen. Andrew was sitting at the table with milk, eating a cookie.

Lynne placed Miranda's laptop on the table next to her. Miranda took a big gulp of grape juice and looked around. The little girl from next door was with Nanna in the sewing room and Miranda could hear them talking. She looked that way as she munched a cookie.

"That's my sister Olivia," Andrew told her, noticing the direction of her glance.

Miranda nodded.

She opened her laptop and started downloading the Spotify and iTunes apps so that she could access her music collection. She didn't like having her music on her laptop. It felt cluttered, like her mother's pile of CD's, but her phone was broken and she needed to do this to think straight.

"Miranda what are you doing. I brought that down so you can use Open Office."

Miranda ignored her mother.

"Come on, you can do that later. I want to call Andrew's father so that he knows where his children are and I want to know what to tell him."

Miranda, lifted one finger in the air. Her index, which her mother knew meant 'one minute'.

Lynne waited and Miranda opened a text file.

_A boy and a girl were hiding around the corner of the portable that I walk past on the way home and the girl pushed me down then the boy grabbed me and held my arms while the girl went through my bag. She stepped on everything in my bag, and the boy pushed me down again. Then they . . .

I can't explain it to her, it's too much bad feelings. If I type it with words that stay it'll make it too real. Miranda thought to herself and then went still.

"Miranda, baby?" her mother urged gently, "'Then they . . . ' what?"

_Ask Andrew.

"Is that when Andrew got there?" she asked gently.

_Yes.

Miranda looked at Andrew's face but she focused on his mouth. Fake eye contact.

"Oh . . . Yeah. No . . . I mean, I wasn't sure when I got there, what happened—in terms of what happened before I got there. Sorry, that didn't make sense." He shook his head like it was an etch-a-sketch. "But what you typed," he gestured towards the laptop, "must have happened when I was walking towards the portables from the school. I could hear something happening so I looked around the corner. I didn't know what I was walking into. They were basically playing pig in the middle with the phone. Miranda accidentally scratched the girl trying to get her phone back and then they, the hoodies, I mean the boy and the girl, got really nasty really fast. The girl smashed the phone and the boy was about to start punching, so I tackled him. I only watched for a few seconds before I tackled the guy. They were being really shitty. I chased them off. They probably think I'm crazy now." Andrew looked up at Lynne.

"Is that what happened Miranda?" Lynne confirmed with her daughter.

Miranda nodded unhappily.

She watched her mother's face cloud with anger and Lynne burst out, "The whole fucking school *knows* she depends on that phone to communicate . . . !"

Miranda grabbed her laptop and bolted up the stairs because she couldn't handle being around angry people and her mother was yelling. Andrew hadn't been angry, when he'd talked to her after. She wondered if he'd been angry when he tackled the guy 'hoodie'. He'd sounded angry when he yelled at the guy and the girl.

Miranda walked into her room and looked around at the dreamy decor. Her Nanna knew her so well. The room was its own world, a Victorian fantasy landscape of gentle colours and textures. Soft blues and greens, velvets and misty embroidered muslins. Mythological creatures, griffons, doves, dragons, and swans, in the lace of the curtains and the carvings on the headboard. Only a ballet dancer could decorate such a graceful room. It was calming and separate from the rest of the world, a beautiful escape from reality, but so very real in that it really existed which never ceased to seem like a miracle to Miranda. Miranda stood and looked out the big west-facing window, at the ocean in the distance and the green rolling hills, which also seemed like a beautiful fantasy after the arid hills of Kamloops. There was a tentative knock and Miranda turned to see Andrew standing in the doorway looking . . . there were too many different expressions, but none of them were anger.

"Your mom sent me up. She's on the phone with my dad and they're calling the principal."

Andrew didn't look strange in her doorway. His presence wasn't an intrusion and didn't shatter or negate the beautiful unreality of her room.

"Is this your room?" he asked.

Miranda nodded.

"It's really pretty," he said, looking up at the embroidered muslin canopy on her bed, then he smiled at her.

Miranda thought Andrew had a beautiful innocent smile, and she smiled back.

"Your mom wanted me to make sure you took care of your knees. She said to ask for help if you need."

She looked down at her pulpy knees.

"I'm really good with band-aids actually. Olivia's not exactly clumsy but, being a hurricane, she does crash into an awful lot of stuff, so I get practice."

Miranda nodded again and she knew it was a vague nod because she wasn't sure what she was communicating.

"Are the band-aids in the bathroom?" Andrew turned and went into the bathroom.

Miranda just stood there.

"I found them," he said, coming back to her doorway with a handful of first aid supplies. "Why don't you sit down."

Miranda sat down on the edge of her bed right next to where she'd been standing.

Andrew pulled up the chair from her desk, opened the bottle of peroxide, and began gently wiping away the dirt and dried blood with cotton rounds till the scrapes and cuts were all that showed. He used cotton swabs to apply polysporin then peeled the paper off the big Elastoplast band-aids. "Straighten your legs partway."

Miranda straightened her legs a little and he applied the band-aids. She looked down at her knees and somehow having the cuts covered up brought the last hour rushing up to her. As if she'd just finally processed it so that she could understand the things that had happened. She reached out and caught Andrew's hands in hers and still looking down she whispered, "Thank you, not just for this. Thank you for everything."

She looked up at him and noticed that he was clean shaven and that he didn't smell like cigarettes. His hair was clean and he smelled like the woods. She remembered what he'd said to her after she'd started coming up from her meltdown. "Are *you* okay?" she whispered, it was the barest whisper, but he was close enough to hear.

"Yeah, I'm okay. Actually, I think that maybe this is the most okay I've been in a long time."

Miranda smiled again and realized she was still holding his hands and let go still feeling the ghosts of his fingers after she withdrew. Shyness overcame her so she picked up her lap-top and opened up a text file.

_Did you quit smoking? She tilted the screen so Andrew could read.

He came around and sat next to her, reached for the keyboard and typed:

_I had the stomach flu and suddenly I couldn't stand the taste of them. So yeah, I quit. Seemed the right time. How did you know I smoked?

_ I have a good nose. I could smell it in the hall at school.

_How did I not notice you at school? I keep to myself, but you're so different from the other kids. I feel stupid that I didn't notice you.

_It's because I'm partly invisible at school. You are now too. Also, I eat my lunch outside the librarian's office and I come in later in the morning than everybody else, so I'm not there as much, not as visible. I don't stay around the other kids and I was always walking too far behind you on the way home, so there was a reason you didn't see me. You're not stupid.

_What do you mean "invisible"?

_When you are too different from the other kids they don't know what to do with you so they edit you out of their reality. Some of them can see us better though.

_That makes sense.

_Where did you move here from?

_Toronto.

_Were things bad there?

_Yeah, they were. You?

_Kamloops. Things were bad there too, but they're mostly good here.

_I like it here. It's kind of surreal actually.

_Yes, surreal is a good word for it.

At that moment Olivia burst in. "Dad's coming soon and we're having dinner here," she said, then she took a look at Miranda's room and gasped.

Miranda looked at the girl. Olivia had a cloud of tight, perfect, nut brown ringlets, bee stung lips, electric sea green eyes, a button nose, and dusty rose tinged skin. She walked in and looked over Miranda's shoulder at the computer monitor. "You're really lucky, your nanna is awesome. She said she would help me make a quilt for my room. We picked fabric and started cutting out the squares."

_My nanna *is* awesome, and I don't mind sharing.

Olivia beamed and sat down on Miranda's other side.

Miranda had a good feeling, sitting there with Andrew and Olivia.

Dinner

James was just seeing the last patient of the day out the clinic door and locking up when the call came through, "This is Dr Warren," he answered, expecting it to be a patient.

"Hi, this is Lynne Hopkins, your next-door neighbour."

"Hi, how can I help you," he responded, still in his GP voice.

The voice on the other end hesitated so he asked, "Is this a medical issue, or a neighbours issue?"

"I'm sorry," Lynne sighed, "It's a neighbours and parents issue—I'm not interrupting anything am I? You don't have a patient waiting do you? This is going to take a minute or two to explain, but don't worry. Everyone is alive and nobody has done anything wrong. At least not our children."

James *did* worry then, "No, all the patients are gone for the day. What is it? Do I need to rush home?"

"No, no. Something did happen though. When my Miranda was on her way home from school today a couple of kids roughed her up pretty badly. Your son caught them and chased them off, then he called me. I just wanted you to know that Andrew didn't start anything. I don't know the kids who attacked Miranda, but I wanted to make sure you knew right away that Andrew was helping, not the other way around. That, and your kids are at my house, which I do hope is alright. My mother is entertaining Olivia in the sewing room and Andrew and Miranda are upstairs visiting. I can send them home to your place if you'd prefer, but I though that you might want to come and have dinner with us when you're done work."

Jim scratched his head in consternation. When he was young he always thought that someday he would feel like an adult but, despite pushing sixty, ever since his wife died, he felt like a big kid making it up as he went along. He wanted to say yes to dinner first, because it was Friday and he was exhausted and the very idea of someone else providing dinner was so spectacular that he probably would have chosen it over the offer of a million dollars at that precise moment. But that wasn't what he should say first, "Should we be calling the principal? I have to admit that while I feel good that Andrew would stand up for your daughter, he shouldn't have to."

"I'm thinking along those lines too," Lynne admitted. "Additionally, I don't want him to face any kind of retaliation from the other kids. Miranda is a target with her communication problems, but as the new kid, Andrew could become a target for standing up for her. I do think it would be better to get ahead of this."

"Did it happen on the school grounds?"

"Yes it did."

"I was going to stay here for another half-hour and try to finish the notes from the last patient. If you call Ms Gilchrist and let her know that there was an incident, let her know that I'm in the loop and want to see her too. I can come as soon as she wants or make time Monday. And I will admit that I would love to accept your very generous offer of dinner." James sighed with relief. That sounded rational, and he had accepted dinner.

Lynne said goodbye, promising to call back as soon as she spoke to the school principal and James went to finish the notes, wondering now, wanting the exact details of what had happened. Andrew had been keeping up the lone wolf act for the last two months, making it curious for him to suddenly emerge and interact with the world. The phone rang just as he shut down the office computer.

"Hi . . . It's Lynne," she hesitated.

James noticed the hesitation, "Call me Jim or James either is fine."

"Alright," he could hear the smile in her voice this time. "Hi Jim. I spoke to Ms Gilchrist. She wants to see us Monday morning at 9:00am. She knows who the two kids are, and she said that there is an ongoing situation and that it isn't as simple as talking to the parent, that it could make things worse. She's calling the RCMP though, the kids are known to them I gather, and asking them to keep an eye out and also requesting a car be present when school lets out for the rest of the school year. She thanked me for calling promptly and said for either one of us to call her or Sergeant Healy anytime if we have concerns. She really said that, '*anytime*'. And she handed out their personal numbers."

"I'm not sure if that makes me feel reassured or worried," James admitted.

"I know, but we've been here for nearly a year and this is the first incident we've had. I only have to get Miranda through one more semester of school after this year, so I can only hope. Dinner will be on the table at about six by the way."

"Alright. I'll be there soon."

Jim had stopped on the doorstep of the blue and white farmhouse across the field from his own house every night on the way home from work to pick up Andrew's schoolwork all week, and a beautiful, slender, middle aged woman with bright eyes and a serene smile had greeted him at the door and given him the homework, wished him and the kids well, and commiserated over the stomach flu. He *thought* her name was Violet. She had brought a tray of muffins to his house when he and the kids had first moved in and he had never properly thanked her. He decided that he must not have remembered her name correctly but, conversely, he couldn't match the Lynne he had spoken with on the phone to the woman he'd met at the door. He pulled into their drive, parked, and climbed out of the Toyota and up the steps to the front door. Lynne's house was the more romantic of the three houses on Josephine Road. Andrew had told him that this house, with its turret, gingerbread, and red brickwork, was a Queen Anne Revival. Their own yellow house, Jim had been informed, with its stone foundation and porch piers—a term he assumed Andrew understood—was a Craftsman. Jim hadn't been to the wooded property at the end of the road but Andrew had walked through the woods one day to see what was there and had told him that there was an immaculately maintained Mid-century house, that looked like a Usonian Frank Lloyd Wright, nestled in the trees. Jim had no idea what Usonian meant.

But this house suited the elegant woman Jim had thought was called Violet. He knocked, and through the bevelled glass window set in the door, he saw a compact thirty-ish brunette approach. "Hi I'm Lynne," she opened the door, smiling.

"Hi . . . Jim," he said his own name and took her extended hand and shook, then followed her into the hall where she took his coat and lead him to the kitchen where all was made clear.

"I think you've met my mother, Violet?"

"Yes, yes. Hi," Jim was irrationally relieved to find that Violet was real and that he hadn't in fact mis-remembered anyone's name.

Violet, who was over the stove, smiled and waved a wooden spoon, "Nothing fancy for dinner I'm afraid. Just roast chicken and veggies, salad and rolls. Gravy is almost done then we'll sit."

"These days, anything I didn't cook myself is fancy."

Violet looked up from the gravy and gave a knowing smile. "The kids are setting the table, just through there. I'll be in with the food in a minute."

James rounded the corner into an old fashioned dining room. Andrew and Olivia were there chattering away with a slim, willowy, girl who looked more like Violet than Lynne. *That must be Miranda,* he thought, inspecting her briefly, noting that she didn't dress like other teen-aged girls and that she had large Elastoplast bandages on her knees. They were spreading a lace table cloth and placing good china and silver around to make up the place settings. "Which side does the fork go on?" Olivia asked moving around with the cutlery.

Miranda came over and pointed to the left side of the plate, then to the knife and spoon, and indicated the other side of the plate. When Olivia put the spoon closest to the plate the older girl reversed them for Olivia to see, then she took candle sticks and matches out of a china cabinet and passed them to Andrew. "Want me to light them?"

Miranda smiled and nodded and finished distributing the plates. Olivia looked up from what she was doing and saw that he had arrived, "Dad!" she yelled.

"Olivia!" he mock yelled back at her. "How are you Pumpkin. How was your day," he asked giving her a squeeze.

"Boring, until exactly three thirty-four PM. After that it was way more interesting. Were you aware that we have cool neighbours?"

"Only vaguely," he admitted.

"Hey Dad," Andrew said looking up once the candle's flame had taken hold.

Lynne came in with the chicken on a platter and Violet called, "Miranda! Come get the buns and the salad!" and suddenly everyone was in the room taking seats, "Here Miranda pass this around. It's just carbonated fruit juice," Lynne told him, passing Miranda a bottle of Martinelli's, "but we always have it for special occasions."

"This is the first time we've had guests since we moved here, so it's a special occasion," Violet explained. "We've been getting to know people very slowly, but settling in somewhere new is a process." She deftly organized the circulation of food as she spoke.

"I hear you. The new routine is all we've been focused on. We're just starting to look up and around."

"You must be meeting people at your practice?" Lynne commented, as she piled roasted carrots and potatoes onto her own plate then helped Olivia dish up.

"That's true. I think roughly thirty percent of my appointments are curiosity appointments. Come meet the new GP. Actually, it sometimes feels like I'm on a small town sit com. I keep looking over my shoulder for a film crew. But a clinical setting is hardly personal."

"My work is the same. I know my staff but they're mostly Phd candidates a decade or more younger than me. Beyond marine biology there isn't much interaction and they all view their presence in St Fina as temporary. They get close to each other, but not the broader community. Actually if this *were* a small town sit com, the research centre could be where all the steamy romantic drama takes place. It's exhausting."

Jim looked around the table and took in his surroundings again. The crystal filled with magenta fruit juice, and the china piled with food. He looked at his children, happily devouring dinner and still talking, laughing at something Miranda had scribbled on a note pad on the table next to her plate. He looked at Violet and Lynne who didn't look to be much more than 15 years apart in age. "You know I assumed on the phone earlier that Miranda is your daughter, but you and Violet are both so preternaturally ageless that now I'm second guessing myself?" he addressed Lynne.

Violet laughed, "You're not the first to be confused but you're definitely the first to double check. When Miranda was born I came to help Lynne out for the first month. Everybody we met at the store or in the park would tell me how helpful my teenager was with my new baby and I would tell them that the baby was hers. They would turn their noses up and walk off thinking I was condoning teen-aged motherhood or, once I began to preface the statement with, 'My daughter is twenty-four', they would scurry off in embarrassment, probably assuming that I'd been the teen-aged mother!"

Lynne laughed, "Even when I was thirty people thought I was a teen-aged mother. I'm forty-three. I think part of the problem is that I've never quite figured out how to dress like a grown up and as a biologist I don't really need to. It's given me a lot of compassion for *real* teen-aged mothers."

Miranda placed a piece of paper in the middle of the table and Violet picked it up and read it then chuckled, "She said the funniest was when she was eight and she was arguing with Lynne. I was with them, and a woman looked at me and told me that, 'If my children wouldn't behave, I should take them home'."

"That didn't really happen did it?" Andrew asked, grinning.

"It did, in a bank. I was cosigning on a mortgage for Lynne."

"I'm never going to live that down am I?" Lynne asked.

"I'm afraid not Dear," Violet patted Lynne on the hand in dramatic consolation.

"Well, all I can say is that getting carded at 43 is not flattering."

"So how did you come to be living in St Fina?" Violet asked James.

"My wife died four years ago and it's been a rough few years. I know they say that you can't run away from your problems, but sometimes a change of scenery is what you need to get your perspective back. You?"

"The same essentially. My husband died, Lynne's marriage was crumbling, and Miranda was very unhappy in Kamloops. I'll say though, that I had a heck of a time choosing between this house and your house. I've always wanted a sleeping porch, but I wanted a turret more!"

They all laughed and Olivia piped up, "I'm glad you left our house for us because we still have a barn and I want goats!"

James nearly snorted his drink up his nose. This was the first he was hearing about goats.

They were finished eating and Lynne looked at Miranda, "Would you and Olivia and Andrew clear the table and do the dishes? We're going to go talk in the living room. Nanna's going make bread pudding in a few minutes so make sure you clean up the kitchen so she has clear counters to work on."

Jim watched Lynne convey the instructions to her daughter and Miranda listened without looking at her mother, then nodded and tapped on Olivia's shoulder. Olivia in turn, practically yelled, "Come on Andrew!" at which Miranda flinched, but smiled. And the kids piled up the dishes and swept out of the room. But in the hour he'd been there Miranda hadn't spoken once.

Yesterday and Today

When they first got home after the evening at the Hopkins house his dad sent Olivia straight up to bed and then they'd talked for a bit. About what had happened that afternoon after school, but also about life. About how, despite the fact that something shitty had happened, they also felt strangely good. Andrew felt full. From dinner yes, Miranda's grandmother was a really good cook and her take on "nothing fancy," was the best meal he'd had in a while. But it was more than just dinner. Laughing around a table with real people wasn't something that had happened since before his mother died and that made him feel like he might cry, but it made him feel like laughing again too. Like he was so full of laughter that he might split open. It was the first time he had ever felt like that and the feeling was maybe a bit scary, especially after a year and a half of barely having feelings at all. There was a sense of division between yesterday and today. A sense that today was a start and yesterday was an end.

Andrew sat in his room looking across the field at Miranda's north facing window. The light was on and he thought about her sitting in that beautiful room looking otherworldly. He opened his laptop and checked his email. He'd given his email address to Miranda that afternoon. In his inbox was an email from pixie-dust-magpie@gmail.com. He clicked open,

_I know I already said thank you, but the kids back in Kamloops would have just watched me get beat up, so . . . Thank you.

Andrew hit reply:

_Are you still up?

_Yes.

_I wanted to thank *you*. You woke me up last week.

_I slept once.

Miranda wrote back.

_What happened?

_Something like today . . . but worse. Why did you sleep?

_After my mom died I got addicted to crystal meth. I was so sad, all the time, and my dad was kind of lost. He'd just checked out. I don't blame him, but I was alone and . . . he'd remarried, one of the hospice nurses. She kind of stalked him and I think he felt like she was holding down the fort, but she was actually abusing me and Olivia, just not in a way that I could tell someone about. I didn't know what to do and I had gotten in with a bad crowd at school and the drugs just . . . I felt closer to my mom when I was high. I hoped I might die every time I got high. Then I caught my stepmom putting bleach in Olivia's juice one afternoon. She was making my sister sick on purpose so that she could feel good about herself for taking care of her. I was really, really high when it happened and I . . . I know if I tell you what happened that you might not want to be friends, but I don't want us to be friends if I can't be honest with you. I don't want pretense. I paid for what I did, and I'm not like that when I'm not high and I will never get high ever again.

Andrew wasn't sure if he should hit send but he did anyway. It was five minutes before a reply came.

_I'm autistic Andrew. I'm autistic and I'm selectively mute. I'm hardly going to hold something that you did when you were high—when you were *addicted* to a drug—against you, when I can't always control my own body. I can't imagine losing my mother. I can't imagine what you've been through.

Andrew wiped away a rush of tears from his face as he read her reply and started typing.

_I don't remember what happened very well because I'd overdosed, and I was on the brink of blacking out. I just got so angry at what she was doing to us, to my family, that I started hitting her . . . and when I woke up in the hospital I was handcuffed to the bed and she had to have facial reconstruction surgery.

Andrew hit send and waited, wondering if this would be it. If this would be the end, and the wait was hard. It was harder than sitting next to her that afternoon when she'd cried in the gravel. It took ten minutes. Andrew opened the email.

_But you're still here in the world, you didn't die of an overdose, and what you did for me today was kind . . . it was very, *very* kind. I can choose how I want to see you and that's how I see you. And you and I are both here in this weird town. And I'm sitting here crying because I've never told anyone that I'm autistic before and you're still talking to me. I don't believe in god but sometimes you have to see meaning in things, and you and I are both here, and I choose to see meaning in that.

If the words hadn't been there on the screen, there for him to see, if they had been spoken and disappeared up into the ether instead, he would have doubted them. But they existed forever, maybe on some server in Nebraska or something, but they existed forever and she'd said them. Andrew hit reply:

_I'm crying too.

He got up and went to his window and opened it, looked out across the field and he could see her there looking back at him out her own window, her elbows on the window sill.

Somebody Who Knows

Miranda wasn't sure how long she'd stood looking out the window, standing in her night gown with her elbows on the sill, looking across the field at Andrew, when her mother came in.

"Hey . . . what are you up to," her mother asked gently, smoothing Miranda's hair over her shoulders.

Miranda turned away from the window and picked up the pad and pencil she had had to resort to using since the loss of her phone. *"Emailing Andrew"*, she scrawled.

"Are you okay . . .? After today?" Lynne asked tentatively.

Miranda knew her mother must be really worried, but too much good had happened that day to cancel out the bad things for her mother to need to worry tonight.

"I wouldn't be . . . but I am," she wrote.

Lynne nodded. "Don't stay up too late okay?"

Miranda nodded and Lynne went out, closing the door behind her.

Miranda sat back down at her desk and hit reply:

_Are you still there? My mom came in.

She hit send.

_I'm still here. Are you going to bed soon?

_Soon, but not right away.

_So you like MGMT?

Miranda laughed.

_My mom likes MGMT. All my music was on my phone. I just needed a wall of sound to regulate myself, to sort of get a grip, you know? That said, there is something random and beautiful about MGMT. They are irreverent and improbable, and yet they exist and perpetuate despite that.

Miranda hit send and laughed out loud at the response that came in.

_Like Olivia, random, beautiful, and improbable! Do you always use music to get a grip?

_ Pain works too, but it's a dysfunctional coping technique that causes as many problems as it solves. Music doesn't cause problems.

_What music do you like?

_I like lots and lots of music, but I seem to lean towards electronic music or music that's a bit out there. Mostly British, Scandinavian, or Canadian. New Order, Depeche Mode, Chvrches, Stars, some Royksopp and Mikke Snow. I like M83 too. And lots of the Canadian indie bands that my mom listens to, and 90's stuff. I like complex music with lots of big feelings and lots of layers. At least that's the best for when I'm on the brink of melting down and I need something to push away the overwhelm. It has to be like a wall of sound. But that's a really limited list of what I actually listen to.

Miranda hit send.

_If I were to listen to just one thing before I went to bed, what should I listen to?

_After today? Chvrches *Clearest Blue.*

Miranda included the password to her Spotify account in her email.

_Will you come over tomorrow and hang out with me and Olivia?

_Do you really want me to?

_I really want you to. I'm going to listen to that song and then go to bed. See you tomorrow.

_See you tomorrow . . .

Miranda hit send feeling like there were a million little birds in her chest trying to get out and she turned off her lights and climbed under her blankets not quite sure what planet she was on.

When Sleep Won't Come

Lynne lay awake thinking. *I wouldn't be . . . But I am.* She knew Miranda meant that she wouldn't have been okay if Andrew hadn't intervened and then stayed with her. Even though Lynne was still furious that Miranda had been attacked and was of a mind to go hunt the kids down, she felt, suddenly, like she might have some community around her too. That maybe, starting today, she'd have some more emotional scaffolding in her life than just her mother. She had no idea what she'd been thinking, that afternoon, sending Andrew upstairs to take care of Miranda, but Violet had been busy with Olivia, who'd been walking past their drive on her way home from school just as they'd pulled in. Andrew had told Lynne that he didn't want Olivia to go home alone . . . that Olivia wasn't alright on her own.

Surely any big brother who would look out for his sister like that, and who had obviously already seen Miranda through a meltdown, could be trusted upstairs with her daughter; even if he did look like a teen-aged Jeff Buckley. But Lynne had started yelling and Miranda had gone dashing up like a scared rabbit. "Would you go upstairs and look in on Miranda. If I go I'll make it worse, I'm so angry right now, and sometimes . . ." Lynne stopped suddenly, knowing she shouldn't share her daughter's history of self injury with a stranger, but just wanting everybody to leave her alone for a minute.

"You don't want her to hurt herself. I'll go up," Andrew had said, as if it were the most normal, rational, thing in the world.

"Can you try to get her to deal with her knees? She might need help," Lynne had asked, feeling a bit pathetic, as Andrew started up the stairs.

But Miranda had come back down with Olivia and Andrew an hour and a half later, happier than Lynne would have thought possible—considering the afternoon she'd had—with band-aids on her knees.

Lynne got out of bed and padded downstairs to look for a light under her mother's door. A soft glow shone out under the crack. She knocked gently, "Can I come in?"

"Yes, do." Her mother looked up from where she was sitting in bed with a book, "You're sleepless as well I take it?"

Lynne nodded and rolled her eyes, "Am I the only one who isn't sure exactly what happened today? I'm angry and happy and way too agitated to sleep. I thought about going for a jog but it's two in the morning."

"A lot did happen today. I'm hoping that it was a little bit of bad and a whole bunch of good. We shall see."

Lynne walked around the big Eastlake bed frame and climbed under the blankets next to her mother. There were more fluffy pillows in that bed than any normal human should need and a lavender filled sachet fell onto Lynne's face as she leaned back into the pile. "How did dad put up with all your pillows," she mumbled.

"With love and patience," Violet answered, smiling.

"Why is motherhood so hard?" Lynne whined.

"If it were easy we'd be cats," Violet answered.

"I knew I could count on you for an enlightening gem of wisdom," Lynne grumbled.

"I'm always there for my girl."

The Fort

M iranda woke up so hard that her heart was pounding. It was like someone had slammed an "awake"
button. It was the kind of awake that she usually only experienced after a truncated falling dream, but she hadn't
been falling in her dream. She wasn't sure she had even
been dreaming. She got up and went to the bathroom,
setting the bath running while she used the toilet, then
getting carefully into the warm water keeping her knees
up so the band-aids would stay dry. Back in her room
she pulled on a dark green, vintage, corduroy, skirt and
a pale yellow t-shirt. It was her favourite outfit because
the colour of her top and the cut of her skirt reminded
her of New Order's *Temptation* music video. Not that
Miranda could ever shoplift a record, but the moment
the video turned from black and white to colour was a
small magic that made her heart skip a beat every time.

She hurried down the stairs, swung around the banister post at the bottom, and headed down the hall to the
kitchen. Her mother and grandmother were sitting at the
table with coffee, chatting, but Miranda didn't sit. She

watched the toaster toast her bread and then ate it with jam, standing silently in front of the fridge. She worried about getting hungry later so she got a dish down and scooped some plain yogurt into a bowl and ate that too, and then she had an orange, still standing in front of the fridge.

She went back upstairs and brushed her teeth and tried to decide which sweater to bring. It was the problem with having two favourites. Downstairs, standing in the entrance way Miranda placed a pencil and notebook and a container of cookies in her bag then carefully tied her shoes. She looked down at the note in her hands. It read: *"Going to Andrew and Olivia's house. Bye."*

Her heart was pounding as she turned back to the kitchen, dashed in, slapped the note down on the table, and then ran out the door and kept running, like there were wolves on her heels, till she was halfway across the field.

She could see Andrew up ahead outside the barn wearing blue jeans and a red and black flannel shirt and she skidded to a halt. He looked up and waved and Olivia came out of the barn and they started towards her, meeting her halfway. They were really happy, Miranda realized. They were both smiling and they started talking at the same time, at length and with volume, so that she had no idea what they were saying, so Miranda just stood there in the middle of the field with them and waited then they started to laugh at each other. Olivia looked at Andrew and said, "You go first."

Andrew chuckled, "Most of what I just said didn't make sense anyway." he scratched his head and looked around then said, "We're building a fort. Do you want to help?"

Miranda said, "You're not wearing black," and then her hand flew to her mouth because the words had flown out of their own volition, as if they were the birds from the night before, escaping up into the blue sky.

"Is that a yes?" Andrew was smiling.

Miranda nodded, irrationally happy about building a fort.

"Black is my loner uniform for school," Andrew explained.

Miranda mouthed, "Ah," and nodded understanding.

"His favourite colour is actually pink!" Olivia almost shouted.

Andrew shoved her gently laughing, and she shoved him back harder, using her whole body, but it didn't have much effect, then the three of them made their way to the barn while Olivia explained what they were doing, at length and with volume.

Miranda loved The Wild Woods as much as Olivia and Andrew did. Part of it must have been an orchard, once upon a time, and the fruit trees were flowering pink and white, leaving petals in their hair. Olivia said that she found all kinds of things buried there. An old iron, silver cutlery, a rusted chandelier. Andrew had spent his week home with the flu googling blueprints for tiny houses and watching carpentry tutorials with Olivia. They had a grand plan and they let Miranda get caught up in it with them. They hauled the wood from the barn to the old foundation in the woods and finished cleaning out the barn, digging through the refuse and throwing rotting saddles and rusted old tools with broken handles onto the utility trailer. They covered the wood with a tarp then sat in the woods eating cookies.

"I'm gonna have to get dad to buy some tools but I figure he'll go for it. We can make it like a pirate hideout, or just a place where we can be . . . kids, I guess," Andrew was saying.

"Like the lost boys hideout in Peter Pan?" Miranda scrawled.

"Exactly. Someplace that doesn't have to make sense."

"But we'll still make it pretty, so that it's a nice place to be, and it'll have a little loft with big pillows where we can read on rainy days," Olivia mumbled around a mouthful of cookie.

They couldn't really build anything that day, not without tools, so Andrew asked if Miranda wanted to see their house, which she did.

"We haven't 'decorated' it," he said putting air quotes around the word decorated as they walked through the kitchen, "We haven't really even unpacked all the way. We just got a big comfy couch at a furniture store in Victoria, and a table and chairs."

Miranda hadn't been in 'The Other House' as she thought of it, probably on account of her Nanna always referring to it as 'The Other House'. Nanna had had her choice of the two houses when she'd first arrived in St Fina. Andrew's house was much like Miranda's though. There was a ten year age difference which was apparent in the slightly more modern sensibility of the fixtures but otherwise it was the kind of house that almost didn't need decorating because it was so well designed and of an age when even the door knobs were tiny objets d'art.

"Some of the original furniture was left behind, somebody told my dad that it's a mix of furniture from both the houses but it ended up here because this house was used as a home a bit longer." There was an old armchair and rocking chair in the living room. "I love the view from here," Andrew told her, looking out the living room window, out over the treetops to the ocean beyond. "I can look at it for hours. There's something about knowing that this is the edge, that sailing to Asia is what you'd have to do if you wanted to head further west from here."

Miranda stood next to Andrew and looked out the window understanding, "I know it's Asia across the ocean, but in my mind, if we sailed there, it would be an exotic fairytale place full of dragons and pearls and beautiful ladies in silk robes." She wished she could get the words out in more than a whisper, but Andrew turned and looked at her nodding, so she continued, "It feels sometimes like we live on the borders of some magical and unknowable place. That's how I feel when I look out over the ocean."

"You said exactly what I wanted to say, but was too shy," he looked into her eyes.

Miranda looked back and tried to process everything but it was kind of like falling. There was so much there and she could just stand there forever but she knew it was socially awkward to maintain that much eye contact without speaking, and it had gotten her punched in the jaw in seventh grade, but Andrew had pretty eyes and he didn't seem as bothered by it as most people.

Olivia came up to them at that moment, "Dad wants to know if we want lunch? He says he can do grilled cheese or pita pizzas?"

Andrew broke off and looked at his sister, "Either one's fine with me." He looked back at Miranda but not at her eyes, "Which do you want?"

Miranda had to resort to the notebook in her bag. *"Are they whole wheat pitas?"* she wrote.

"Probably not. Olivia doesn't like them," he said.

Miranda smiled and almost laughed, because she didn't either and it was a pleasant change to be saved by the eating habits of a fussy twelve year old. *"Then either is fine,"* she scribbled, and Olivia yelled, "Either!" at her dad in the kitchen.

"Do you want to see upstairs?" Andrew asked, then turned to Olivia, "Do you want to show Miranda your room?"

"It's not much yet, I mean it's still the nicest room I've ever had even if all I've got is a mattress on the floor," she said leading them up the stairs, "but it'll get better.

Dad said we'd go down to Victoria to get more furniture once school's out."

Miranda looked out Olivia's window, at her view of The Wild Woods, "Andrew wanted to see the ocean but I wanted to see the woods so it worked out. Dad took the room with the porch."

They had walked past Andrew's room but it was strewn with clothes and books and he'd closed the door saying, "I never really think about what a disaster it is in there but now that you're looking at it I'm slightly mortified."

Miranda smiled. She looked at the doors in the hall then up at the ceiling. *"Do you have an attic?"* she wrote down on her pad.

"An attic?"

"That space between the ceiling of the top floor and the roof," she wrote, then drew a smiley face.

"Yeah no, I know about attics," Andrew laughed at himself. "I just hadn't even thought about ours. There isn't a door, that I know of, so it just hadn't occurred to me."

Miranda had noticed windows just below the gables but couldn't see where they were inside. She walked to the end of the hall and opened the door there.

"It's just a linen cupboard," Olivia said.

Miranda looked up to the top of the cupboard and saw a latch though. She pointed up to it and Andrew and Olivia started talking at the same time again loudly and excitedly, "Stop talking Olivia! Here let me boost you up!" Andrew yelled, then squatted next to her and grabbed her around the thighs and lifted her up so she could reach the latch and she reached up and unhooked the latch so that the shelving swung open into the bottom of a narrow stairwell.

Miranda couldn't stop from hopping up and down on the spot and flapping her hands because secret passageways and hidden attics were the stuff dreams were made of.

"Holy shit!" Olivia yelled.

"I had no idea this was here! How did you know?" Andrew asked, totally gobsmacked.

"Windows under the gables. You can see them outside," she whispered.

Just then Andrew's dad came to the top of the stairs. "Hey! I've been calling. Pizzas are out of the . . . I see you've found the attic. Come eat before you go up there. I have some rules for the attic," And he turned around and they trailed after him back to the the kitchen while Andrew and Olivia talked at the same time mostly yelling things like, "You knew!" and "Why didn't you tell us!"

They got down to the kitchen and even Miranda was waiting on the edge of her metaphorical seat for an answer.

Jim, very placidly, placed the tray of food on the table, pita pizzas and chopped veggies, and they ate but sat there looking at him expectantly. Miranda wasn't sure what to think of Andrew and Olivia's dad yet. He was one of those dads who starts going just a little bald and then shaves all their hair off. She thought he seemed pretty chill, and pretty nice so far.

It was Andrew who lost patience first, "So, the attic Dad?" he prodded after eating a pita.

Jim smiled, "I've been waiting for you to realize there's an attic for weeks. I thought you would find it right away."

"Miranda found it," Olivia admitted, a little dejectedly.

"Good work!" Jim held his palm up for a high five and Miranda ducked. "That's cool, no high five," he said.

"Okay, but what's up there?" Andrew asked, ignoring his dad's dorkiness.

"I've only gone up once for a brief look," Jim admitted, "and when the house inspector went up he said it was very, *very* dusty, so if you guys are planning on going up you need face masks and goggles for the dust, but when these two houses were shut up for good ten years ago, the caretaker moved everything that was left up to the attic, and then built the secret door so that vandals wouldn't find it in the event of a break in. I don't know exactly what's up there, but there's lots of it."

"Can we go get some masks at the hardware store?" Andrew asked.

Jim opened a broom closet and reached in for a box of masks and eye protectors which he placed on the kitchen counter. "Knock yourselves out," he said.

"Is that like 'go nuts'?" Miranda whispered in Andrew's ear.

"Yeah . . ." Andrew paused thoughtfully, "It's pretty much the same as 'Go Nuts'. There might be some different nuance, depending on the context of the situation and opinion of the person saying it. But in this situation it's the same as 'go nuts'."

"So Dad, you said rules?" Olivia asked.

"Yes. You guys can't bring things down from the attic willy-nilly and fill the hall with clutter. It has to be dust free if you bring it down, and it has to have a home to go to. I want you to bring a broom, the vacuum, and some dust rags up with you. You can dig all you want up there but clean as you go alright?"

Miranda nodded along with Andrew and Olivia, even though it wasn't her attic.

The Attic

A ndrew got out of the bath and looked down into the murky water. When he was little his mother would always say, the dirtier the bathwater the better the day. He smiled at the memory. He almost forgot to shave but then he went back to the mirror and got it over with, then pulled on his pyjamas and went to his room. He knew that his pleasure wasn't irrational when he walked in, but having feelings again made it feel a bit out of proportion to be *that* happy about having a clean room with furniture. He flopped down on the bed and reached his hand up to feel the smooth turned wood of the—*what had Miranda called it?*—he tried to remember, *spool bed*, headboard.

When they'd climbed up to the attic that afternoon Andrew had carried the vacuum cleaner up the narrow staircase and looked around. There was light pouring in the windows illuminating the dusty drop cloth covered mountains of furniture crammed in the small below height attic. He'd moved further into the attic to make room for the girls and then looked down at his footprints in the dust. It was a good thing they'd worn their shoes up. The dust was so thick it was almost like snow. He'd been right in assuming there wouldn't be an electrical outlet up there and was glad he'd used an extension to plug in the vacuum at the bottom of the stairs.

"I'm going to see if these windows open," he'd said, and managed to open the stiff latch and push the window open.

The girls carefully lifted the drop cloths off the piles of furniture and trunks and threw them out the window while Andrew vacuumed around them and used the hose to suck up the cobwebs. They cleaned and dusted for about an hour exclaiming as they went, at all of the things they could take down and use.

There were bed frames, two desks, a thing like a desk that Miranda called a secretary, chairs, trunks, chests of drawers, lamps . . . He and the girls moved all the furniture down that they could carry. There were two twin sized beds. Andrew had wanted the spool bed and Olivia wanted the brass bed—with pink painted porcelain details—so they took them down to their respective rooms. Andrew had forgotten again that his room was in a state as he and Miranda had manoeuvred the headboard down the hall and carried it in, but then Miranda had whispered, "If we bring down a chest of drawers then you'll have a place to put your clothes. I saw a book case up there too." And then she headed back to the attic like she hadn't noticed the mess. Andrew had looked around briefly and made sure there was no dirty underwear lying around and then followed her up for another trip. By the time Miranda's mother called to say she had to go home for dinner she'd helped Andrew and Olivia put their rooms together so that they looked like they actually lived there. Andrew had watched Miranda walk back across the field through his south facing window, sort of wishing she could stay. He'd noticed that she seemed a little reluctant to go, but she had written on her note pad, *"Come do homework with me tomorrow?"*

"I'll come right after breakfast," he told her, and she smiled and they looked at each other saying nothing for longer than most people would find comfortable, but Andrew had decided he kind of liked it, then she'd turned abruptly, hair swinging around, and headed across the field and Andrew had gone back upstairs to work some more on his room.

After dinner as Andrew helped clean up—he'd told Olivia he'd do her share of the chores and she had gone upstairs for a bath—he'd asked his dad, "Do you know much about autism?" he'd tried to ask it like it was just something he was casually curious about.

His dad had sat there thoughtfully for a moment, "Not a lot, but more than some. Probably more than most GPs. Your mother had quite a few clients who were on the spectrum."

Andrew's mother had been a social worker. He nodded.

"Are you asking . . . about Miranda?" his father asked hesitantly.

"Did Miranda's mom . . .?"

"No, she didn't tell me directly but she said enough for me to read between the lines," Jim admitted.

Andrew nodded, feeling better that he wasn't telling his dad anything that he didn't already know, "She knows I had a drug problem, I told her . . . and she told me she's autistic. I remember listening to mom talk to you about people she'd worked with, but it didn't mean as much when I was twelve. Miranda seems pretty normal in a lot of ways, but she's also kind of uncanny and easier to be around than most people. It's like she isn't wasting energy trying to be something she's not."

Andrew's dad smiled and nodded, "It can take a lot of energy to mask what she's going through. Lynne said that Miranda is happier as she is. I gathered from what she said, that there were problems back in Kamloops." Jim paused for a moment, obviously thinking deeply, then said, "Don't limit your expectations of Miranda just because she has a diagnosis. Your mother used to get very angry at the world on behalf of her autistic clients. People hear the word Autistic and make all kinds of assumptions but, especially for women on the autism spectrum, the assumptions are often wrong. Just take Miranda at face value, meet her where she is, and you'll be fine."

Andrew thought about the things he knew about Miranda so far, how observant, thoughtful, and intelligent she was. How deeply she felt things. And she had called Andrew kind, but when she'd told Olivia that she would share her grandmother Andrew had thought that was incredibly kind. Andrew knew he would forever be her loyal friend after that, because for all that Olivia was resilient, the last four years had taken their toll on her too, and anyone who would share their beloved grandmother with his little sister was incredibly kind.

Andrew nodded, then went upstairs to have a bath and do some reading for school. It wasn't till he lay down after his bath that he realized just how much physical work they'd done that day, but he looked around his clean organized room again and smiled. It almost had as much character as Miranda's room now. He turned on the hand painted lamp they'd placed on his bedside table and picked up the novel he was reading for school, but he didn't start reading right away. He just looked around the room a bit longer feeling content. It was worth the work.

Goats

Olivia ran up the stairs after dinner with her dad calling after her, "Olivia! Bath first! Room after!" She got to the bathroom, looked in the mirror, smiled at the dirt smudges on her cheeks and then ran the bath and smiled again when the water turned a cloudy light brown as she rubbed the grime off her skin in the big old fashioned bathtub. Olivia got her hair wet with clean water from the tap and then worked a big handful of conditioner in and carefully combed it, then rinsed it and wrapped it in a special soft towel. She pulled on her pyjamas and then went to find Andrew who was just coming down from the attic with another lamp. "Here," he said. "I found a lamp for your bedside table. I'll go get a light-bulb."

Olivia took the lamp to her room and placed it on the bedside table. The shade was glass with pink flowers painted on the inside of the shade. Andrew came in a moment later and screwed in the light-bulb then plugged it in and turned it on so that the rosy glow filled the corner of her room. She looked at her brother then asked him, "Would you do my hair?" She hadn't asked in a long time. Some time over the last six months she had realized that most twelve-year-olds dealt with their own hair, but she had a sudden urge to not feel so big.

"Of course I'll do your hair," Andrew answered, obviously a little surprised at the request, and sat down on the edge of her bed and she sat cross legged on the floor while he pulled the towel off her head and then carefully finger curled each curl so that it would dry separate without going frizzy. "So, did you leave me any hot water?" he asked, carefully parting her hair along the side with the comb and lifting and separating the curls

"There'll be more by the time you're done," she told him and turned to smile up at him.

"You're cheeky," he told her.

She sat and remembered when she was eight and Andrew was thirteen. She'd come home from school indignant and maybe a little hurt by one girl calling her hair freaky and another condemning her for not knowing how to do her hair right. Her mother had done her best to make her feel good again with toast and tea and a hug and had said she would try buying another anti-frizz conditioner, but it was Andrew who had said to their mother, "You can't *just* buy new conditioner. Olivia doesn't have white people hair. Here look up a YouTube tutorial." He'd gone to the family PC in the living room and started to google curly hair. "There's a girl in my class with hair like Olivia's. She doesn't wash it so much and she does different stuff to it. I heard her telling the other girls."

It was Andrew who had learned what to do with Olivia's hair to give it some shape and make it look pretty, so that the other girls wanted hair like hers. He'd given their mom a list of deep conditioners and styling tools to pick up at the store. He'd looked at Olivia and told her, "Sometimes parents are hopeless."

Olivia thought about her birth mom, the source of the profuse curls. Unlike Andrew's biological mother, who had abandoned him at a hospital just hours after his birth, Olivia had lived with her birth mom till she was nearly four. Her early memories were fuzzy and a bit chaotic and the only thing of clarity that existed in those memories was of suddenly having the most incredible, attentive, and exciting playmate. Andrew. She remembered that her birth mom wasn't around as much after that but she couldn't remember the apartment where she'd once lived, only the townhouse where she'd lived with Andrew and her adoptive parents. Officially, Olivia had been a foster child till she was six, when her birth mom had come to terms with her schizophrenia. Her birth mom, Isabella. It was such a beautiful name for such a beautiful girl. It was strange to think of the chaos inside Isabella's beautiful head. It was an open adoption and Olivia still talked on the phone with Isabella. Apparently Olivia's biological father was a Scandinavian exchange student who didn't know that Olivia existed.

It had taken a few years for her to love her adoptive parents with the same intensity with which she loved Isabella and Andrew, but she'd gotten there, and then Cheryl, her mom, had died. But Isabella had been there for her, as much as she could be. And when it had come time for Olivia to leave Toronto Isabella had said to her, "You'll love it where you're going. Take it from me, I know a thing or two about islands. It will be beautiful and you'll be close to the ocean. When I'm in a good head space I'll make it out there for a visit. See it as an adventure my love. Just keep looking forward."

So Olivia had held her chin up and wiped away her tears. She reminded herself that her friends didn't understand her anymore anyway, not after everything that had happened, and she wanted to go on an adventure.

Olivia held up her phone and took a picture of the pretty lamp on the carved Victorian night stand with the stained glass window above and the corner of the brass bed frame showing.

"Are you sending that to Isabella?" Andrew asked.

"Yeah, she'd like it, it's so pretty. She always likes stuff like that, and seeing what it's like where we are now."

"Yeah, she would like it," Andrew agreed, working serum into the ends of her hair then blow drying it a little with the diffuser. "There, done," he said, wrapping the cord around the hair dryer, then he looked at her out of the corner of his eye. "Everything okay?"

Olivia thought for a minute, "Everything is good, but in a sort of bitter sweet way that makes me want to be a little kid again."

"I know what you mean. I think it's this place. I haven't taken baths in a bathtub since I was ten years old, or thought about building a fort, or been disappointed that my friend had to go home for dinner, in a long time."

"I like Miranda. I'm glad we've got interesting neighbours. They're kind of weird, like us."

"Weird like us huh?"

"Well you gotta admit . . . we're not too normal?"

"No, not *too* normal," Andrew chuckled, and then headed to the bathroom for his own bath.

Olivia went to her window and looked out through the leaded pane. She looked out over The Wild Woods and at the barn. It was just so easy to imagine goats.

Under the Cherry Trees

There had been a police car parked across the road from the school Monday afternoon when she and Andrew left for the day, and a group of men emptying the portables. A mac truck sat waiting to haul them away. Miranda had felt a bit self conscious at school that day, looking around her to make sure that 'The Hoodies', as Andrew called them, were nowhere to be seen. It had been a strange day in other ways too. She had sat with Andrew in biology and math which had drawn attention. Suddenly they weren't invisible. As if together, somehow, they couldn't sustain invisibility. And Andrew had eaten lunch with her and they'd gotten half their homework done over the lunch break. Andrew was much better at math than Miranda, not that she couldn't do math, she just found it so painfully boring that she had to drag herself through it like it was barbed wire, but Andrew thought it was fun and his enthusiasm for it made it less excruciating.

Miranda walked slowly along the dirt road that lead home that afternoon, lingering on the last crossroads with Andrew as they waited for Olivia to join up with them on her way home from the elementary school, so the three of them could walk the rest of the way to Miranda's house together. The newness of having friends was exhilarating and anxiety provoking, almost overstimulating. Everything was brighter and more vivid. When she looked up at the late blossoms in the trees her skin tingled and she felt the colour sweep through her as the spring breeze whipped the petals through the air. "Do you feel how beautiful they are?" she whispered, looking up through the blossoms to the blue sky beyond, only half meaning to have spoken.

"Do you know what anhedonia is?" Andrew asked in return.

"An—a prefix; without. Hedone; the Greek goddess of pleasure . . . I would assume it means, without pleasure?"

"Yeah. The drugs caused it, but it started wearing off about a month ago. Every time I look at the trees I feel like I'm going to explode. Small things that I would have taken for granted five years ago make me so happy that I'm not sure how to express it. When you found the attic on Saturday it felt like the adventure of a lifetime. I *feel* how beautiful the trees are." He smiled looking up into the branches.

Miranda felt the smile spreading to her face, "There are so many things I don't say to people because I can't expect comprehension. You're the first person I've spoken to in more than a whisper in nearly a year."

"So, nobody else here knows what your voice sounds like when you talk?"

Miranda nodded.

Olivia came running up then, "I'm done all my homework. I did it at lunch so I can work on the quilt with your nanna!" she shouted when she was still far enough off that her volume wasn't too much.

They turned and headed towards Miranda's house. When they came in the door Miranda's nanna had just pulled a zucchini loaf out of the oven and was slicing it up. They stopped at the kitchen table and ate then Olivia ran off to the sewing room. Miranda felt a bit uncertain for a moment because she would normally have gone upstairs and listened to music for a bit just to get her feet back under her, to unscatter herself, and she didn't want to break her routine. It was what she did everyday and it made her feel like she was going to cry when she tried to tell herself that she could break her routine. She felt like she just needed a few minutes of music . . . but surely Andrew wouldn't mind that, and her laptop was in the living room anyway, plugged into her mom's stereo.

Andrew followed her to the living room and she woke her laptop and opened a text file:

_Do you mind if we just close our eyes and listen to music for a bit? I always feel dysregulated when I get home from school.

For some reason if Miranda typed Andrew always typed back to her which Miranda liked. No one else she knew bothered, they just did the easiest thing and spoke out loud, but when Miranda and Andrew had done homework together on Sunday they had barely spoken out loud which was so peaceful. Miranda had saved the text file and read their conversations again later. She'd copied the file and emailed it to Andrew after dinner and they'd kept talking via email for another hour before going to bed. She'd looked out her north facing window just before turning out her light and he'd been looking out too.

_Go for it.

Andrew typed,

_I've been so out of sync with the world that I haven't listened to music much lately. It didn't sound right for a while. Put on something that sounds beautiful.

_Okay.

Miranda actually had a playlist called *Beautiful* so she selected it, hit shuffle, and lay down on the settee as Gabrielle Papillon's *Deep in the Earth* pushed the chaos out of her body. It was almost like dreaming, then the strange contradictory bliss of Morrissey's *Every Day is Like Sunday*, followed by Chvrches *Down Side of Me*.

Four songs in she opened her eyes and looked up at the ceiling, feeling like herself again. She looked over at the chesterfield where Andrew was still lying with his eyes closed but he smiled and then opened his eyes and looked over at her as if he'd felt her gaze with his skin.

Miranda turned the volume down a bit and Andrew came over to the settee and typed:

_It's like punctuation for the day, stopping like this and not worrying about getting on to the next thing. Just stopping and letting the music be a buffer, like a period or a comma in writing. Or a new paragraph. Like taking the time to feel all things we're not allowed to feel at school.

_Yes! I find school stressful and the music is the thing that tells me that it's done for now, like punctuation. I think I hold a lot in at school. If I don't stop I break down eventually.

_School *is* kind of stressful. I don't know how to be around other kids anymore and I don't really want to be there, but I also kind of like going to classes. I don't mind *school* I guess, but I *do* find it stressful being there.

_Same for me. I've never gotten along with other kids. I'm always interested in things that they don't get. I like history and mythology and art and thinking about the nature of beauty. I couldn't really have conversations about those things with the kids at school.

_I agree, I couldn't tell them about rehab.

_They wouldn't understand meltdowns, perseverations, or catastrophizing either.

* * *

On Tuesday Miranda's father showed up. She didn't mind when he came to visit, Miranda supposed that she loved him, but he was very concerned with appearances. Miranda knew that he was desperately trying to compensate for his own insecurities and perceived shortcomings and that he was projecting them onto her. She didn't care how people saw her as long as she could breathe, and actually look at herself in the mirror and see the things she liked about herself. Her father had very specific ideas about the world and when he arrived just before dinner she was still sitting at the table finishing studying for the biology final with Andrew while Olivia worked on her quilt. Her father looked at her not saying anything. Miranda's nanna came out to the kitchen, "Jeremy, we didn't think you would be here for another hour or so."

"The roads were good," he said, and then, "Hello, Miranda."

Miranda lifted an hand in greeting and then typed to Andrew,

_This is my dad, Jeremy.

Andrew lifted a hand tentatively and said, "Hi."

"These are Miranda's friends, Olivia and Andrew," her nanna told her dad, as Olivia followed her out of the sewing room, curious.

Miranda could trust that her nanna would realize what needed to be done to keep people from feeling uncomfortable. Miranda had been unable to talk around her father for months. She looked at Andrew and smiled, feeling a bit lost and she rested her hand on Andrew's for the briefest moment hoping that it would mean, "I'm sorry if I'm awkward," and hoping that he would understand it that way.

Miranda looked up at her Nanna who looked back at her granddaughter and Miranda's nanna nodded to her and smiled, "Miranda, why don't you pack up your homework and you, Andrew, and Olivia go upstairs and visit in your room till Jim calls."

Miranda's whole body flooded with relief and she put her books in her bag, grabbed her laptop, gave her dad a quick perfunctory hug and then ran up the stairs after Olivia with Andrew bringing up the rear. They closed the door behind them and Miranda and Olivia flopped down on the bed and Andrew took the velvet parlour chair.

"Your dad looks like Lord Business from the *The Lego Movie*," Olivia announced.

"Olivia! You shouldn't say that," Andrew scolded his sister. "Plus I bet Miranda hasn't seen the Lego Movie."

Miranda shook her head. She hadn't seen it. She had no idea what Olivia was talking about, but her dad *was* rather businesslike and in his dark suits he did look rather serious and commanding.

"He's a data analyst," Miranda whispered. "He can be very serious. Your dad is . . . warmer."

"He did look pretty serious," Andrew mumbled.

"He doesn't understand me," Miranda admitted in a whisper so soft Andrew and Olivia had to lean in. "It's partly why my parents divorced. His job means a lot to him. He kind of forgets about us."

"So Olivia's kind of right?"

Miranda nodded.

"I like our Dad," Olivia said to Andrew.

The Noise

Lynne had taken Miranda for granted. She felt terribly guilty for it, but if having the Warren kids from next door over taught her anything, it was that she loved her blessedly quiet daughter. How could two kids be so loud? She tried complaining to her mother but Violet laughed at her and told her that she was in no position to talk.

But at the same time, Lynne relished the noise because even though she got no peace until the Warren kids went home, for all their noise, they fully embraced Miranda exactly as she was. And there was a sort of beautiful harmony to the way the three of them ran together, in and out from the Warren house to the Hopkins house, to the woods and then back to raid the snack cupboard. Olivia had no sense of vocal modulation, and Andrew was at least five foot ten and sounded like a whole heard of buffalo on the stairs. It was nice to see Miranda sitting at the table doing homework with him after school and it was nice for Miranda to have a friend who was similarly studious. It was also nice for her mother to have a little quilting apprentice.

Jim had stopped by mid-week holding an envelope containing three twenty dollar bills, "Andrew eats at least three times as much as Miranda and this is how much less I've spent on groceries this week as compared to last, so I have to assume that he's eaten sixty dollars worth of food here."

Lynne cracked up and took the envelope. "Olivia can pack it in too," she told Jim.

On Monday morning she and Jim had both gone to the meeting with Ms Gilchrist, the school principal. "It's a delicate situation I'm afraid. And this being such a small town makes things more complicated. Misty and Robin's mother left about three years ago and their father hasn't coped well. He drinks, and he can be heavy handed. We just keep hoping that if we can get the two of them through high school that maybe they'll turn around and start making better decisions once they are just a bit older and have some more independence."

"I'm not sure what you're trying to say to me," Lynne had almost snapped.

"I'm telling you that I can officially suspend Misty and Robin Macintosh from school for the week and ask their father to pay you back for the phone, but they have no money. If their father finds out what happened he'll be angry which turns into a cycle. The kids get unfairly punished by him and then act out more. Family services are involved, but Macintosh is on thin ice with them. If Misty and Robin get put into foster care it will remove them from the supports that they *do* have here, their grandmother and cousin. There isn't a foster parent who can care for them in the community, and their grandmother can't take them full time. She's ill and the cousin is her full time carer. If they're put in foster care they'll be separated, sent to Victoria, and possibly put in a hotel."

"You realize they would have beaten Miranda if Andrew hadn't stepped in?" Jim asked.

"I know it seems like I want to do nothing but I assure you that's not the case. I have spoken, off the record with Rob and Misty, and their grandmother, and they have agreed to go to her house for the week during the school day, and Sergeant Healy knows what happened and is making sure they show up there each morning. I've given them each a project to do. They know this is their last chance. You know what happens to kids like them in the foster system."

"I know," Jim sighed heavily. "They age out and then end up on the streets. Often addicts."

Lynne put her head in her hands, "God I hate this. Why do vulnerable kids hurt other vulnerable kids? It doesn't make any sense."

"Often children who have been bullied become bullies," the school principal murmured, almost to herself. "I *have* convinced the school board to have the portables hauled off the school grounds. It was a prime spot for an ambush."

Lynne and Jim made sure that Andrew and Miranda would walk home together and wait for Olivia at the cross roads just to be safe.

On Tuesday Jeremy arrived. Lynne didn't enjoy visits from her ex. He actually behaved reasonably, he was considerably more engaged in what was going on around him than he had been for the last three years of their marriage, but he drove her crazy. When he showed up on Tuesday he was an hour early which was unlike him. If he said six o'clock he showed up at six o'clock. Lynne almost suspected that he was checking up on her. He pestered her with questions about everything and persisted in trying to get Miranda to talk. Of course Miranda got quieter every time he visited. And he couldn't seem to be pleased that Miranda had friends. He did however bring Miranda a new phone and he only stayed for two days before he got bored and left to go back to work. So it could have been worse, and after that the next two weeks were metaphorically quiet.

Ten days before the May long weekend Jim called late in the evening just as Lynne was thinking about going to bed.

"Hi," he said, sounding as tired as she felt. "I'm trying to solidify plans for the long weekend and Olivia and Andrew have some . . . new ideas, about how they want the weekend to proceed. I promised them I would talk to you."

"Alright, I feel silly talking on the phone when I can see you out the window though. I'll be right over."

Lynne walked across the field and sat down on the porch swing next to Jim who had an extra glass next to him, "Do you partake?" he held up a bottle of tequila. "Once a week is my quota, just those nights when I have a yen to be philosophical in the dark," he told her.

"You sound like my mother," Lynne told him dryly. Then, "Yes I partake."

Jim poured her two fingers and she knocked half of it back then sighed and stared contemplatively out into the dark woods, "Maybe I oughta spend more time being philosophical in the dark."

"It isn't productive, but I think our society is overly preoccupied with productivity."

"Mm," Lynne nodded and sat quietly for a few more moments before asking, "So how are you and the kids settling in?"

"It's starting to feel like we live here. Did Miranda tell you about the attic?"

"Yes! She practically wrote an essay!"

Jim laughed, "She's a good influence on my two."

"After the year we've had it's deeply gratifying to have another parent say that about her, but the truth is that Andrew and Olivia are a good influence on Miranda too. She still doesn't talk to me unless it's in a whisper, and she still mainly types, but sometimes I hear her *talk* to Andrew. I hadn't heard her voice in so long . . ." Lynne hadn't expected the tears that came hot and fast down her cheeks and she wiped them off her face with her hands and laughed.

"Andrew . . ." Jim hesitated for a long time before restarting, "Andrew almost died from a crystal meth addiction two years ago. I can relate to that fear, that somehow you are losing your child, and the relief at getting them back. I feel like I'm betraying him when I have to tell people that he was an addict, but if Miranda was my daughter I would want to know who her friends were."

Lynne was silent for a moment, digesting what Jim had said about Andrew, and deciding how she felt about it, but she instinctively trusted the kid and she wasn't going to let the new insight into his history poison the way she saw him, so she told Jim, "I feel similarly about disclosing Miranda's autism. Autistic is a weighty label, like 'addict', and the moment it's out of my mouth people treat me like my daughter died or something, when she's not dead she's right there and there's nothing wrong with her!"

"Do you ever feel like ending up here was . . ." Jim stopped for a moment and chuckled and Lynne saw that he too was feeling a bit emotional as he wiped his own eyes and shook his head at himself.

"Preordained? Destined? Providential . . .?"

He nodded, "Something like that."

"All the time," Lynne laughed, then asked, "Is Andrew alright now? Meth is nasty stuff."

"He'd only been using for about three months and he was self-medicating for a pretty deep depression. There were other issues too. I didn't really cope myself after my wife died, and I'd remarried which was a disaster of monumental proportions. She was a nurse at the hospice where my wife died, but she's in prison now. I'll tell you the whole story some other day . . . With Andrew though, we were very lucky that there wasn't any irreversible cognitive damage. His brain fully healed, and once he was clean and we started to work on fixing the problems that lead to the addiction in the first place, he gradually turned around. He's an A student. He does weekly voluntary drug tests. He's pretty open with me and he's said that he can't imagine going back to that."

"God, you must be relieved," she told Jim, understanding now, the sense she'd had that perhaps Andrew was different, somehow, from other teenagers.

"Very profoundly. I don't take his recovery for granted."

Lynne nodded again, then told Jim, "Miranda doesn't always share with me in a linear fashion. If I ask her a question she often responds with something that's only half related so it can be difficult to have an exchange with her. It's almost like two parallel monologues and only after will I realize that she actually did answer my questions, just in such an oblique way that I have to look from a distance to see where we met up." Lynne smiled at herself, over-explaining, "The reason I told you that, is because I wondered if Andrew talks to you about their friendship. Do they know about each other?"

"They disclosed to each other the day they met. Their whole friendship has been built knowing about each other," Jim told her, and she could hear in his voice that he found it profound, and she had to admit that she did too.

Lynne nodded, deep in thought. "What about Olivia?"

"I think that maybe, somehow, fate placed an incredibly loud angel in my care. I don't think that Olivia understands that Miranda is autistic, but even if she did, it wouldn't change things. Olivia's birth mother had to give her up when her schizophrenia became more than she could cope with, and instead of making Olivia bitter, it's made her incredibly accepting and compassionate."

"Her own father thinks she's loud!" Lynne threw up her hands in mock drama, "And here I was thinking that Miranda's silence had left me unable to cope with a normal child's volume," Lynne laughed.

"Olivia and Andrew *are* loud, especially when they talk over each other which I thought they would outgrow," Jim laughed and shook his head.

"Is Andrew adopted too?"

"Yes. I had the mumps as a kid and Cheryl was 38 when we met. Getting pregnant wasn't in the cards. There are so many kids in the world who need homes. It was a no-brainer to adopt."

Lynne looked out into the woods again, sipped her drink, and sighed, then shook her head and laughed, "Life is so strange isn't it?"

"You can say that twice," Jim agreed, then asked, "Has Miranda always been selectively mute?"

"Not the way she is now. It got much worse almost a year ago. I think something happened to her to trigger it but I've never been able to find out what. There were other factors too. Miranda's father isn't understanding and he pushed so hard for her to be normal that she reached a breaking point. I went along with all the therapies and interventions for the sake of the marriage but I should have left him sooner. Her anxiety and moods improved so much when we just backed off. She might be virtually silent, but I can tell that she's at least content now."

"When did you realize that she's autistic?"

"The summer she turned twelve. She didn't mature in the same way other little girls do. She became serious and intense, although she'd always been a little professor. She somehow got her hands on a copy of Collectors Weekly and then learned as much as she could on the internet about Art Nouveau porcelain and pottery. She dragged me to every thrift store, garage sale, rummage sale, pawn shop, and church bazaar she could get me to. You name it, we went there. We even drove to garage sales in different towns. Then Mom came to visit and she went up to Miranda's room to say hi. When she came out she looked at me and said, 'Lynne, you do realize that Miranda has roughly twenty-thousand dollars worth of antique porcelain, china, and pottery in her room, don't you?'"

Jim gasped and laughed, "Not really!"

"Yes really! I have it all listed on my home insurance policy!"

"What did she say when you asked her about it?"

"She said, 'I didn't know that you didn't know,' but the fact that she can spot a three-thousand dollar Moorcroft vase in a pile of junk from thirty feet away? Most twelve year old girls are having first crushes and getting into makeup. Not Miranda. Nope. She became an expert on Art Nouveau pottery. The crazy thing is that she used her allowance and only spent about thirty dollars for her five favourite pieces, a figurine, three vases, and a bowl. She told me afterward that she estimated that there was another twenty grand in collectibles that she could have had for about eighty dollars."

"God that's remarkable. No small wonder she found the attic," Jim shook his head again this time in amazement.

"My ex refused to see the autism, and he's a bloody data analyst! He was in denial, refused to let me have her diagnosed even though she already had nonverbal learning disorder, developmental coordination disorder, sensory processing disorder, *and* generalized anxiety disorder diagnoses. The first thing I did when I divorced him was take her to a specialist who understands autism in girls and she confirmed it. All Miranda's other diagnoses were removed and now that we aren't constantly treating her like she's broken she's doing so much better."

Tequila and Porch Swings

Jim talked to Andrew before he called Lynne and he told his son that, if they were going to ask Lynne if Miranda could come on a trip with them, that he was going to have to tell Lynne about Andrew's history with drugs. Jim knew there was a chance that Lynne already knew from Miranda, and he really did believe that Lynne would be able to accept it without curtailing the kid's friendship, but it wasn't a guarantee, and he saw Andrew nod and watched as the bruised look that had almost disappeared came back into his son's eyes.

"Tell me what she says right away dad. Miranda understands me and I know I haven't known her long but if Lynne says she doesn't want us to be friends . . ." Andrew left the room suddenly, pounding up the stairs then slamming his bedroom door.

Jim felt heavy and exhausted as he took his phone out to the porch swing and poured himself a drink, hitting the little green call icon next to Lynne's number.

He watched her walk across the field and then poured her a drink when she accepted his offer. It was easier than he thought it would be in the end, telling Lynne about Andrew's drug use. It had the same feeling behind it as seeing the medical practice for sale and walking into their house for the first time. Providential. He got the feeling that Lynne was, likewise, relieved to be talking to someone who knew what it was like to have a child who would likely be stigmatized by the average person.

They talked for about three quarters of an hour before Jim suddenly remembered why it was that he had called Lynne in the first place.

"I have a dilemma. I'm supposed to be going to a physician's seminar in Vancouver on the Saturday of the long weekend 'Managing Medical Needs in Remote Communities'. I was going to take the kids with me and they were going to go to the Museum of Anthropology while I was at the seminar. They love that museum . . ."

Lynne cut him off, "Your kids love the Museum of Anthropology too? I mean I get Miranda loving it but . . . she is autistic."

"They love it. We first visited the museum when we arrived on the west coast, and they had an opportunity to go to Science World on our last day in Vancouver, but they opted to go back to the museum a second time instead. I told them that they could go again on the long weekend and they *were* looking forward to it, but now they . . . want to know if Miranda can come too, or if they can stay at your place while I go to the seminar alone.

I was going to take them out for dinner at the rotating restaurant, and we were going to go out for curry . . . I've made all the reservations. I don't mind bringing Miranda along, she's no trouble and it won't put me out at all. It's the first school holiday since we arrived and they are *so* thrilled to have a friend that they don't want to miss out on that. I told them I would ask you."

Lynne smiled, "It's been a while for your kids too, hasn't it, since they last had normal friendships?"

"It has."

"Well, since *your* kids are probably going to be breathing down your neck for an answer, you can tell them that it's, 'Very Probably'. I'll have to discuss it with Miranda, and I'll have to clear it with her father," Lynne said that last with an air of resentment. "I don't want you to miss a weekend away with your kids, but if Miranda goes with you, you have to be careful not to overwhelm her. Bring her noise cancelling headphones and make sure she has a few chances each day to step away from it all."

"Absolutely. I'd already booked one of the family suits at the Sylvia Hotel so she'll have space. She can close the door of a bedroom for an hour before dinner if she needs to. The plan is to leave on Friday right after school and have dinner on the ferry, then come back late Sunday afternoon."

Lynne nodded, "I think Miranda will want to go. It's been two years since she's been to the museum and when she was small and I was in grad school it was her home away from home. I'll talk to her. In the mean time," she sipped the last drops of tequila, "I'd better get home. I'll talk to Miranda in the morning. And your kids can stay over with us any time you need. I get the feeling you don't have any family to help out."

"I don't. Cheryl and I were only children and our folks have all passed. It's just me," Jim told her. Then, "Look, it was good talking to another parent who has a similar perspective. We went to support groups in Toronto but . . ."

"I understand. People are judgmental, but the fact that you've gotten your kids through the things you've been through, gives me more confidence in your ability, not less."

Jim watched Lynne walk back across the field. She was an incongruous woman, in her jeans and concert t-shirts, her trendy haircut, and immaculate no-makeup makeup. For all that she looked no older than thirty, when she spoke she had a very casual sort of hyper-intelligence that left him unsurprised that she would hold a PhD and run a research centre, and she was the odd one out between Violet and Miranda.

Upstairs Jim knocked on Andrew's door, "Yeah, come in," came muffled through the solid wood of the door. Jim opened the door and Andrew sat up on the edge of the bed, placing his feet on the floor and his elbows on his knees and looking at Jim with very serious eyes, "What did she say?"

Jim could sense Andrew bracing himself for the worst so he told him without preamble, "Lynne say's 'Very probably,' about Miranda coming with us, and 'Yes', to you and Olivia staying over if that's what you want."

Andrew let out a long breath and swayed slightly, closed his eyes and pressed his lips together, "Lynne's okay with everything?"

"Lynne is an intelligent and caring mother. I didn't think it would be an issue, but it is better to have it out in the open and know where she stands. She's going to talk to Miranda in the morning about the trip," he patted Andrew on the shoulder and looked around the room. "It's very clean and organized in here." Each time he came into Andrew's room over the last three weeks he couldn't help notice the neatness, the way it had been arranged for optimal flow and convenience, and that the surfaces were clear and free of dust.

"Miranda helped me organize it so that it doesn't really get messy anymore. Her room is so . . ." Andrew stopped and smiled. "Have you seen it? You've been up-stairs in their house right?"

"Yes, I've been upstairs and I did walk past. It's a very atmospheric room."

"Well, I can't hang out with her at her house, hang out in her room, and then have her over here and inflict a mess on her. So I asked her to help me with it."

"You guys did a good job. It's a very gentlemanly, intellectual room now."

"That's sort of what I was going for. Miranda knows a lot about old things. Not just antiques but about old ideas and the way people used to think and how they lived and why they liked or did what they did. It helped make the furniture look right in here, and we found a trunk of lamps and framed lithographs and early prints in the attic too." Andrew gestured towards the framed print of European woodland birds above the desk.

That reminded Jim of something that Lynne had said earlier and he asked Andrew, "Has Miranda ever said anything to you about her muteness? Do you know if something happened to trigger it?"

Jim watched Andrew's face and he could tell that Andrew did know something, "Doesn't Lynne know?" Andrew asked.

"No."

"I don't really know either . . . It's just something she referred to once, but sometimes Miranda . . . she speaks sideways. If you look straight at it you won't understand. I won't inform on her though. If she tells me and asks me to keep it to myself I'm not going to come running to you guys with it until she's ready. I get it that she's got some issues, but she's my friend and she trusts me."

"I know Andrew. I wouldn't ask you to betray your friend. I just wondered, that's all. I suspect you'll find out from Miranda whether she wants to come on the trip with us tomorrow in biology."

Jim headed to the end of the hall and checked for light under the door and listened for a moment to make sure that Olivia was really asleep, and then went to his own room. The kids weren't the only ones who had ended up with furnished bedrooms after the discovery of the attic, Jim however, did not end up with a clean neatly arranged room. A dresser and bed frame were propped in one corner and his mattress was still on the floor next to a row of boxes and an antique secretary. He thought about tackling the mess for a moment but then decided he'd pay Andrew and Miranda to do it on the weekend, and then laughed at himself for it. He went out onto the sleeping porch. He hadn't known, until Violet had named it, that that was what it was, but now that he knew he was almost looking forward to summer, so he could sleep under the stars like a kid. The feeling of looking forward slipped into place with an audible click, and Jim realized that he was doing alright.

The Drawers!

Miranda woke suddenly as her mother sat down on the bed next to her and smoothed her hair back from her brow.

"Sorry baby! I didn't mean to give you a start," her mother said, and Miranda rolled and wrapped her arms around her mom's waist as her mother kept stroking her hair.

Miranda looked up at her mother and gave her a look with eyebrows raised expectantly, wondering what she was doing there, not that she minded.

"You really don't *need* words sometimes, do you?"

Miranda smiled and stretched like a cat wondering what her mother was up to but unwilling to give her the satisfaction of too much curiosity, except to make sure her mother knew that Miranda knew, that she was up to something.

Her mother chuckled and caved first, "You've been invited to go to Vancouver with the Warrens on the long weekend to spend Saturday at The Museum of Anthropology with Andrew and Olivia. Would you like to go? It's okay with me, I just have to check with your dad."

Miranda scrambled up to a sitting position, "The drawers make me so happy!" she said, almost as loudly as Olivia and clapped her hands over her own ears.

Her mother smiled deeply, "I know, it's a fun museum and you love it. Does that mean you want to go?"

Miranda thought about it and a part of her really didn't want to even leave the property, but she did that five days a week for school and if she did it for school she could do it for . . . All of a sudden she realized that she would be going with Andrew and Olivia . . . which her mother had of course said, but hearing it and knowing it were different, and it would be so much better with them than it was with her mom who really just humoured her when they went . . . "Do Andrew and Olivia like the museum?" she whispered.

"According to Jim they love it. They went twice in one week a few months back and they want to go again, but they don't want to go away for the long weekend because they've been enjoying spending time with you, so their dad gave them the option of inviting you along."

Sometimes Miranda wished transporters were real because if they were she would probably go to the museum every other day. But she liked riding the ferry, and she would be with Andrew for three days straight . . . which gave her that beautiful birds fluttering in her chest feeling. Andrew and Olivia and the museum at the same time.

"I'm going to go down and eat breakfast, you think it over, but something tells me that Andrew is going to be waiting for an answer when you get to school."

Lynne left the room and closed the door behind her. Miranda sat in her bed and looked out the window at the ocean which always made her think of Andrew now. She rested her chin on her knees stroking the velvet coverlet and thinking. She was pretty sure she wanted to go. There was a part of her that was afraid of all the little things that could happen and another part of her that was so happy at the idea that she felt physically a little ill. She listed the things that could go wrong and reminded herself that it was statistically unlikely for the ferry to sink, and that she knew she wouldn't accidentally jump overboard, and that she could tell Andrew and Olivia that the railings make her nervous and that they would be understanding. There might be a car accident but it's hard to avoid cars and Jim's car was a new, well maintained, Toyota hybrid, so it was probably pretty safe. All the little things crowded in on Miranda and she cried for a minute or two but then remembered that going out into the world was life and that she wanted that. To be with people and have adventures. And Olivia and Andrew liked the museum too. She took a deep breath and got out of bed, pulled her wardrobe open and looked at the dresses. She chose a vintage emerald green cotton dress with tiny pink rosettes printed on it. She washed her face in the bathroom, brushed her hair, and then went down to the kitchen.

"Did you decide?" Lynne asked.

Miranda didn't look at her mother.

"She'll say when she's ready Lynne," her nanna said.

"I know," her mother grumbled, but then said, "You know Jim is all alone with those two kids. He doesn't have any family at all. I was thinking, it wouldn't put us out any to give them a standing invitation to dinner Sunday nights would it?"

"I certainly wouldn't mind. Olivia was asking me how to make bread. She might have fun helping. From what I hear Jim is a pretty basic cook," Violet replied to Lynne.

Miranda listened and thought, *Olivia would like to help.* She was always asking how to do things and how things are made and asking Jim questions that he couldn't answer like, "Do donkeys make good pets?" Miranda's nanna had a donkey, "Back in the day." She knew donkeys were loud and stubborn.

"I'll tell Andrew at school," Miranda said, and her Mother and nanna went silent.

Miranda ate her toast and didn't look at them. She finished eating and then went up to her room to finish getting ready for school. She sat down at her dressing table and looked around, trying to get her heart to slow down a little. The beauty and the order and the familiarity of her room brought her down a notch and she went back downstairs with a sweater and her phone. She grabbed her book-bag and went out to the car to wait for her mother.

Lynne got in the car and Miranda whispered, "You have to make sure that Dad says yes."

"I'll make sure he says yes," Lynne promised, smiling.

At school Miranda hurried to class and sat in the desk next to Andrew's. He looked at her and she snuck a quick look at his eyes and then looked down right away to keep from getting stuck. She smiled though and she felt her cheek muscles aching.

"You're coming?" he asked, and she looked back up and nodded.

_My dad might say no, but my mom said yes, and I want to go. My mom said she would make sure my dad says yes.

She typed into her phone and held it up for Andrew to read and he smiled.

"I can't wait to go," he whispered.

Miranda looked up at Mr Lawson, the biology teacher, who was scowling at them. He said nothing though, as it was the end of the year and Miranda and Andrew were his top students.

It was misty and cool the afternoon they left for Vancouver. Miranda, Andrew, and Olivia ran home from school. Miranda had packed slowly over the week so when she got home all she had to do was change her clothes, grab her suitcase and purse, then run across the field. She pulled on her green corduroy skirt and the yellow t-shirt, then pulled on a new hand knit cardigan that her nanna had knit for her, along with the matching tam. She clattered down the stairs and hugged her nanna tightly and then ran across the field on the dirt path that she, Andrew, and Olivia, had worn into the grass, to the waiting car. They piled in, Olivia crowing because Andrew had let her have the front passenger seat for once while simultaneously arguing that she should have been the one who got to sit with Miranda in the back. And then they were off.

As the car took them down the highway Miranda felt good about her decision to go. Jim put Simon and Garfunkel on the car stereo and they played twenty questions on the long drive to the ferry terminal.

She had almost changed her mind about going when her mother called her father to let him know about the invitation. When her parents were still together there hadn't really been any fighting because her father always refused to engage. If he caught even a whiff of disagreement he would leave the room, leave the house, go to work, leave on a business trip. It was horrible because Miranda's mother was left in a constant state of irresolution. Miranda didn't get angry easily but she was angry on her mother's behalf and she felt a simmering resentment towards her father as a result. Now her parents fought openly because it was harder for her father to walk away from his mobile phone. It went everywhere with him. So now Lynne could scream at him over the phone. The call had started out reasonable, but then she could see in her mother's posture as she stood in the living room, phone to her ear, that her father was already raising objections. Her father was the king of finding reasons not to do things, "Don't be ridiculous Jeremy," Lynne had said, patient at first, then she'd said, "It's perfectly normal for kids to go on trips with their friends families."

"She'd be going with the village GP and his kids. I've been in their house they eat dinner with us. She'd be as safe as if we took her ourselves."

"They're used to Miranda and, unlike most people, Jim actually has half a clue when it comes to autistic kids."

"No Jeremy, it's not like that."

"Even if it was, she'll be sixteen in a matter of weeks."

"For crying out loud!"

Miranda bolted and ran across the field barefoot in her night gown. She'd knocked on the Warren's door and Jim let her in. She crept past him up the stairs to Andrew's room and knocked softly. "Come in?"

Miranda opened the door and crept through. Andrew was reading in bed and was surprised to see her.

"Are you okay?"

Miranda was shaking from too much adrenaline from the fighting. "My parents are fighting," she whispered.

He sat up and pulled up the comforter that was across the foot of the bed and offered it to her and then patted the foot of the bed. Miranda took the blanket and wrapped herself up in it and sat cross legged on the foot of the bed.

"I hate it when they fight. I wish my dad wouldn't make everything so hard. It makes me more afraid of doing things and going places."

"I guess I was pretty lucky. My parents never fought when my mom was alive. They met late and always said they didn't have time to fight. And my mom always said you have to step out the door to come home again, so doing new things and going new places always felt safe."

"Was it very awful when she died?" Miranda asked, still whispering.

Andrew nodded and was silent for a moment then said, voice thick, "When I think about her, I can understand why you're mute sometimes. It's like I can't speak through the grief."

Miranda nodded, got up trailing the blanket on the floor, and picked up Andrew's laptop and passed it to him. He turned it on and opened a text file.

_I Wish she was alive, but I know that her death was the thing, the catalyst, for us being here, where we are now. I know that I can't go back and reverse things. Sometimes I talk to her and imagine what she would have said to me, but I have to do it in my head, because . . . I can't do it out loud.

_It's like there's a ball of emotions stopping my throat up. I don't have very good emotional regulation so my voice gets stopped up by most emotions, sometimes even happiness. I wish I could meet your mom.

_She would have liked you. She was the kind of person who believed everyone had something of value inside them and that it's always worth looking.

* * *

Miranda had woken up the next day to Jim shouting up the stairs, "Pancakes! Eggs! It's almost ten o'clock!" She looked around confused. The door to the hall hung open and she was still at Andrew's house. Andrew was sleeping on the floor in a sleeping bag on a camping mattress, and she was sleeping on his bed still tightly wrapped in the thick blanket. Suddenly she remembered running across the field late the night before and spending half the night typing with Andrew.

Andrew opened his eyes blinking and Jim was standing in the doorway, "Olivia made breakfast and she's getting impatient. Violet brought your bathrobe and some clean clothes over. Come on, up you get sleepy heads!" Jim placed a little carryall from Miranda's house on the foot of the bed.

Miranda pulled on her bathrobe and got up. She and Andrew went downstairs to the kitchen in their pyjamas where Olivia was standing looking the table over making sure everything was there. "I made pancakes from scratch. I can't figure out why you always use a mix Dad. It really wasn't that hard."

Olivia was still in her pyjamas too and Miranda realized it was Saturday morning.

"Next time you guys have a sleep over don't leave me out!" Olivia told Miranda and Andrew very seriously.

Miranda felt bad. She hadn't meant to leave anyone out and she leaned towards Olivia and whispered, "I'm sorry."

"Miranda was upset last night. She didn't know she was going to come over. You were already sleeping. Next time we'll plan for it and set up the tent in the living room okay," Andrew told her, and Olivia accepted it.

That was last weekend and now they were sitting at a table on the six o'clock ferry eating dinner. After they ate Miranda, Olivia, and Andrew wandered the ferry talking.

"I know the ferry doesn't look magical. Maybe it's all the boats in mythology that makes the ferry *feel* magic, or maybe it's that the ferry takes us home, but I love ferries," Miranda murmured, looking out towards the sparkling city as they made the approach in the setting sun.

She watched the wind play havoc with Olivia's hair and smiled as Olivia slung her arm over the top of her head like a headband of flesh and just left it there, "I think it's because the ferries take us where we want to be and keep us fed and comfortable while we get there. I know the grownups complain that it's expensive, but I feel kind of like the ferry wants to take care of us."

Andrew started to laugh but not in a mean way, "Which ferry are we on?" he asked.

"Queen of Cowichan," Miranda and Olivia answered at the same time.

"It would be so easy to make fun of you guys right now except that I feel the same way so I'd be a total hypocrite."

The Drawers! II

The rest of the museum was great too, but there was something about the large area with all the drawers. The Multiversity. Nine Thousand objects in 14, 500 square feet. There was something about the discoveries you made as you took the handles with your hands and pulled. Sometimes something beautiful was inside, ancient Chinese pottery for instance, and it had once had a purpose, but it was now obsolete. Or it was an object that looked so simple, almost boring, but was once indispensable. Sometimes it was something that we still use today but was completely unrecognizable. And once he'd opened a few drawers the sense of pulling, and the glide of the rollers, got tied into his intellectual curiosity and the satisfaction of discovery. It was the healthiest addiction that Andrew could think of and suddenly he was there with Miranda, and she got it. She absolutely understood the fascination. He'd been thinking that he and Olivia were just weird.

That morning when their alarm went off at the old and slightly shabby—but incredibly comfortable—hotel, they had eaten a room service breakfast—the best he'd ever had at a hotel—and sat at the breakfast table looking out over the ocean. His dad had said goodbye triple checking before he left for the seminar, that they knew which bus to take, and had cash enough for a taxi should they need it, and had every phone number that they could possibly need, and had the key card for the hotel, and then he told them to have fun. The museum didn't open till ten o'clock so they hung around the hotel suite for an hour before leaving. The suite had a kitchen and two bedrooms. The girls had taken the one with the king sized bed and Andrew had shared the room with the twin beds with his dad. It was interesting to look around in the light of day as they hadn't gotten in till late the night before. The hotel had the same 'outside of time' feeling as home did.

"I like it here," Miranda had said, as they sat watching a sailboat sailing out to sea.

"We stayed here when we first came to the west coast," Olivia told her. "Dad said him and Mom spent their honeymoon here."

"Apparently people used to live here in the hotel back when it was first built in nineteen-twelve," Andrew told them.

Andrew didn't know Vancouver well but he had grown up in Toronto so he was comfortable navigating a city and Miranda still remembered a lot of landmarks from when she had lived in Vancouver, so they made it to the right bus stop with no issues. He hadn't known that

Miranda had basically grown up on the UBC campus until last week.

_I was eight when we left. All my mom's friends still live here. We left because of my dad's work, but we used to come back to visit.

She had typed into her phone while they were on the bus to the university.

Even though Andrew loved living the small town, island life, they'd adopted, in a way, to be away from St Fina, in a real place, was exciting. Andrew had almost begun to feel that he had wandered into a sort of Brigadoon, and somehow the people there wouldn't exist away from the strange little town. Andrew watched Miranda take Olivia's hand as they got off the bus at the university and lead her through the campus towards the museum. They were real and solid, walking along the sidewalk ahead of him, their hair shining in the sun, Olivia's bouncing and Miranda's swinging. Miranda told them that it was a bit of a walk from the bus loop, but that didn't matter because the museum wasn't going to open for another half hour anyway, and the sun had come out and burned away the clouds. Once they had gotten in and payed their admission they made their way slowly through the exhibits of First Nations wood carvings and artifacts; reading the plaques and whispering to each other, delaying the gratification of the drawers. Andrew, Olivia, and Miranda spent two hours opening drawers and marveling, with more excited whispering, their minds wandering through history. Afterward, in a bit of a trance, they stood in the shadows gazing into the pool of light illuminating Bill Reid's *Raven and The First Men.* "I could imagine that raven landing on our beach," Miranda whispered.

"Totally," Andrew and Olivia whispered at the same time.

They walked out of the museum at one o'clock and a very colourful woman was standing there waiting in the sun. Lynne had arranged for Miranda's godmother to take them for lunch and then bring them back to the hotel. "MIRANDA!!!" the woman yelled, and then came running and hugged Miranda in a swirl of pink hair and bright green and purple chiffon that were at odds with the combat boots.

"You're Andrew . . ." she was a hugger, "And you're Olivia!"

Andrew knew Olivia was going to like this woman.

"I'm Nadine!" She turned to Miranda, "Your mum says you're still being mysterious?"

Miranda nodded, and held up her phone,

_Mostly.

"Only mostly! Well come on. I've got a reservation at a really hip place on The Drive." And she drove them to a part of town where stretched earlobes and burgundy hair were the norm and graffiti was seen as a culturally relevant art form.

Nadine was the wildest grownup Andrew had ever met, but for all that she was very young at heart and passionate, she also had her shit together. She ran a non profit that helped marginalized women get access to higher education and volunteered at her local SPCA. She talked to them like they were her equals, as if their opinions were as valid as the people she worked with, and she prattled away to them as they rode in her lime green Honda across the city and peppered them with questions, "So you'll be done with high-school next year, are you going to take a gap year?" she asked Miranda.

"I don't know. It depends on if I get obsessed with something. I don't know what to do really, I don't know if there's a degree in what I like," Miranda wasn't loud but she was talking.

"You spent the afternoon at the museum. It's safe to assume you still like old beautiful things?"

"Mostly . . . yes."

"You should do Art History, although, some people might say it won't get you a job," Nadine smiled brightly, "My women's studies degree really bugged my uncle for just that reason."

"What about you?" she looked over her shoulder at Andrew.

"I've only got one semester left too. I'll be done same time as Miranda, but I don't know if I want to take a gap year cause I'm graduating late."

"And you're twelve right? That's grade seven isn't it. I hated grade seven it felt like an incredible waste of time," she said to Olivia.

"Grade seven kinda sucks," Olivia agreed. "It feels like a nonsense year in between elementary school and high school."

"Exactly. Nobody gives twelve-year-olds the credit they deserve."

They ate at a restaurant as out there as Nadine, "So I figured you guys would like this place because, what teenagers spend the day at the museum when let loose in the city?"

Nadine had them back at the hotel by three pm and she said goodbye, giving Miranda a parcel and telling her, "I found it at a thrift store in Sweden. Don't open it till you get home and don't leave it sitting out in an obvious place in the hotel room." Then she started hugging again, "I will see all you guys again in August because I'm coming for two whole weeks!"

Back in the room Andrew and Miranda read books while Olivia took pictures out the window of the Burrard Inlet with Miranda's phone and then tried to lure a seagull inside.

"Olivia . . . Probably not the best idea," Andrew told her.

Then she started bugging them, "Can I watch TV?"

"I have to read this for school and Miranda needs some quiet time. Didn't you bring a book?"

"I took it out of my bag to read in the car and forgot to put it back in."

"Well, you'll have to find something quiet to do."

"Can you read your book out loud to me?"

"I don't think you'll like it. It's Margaret Attwood. And it'll make it hard for Miranda to read if I'm reading out loud."

Olivia was quiet for another ten minutes. "Miranda? What's your book about?"

Andrew looked up and watched Olivia and Miranda out of the corner of his eye, worried that Miranda might be tired, or near the end of her social reserves, and not wanting Olivia to push her over the edge. But Miranda turned back to the beginning of her book and read the character description of the main character out to Olivia, "Elnora, who collects moths to pay for her education, and lives the Golden Rule . . ." and she continued and read the other characters. Olivia was obviously inter-ested but Miranda stopped and said, "But Andrew has to read his book for school so we should be quiet."

Olivia nodded and sagged. Miranda smiled and asked Andrew, "If I give you my headphones and some music to block out our voices will it bother you if I read to her?"

Andrew was surprised, "No. Not at all. If I can block out your voice I'll be fine. Go ahead, but not if it's going to wear you out?"

"I'm okay. We're not going for dinner till seven. We can just lie here and read. I've read this book four times. It'll be fun to read it to Olivia."

And that was what they did, and Andrew had to admit that listening to music made the school reading a little less onerous, but every so often he'd stop the music and take off the headphones and listen to Miranda read to his little sister.

The Green Phone

Violet loved rotary phones. She still remembered how it took a little time to make a call and how with the first swing of your fingertip around the rotary you were already anticipating the voice on the other end. She liked the feel of the ear piece pressed between her shoulder and ear and twirling the cord around her finger, so when she'd first viewed the house she'd been tickled and delighted to find an avocado green rotary phone in working order still installed in the kitchen. It was like a friend from a time long gone. Her first day in the house she had called her childhood friend on it and it had felt like going back in time. Of course her friend, Dianne, had said, "You are batty Violet, but that's why I love you. You enjoy your rotary phone."

The phone was ringing now and Violet loved the old fashioned sound drifting through the house. It was certainly preferable to the sound of Lynne arguing on her smart phone with Jeremy in the parlour. It was late for someone to be calling. The stove clock said quarter to eleven as she walked past in her dressing gown. "Hello?" she lifted the receiver, wondering who it would be.

"Violet, I tried Lynne first but I was shuffled to her voice mail."

"Hi Jim," she said, recognizing his voice now, after weeks of calling back and forth after the kids.

"Is everything alright over there?" he asked.

"More or less. Why?"

"Miranda just showed up on my doorstep in her pyjamas and she looked spooked. I let her in and she's upstairs talking with Andrew. I wanted to check in with you, nothing's wrong?"

"Oh, dear. I'm sorry," Violet sighed, knowing what had happened. "Lynne is on the phone fighting with Miranda's father and Miranda has trouble with angry people. Nothing is wrong, Jeremy always has to be convinced to give Miranda a little leeway though. She finds it incredibly stressful when her parents fight. When she bolts she doesn't always think, she just goes where her feet take her."

"The fight isn't over the Vancouver trip is it?" Violet could hear in Jim's voice concern that perhaps he had caused unnecessary strife in making the invitation.

"Yes, but no. If it wasn't the trip it would be something else. Jeremy is not father material and he quite happily let Lynne have custody. He had trouble fully engaging with Miranda and really understanding her needs. Not to suggest that he doesn't love her, but the autism genes run strong in both Miranda's parents, and Jeremy . . . has trouble."

"Not that I'm saying that parenting alone is easy, but I don't envy people who have to co-parent with an ex-spouse they don't see eye to eye with. Miranda is fine here, by the way. If you'd prefer to come get her that's fine, or we can just leave her where she is and Andrew can sleep on the floor. Maybe just run some clothes over for her, and a bathrobe."

"Will do Jim. Thanks for letting me know you've got her. I hope she didn't wake everyone up, and Lynne is still on the phone with Jeremy so if it really won't put you out to keep her, I'd appreciate it."

"Not a problem Violet, Andrew and I were still up. I'll see you tomorrow."

After dropping an overnight bag for Miranda at the other house, Violet made a cup of herbal tea and listened to Lynne reason with Jeremy for another half hour. She was proud of Lynne for the way she was dealing with the divorce, and she did have some compassion for her ex-son-in-law. Lynne didn't have to clear things with him and she did it so that he could stay connected with Miranda, if only in a small way, but it was exhausting to listen to.

Lynne walked into the kitchen looking tired, "I wish I didn't have to start screaming for him to understand when things are important. I wouldn't stop Miranda from going at this point. I just want him to say, 'Sounds great! Tell her to have fun,' and not lecture me about how

I should wrap her in cotton wool. There's a difference between keeping her safe and stopping her from living. God!"

"Miranda bolted. She's at the Warren house. Jim said he'd keep her till tomorrow," Violet told her daughter.

Lynne banged her head on the table. "Next time I'm skipping the pretense of checking with him altogether and I'm just going to email him and tell him what's happening and why and let him deal."

Miranda was home by eleven the next day with Andrew and Olivia in tow. Olivia stood beside Violet quietly watching her rub the tarnish off a silver candlestick holder before asking, "Can we work on the quilt?"

"Of course!" Violet brought down Olivia's quilt basket and watched as she sat down at the sewing machine, changed the thread, then, with great care, began assembling her next square.

Violet really wasn't helping Olivia much anymore. The little girl was quite industrious and had a flair for kaleidoscope colour combinations. Violet didn't use traditional fabrics in her quilts and she had stacks of old silk dupioni, velveteen, and jacquard. She had purged her collection just before the move but had some special fabrics that she had been holding onto for the right project for years and she had bought all kinds of exciting fabric from Charlotte. Olivia's quilt would be frosty lilac and peach velveteen with vintage yellow and chartreuse chinoiserie jacquard and a turquoise and purple floral print from the fifties. All the colours of a summer sunset. "If you finish the last three squares today we can start putting it together tomorrow. We'll be done by next weekend."

Olivia beamed up at her.

"You know your squares and very well constructed. What do you think of entering this in the fall fair?"

"We have a fall fair here?"

"A small one," Violet told her.

Olivia beamed harder.

On Sunday morning Violet supervised as Olivia assembled her squares and then taught her how to make bread. Mid-afternoon Jim came by and he sat at the kitchen table with a cup of coffee watching, and when Olivia rolled the big ball of bread dough into a bowl to rise and then skipped off, back to the sewing room, he asked Violet, "Are you sure you're alright having her around so much?"

Violet laughed, "I have two grandsons in their twenties and I've got Miranda who is perfectly happy to write an essay on why a quilt is beautiful, and to sleep under one, but she isn't a doer. She's a thinker. Olivia is a doer," Violet said with conviction, "and the children we nurture don't have to be our own flesh and blood. I'd always envisioned passing on all of the things I know how to do, one day. I'll pass them on to Olivia. Has she talked to you about goats, by the way?"

Jim blanched at the mention of goats and Violet laughed.

Violet had finished knitting a new cardigan with a matching tam for Miranda who was growing up, but not out, and every time Violet thought she was going to be done soon she had to add an extra quarter inch to the cuffs. And no sooner had it finished wet blocking, it seemed Miranda was pulling it on and running off with her suitcase to spend the weekend with the Warrens.

The weekend was eerily silent but late on Saturday afternoon Lynne crept up to her with her phone outstretched, "Mom, look," Lynne was white and looked like she'd been crying.

Violet looked at the phone, below a text from Jim that said,

_Just got back from the seminar, they haven't noticed me yet. Didn't expect this

there was a video, Lynne pressed play. The kids were lying on a chesterfield together, Andrew reading with Miranda's headphones on and Miranda reading out loud to Olivia who was snuggled up to her side.

"I was so scared that I was going to regret letting her go," Lynne said with her voice shaking. "Look at the text I got from Nadine." Lynne scrolled to a picture of the three kids grinning in front of some graffiti accompanied by the words,

_So glad to hear Miranda's voice again, no matter how little.

"I'm so relieved Mom."

"Oh Lynne, so am I. So am I."

Every Day Is Like Sunday

Jenny sat on the plane, bored. She'd painted her nails, glossy black, touched up her eyeliner three times, brushed her hair—inspecting her thick black fringe to make sure it didn't look greasy. Her brother slept. It always made Jenny mad the way he could do that. Just sleep anytime he needed or wanted. She decided to check the plane's database of movies and she plugged in her earbuds. She didn't know what she expected, it was a plane after all, and at least Mission Impossible III had eaten up some of her time, but would it kill them to get some *thoughtful* movies? Jenny opened her compact again and made sure her black eyeliner still looked alright and looked over her black outfit to make sure she hadn't picked up any lint. Her mother never exactly hassled her, but for most of the six month trip Jenny had been made aware that it would be appreciated if she would try not to be so gloomy. But gloomy was easy for her. And none of them had a sense of humour about it. She was fifteen, of course she wasn't really *this* dark, she had perspective, she certainly wasn't a nihilist. She wasn't depressed, she was just realistic.

And she liked her own company so the knowledge that she was going home to spend the summer alone wasn't that bad. She had a pile of books, and the internet, and music. And she always had Willy. She was never *really* alone. And the introspective part of her, that really did like solitude, enjoyed the way it felt when one day blended into the next. But it was a bit predictable. Why did they act like she was being so dark when she was just being honest about the fact that she was about to spend ten weeks alone in her room listening to music. That's what you do during the summer holiday when you live in a ghost town. That and wander the forest alone. Because she wasn't going to put up with the aggravation of trying to make friends with one of the roughly twenty kids in St Fina who were her age. She'd known them her whole life and they had yet to do or say anything to make her think they were worth her energy. The only kids worth her time had either moved away, or they had changed.

At least Jenny would be home soon. That, at least, was something. Back in their own house, in her own room, her own bed, where she could breathe. It was something big to be away for half a year and now she could barely wait to be back in their own home. It was like an embrace she was waiting for, and wouldn't feel right in her skin until she'd had.

She looked next to her at her sleeping brother. He'd started getting taller this year and now he was three inches taller than Jenny was. They'd been the same height for most of their lives. Willy was getting more masculine looking too. He'd been very pretty till recently but his jaw was developing and his voice had dropped. He looked like a guy these days. They used to swap clothes and then wait to see how long it would take people to notice, they'd gotten through a whole school day once, but then Willy had cut his hair off and Jenny had gotten bangs and it didn't work after that. At least not as well, although Jenny still had to snicker at the time they'd made it through the first hour of the school day. Willy's English teacher hadn't looked closely enough at him to realize that it wasn't him. Jenny's math teacher really believed she'd cut off all her hair. It definitely wouldn't work now. Willy almost needed to shave. He'd bought all his new clothes in Japan too so now the two of them were going to stick out even more than they used to. Japanese street style would not go unnoticed in St Fina.

Jenny looked at her phone. Three hours left. She plugged in her ear buds and scrolled through her music. Past The Cure, Placebo, The Twilight Sad, Iskwe, and into Morrissey/The Smiths.

She selected *Every Day Is Like Sunday* and then pulled out her journal, listened to the song on repeat, and wrote until the captain announced their descent.

The Beautiful
Wild Summer

A ndrew and Miranda walked to school together on
the last day. They'd wanted to skip out on the Last-
Day-of-School school picnic but their parents had made
them go. They looked at the lineup for hotdogs and
glumly, silently, indifferently, joined the queue. "I don't
like hotdogs," Miranda whispered in his ear and Andrew
snickered.

"Not boiled wieners with no onions or sauerkraut
anyway," Andrew whispered back.

They looked down at their boiled wiener hotdogs
and then looked dubiously at the tables for a place to
sit by themselves when a voice called out, "Hey losers!
Strength in numbers! Come sit with us!"

Andrew looked towards the voice. A boy and a girl
with black hair and dark eyes that Andrew didn't recognize sat at the only table with empty seats. He and
Miranda walked over to the other kids, bewildered, and

Miranda whispered, "Why does he want us to sit with them if he thinks we're losers?"

"I can't tell if you're being intentionally rude, or if that was an incompetent attempt at friendliness," Andrew said to the boy who had called out, bristling slightly.

"He's trying to be nice, he doesn't mean 'losers'. Sit with us," the girl told them.

"Except I kinda do, with them we'd totally be a Loser's Club!" the boy said.

"We're gonna go," Andrew said turning away.

"No don't go, sit with us. Don't you guys read Steven King for god's sake? He means it as a compliment," the girl said hurriedly.

There wasn't anywhere else to sit, so they sat.

"We're your neighbours, by the way. I'm Jenny, he's Willy. We live in the big house at the end of Josephine Road."

"The Mid-century one. Did you guys know that it's actually a real . . ."

"Willy they aren't even going to know who you're talking about," Jenny was obviously getting frustrated with her brother and she shook her head and covered her face with one hand, turning with a hard done by slouch.

"Frank Lloyd Wright?" Andrew and Miranda said at the same time and Andrew turned to Miranda, "Hey! First time you used your voice at school!"

And then Willy threw his arms in the air and yelled, "Oh! You guys so totally *are* beautiful losers!"

"Willy! Enough!" Jenny said plaintively.

"Look," Andrew levelled his gaze at Willy, "This is an ambiguous and socially confusing thing you've got going on here, and if I'm confused you can bet that Miranda is lost, so if you're trying to be friends would you cut the crap!"

"Sorry," Willy said, "It's just that new kids never move to town and we've been in Japan with our grandma since November. And now that we've gotten back and had a chance have a look at you, you look kinda . . . weird, like us."

"We don't fit in either is what he's trying to say," Jenny explained, taking pity on her brother and giving his shoulders a squeeze.

"You guys are Japanese?" Andrew asked, really looking at them now. They were quite good looking, and dressed like no one else in town, but they didn't really look Japanese to him.

"Half. Our mum is Haida and our dad is Japanese so the native kids think of us as Asian, Japanese people think we're Filipino, and white kids think we're native. Plus our last name is Araya which is also a Spanish name so some people think we're Mexican," Willy explained.

Andrew didn't think they looked Filipino either.

"You're not even part of the local band, so you don't fit, even partially, into any one group here," Miranda whispered.

Andrew looked at her. She'd been much less skittish since the Vancouver trip.

"Exactly, even though our family has been here for seventy years," Jenny said.

"We heard about Misty and Robin attacking you. That must have sucked," Willy said.

"WillEEyyy! Just a dash of tact! They might not want to talk about that!" Jenny was getting panicked. "We'll see you around maybe. We'd better get home," Jenny pulled Willy away from the table, knocking over chairs, leaving her hot dog untouched, and stomped away across the field in a swish of black hair and filmy black fabric as her brother pushed the end of his hotdog into his mouth following after her.

Andrew stared after them in total confusion, then looked at Miranda who was looking back at him and he could see her trying to talk and being all stopped up with emotions. She took his hand and dragged him away from the table after Jenny and Willy, running and tugging on his hand to catch up to them. When they did, and the siblings turned to look at them, Miranda shook his arm and hopped up and down looking distressed.

"You want me to say something nice to them? Like invite them to hang out or something?" Andrew whispered in her ear and she nodded emphatically.

"Okay." He turned to the siblings, "Those were shitty hot dogs. I didn't even finish mine. Want to come to my house and have nachos with us?"

That was the first day of summer vacation. The moment Olivia came home from school and met the twins —Jenny and Willy were, it turned out, fifteen year old fraternal twins—she took an instant shine to them and dragged them out to see the start they'd made on the fort. "This is pretty good!" Willy told them looking at the frame they'd gotten up. "Do you want help? My dad's a contractor. I know what I'm doing."

"That'd be great. I need somebody stronger than those two," Andrew waved at Olivia and Miranda, "to help me with the roof."

And from that point on it was like they were wild children, living on the edge of reality. They built their little universe from the ground up and ran with the wind. They spent days on the beach and woke up browner each morning. They swam in the ocean like fish and they lay in the grass of the field and waited each night for the stars. They started to forget what shoes were.

"Where are your ancestors from?" Jenny asked one night, of no one and everyone, lying in the dark staring up into the sky.

"Nobody knows who my biological parents were. I wonder sometimes," Andrew answered back, almost in a trance, staring up into the sky. "I look pretty white. They're probably some generic Europeans."

"My biological mom, Isabella, is from the Caribbean and my bio dad is from Iceland. They were teenagers and he was an exchange student in Toronto," Olivia answered.

"You're an island girl, like me and Willy," Jenny murmured.

"I'm not an island girl Jenny," Willy told his sister, and they laughed.

"What about you Miranda?" Andrew asked.

Miranda took a couple of deep breaths, "Scotland, Wales, Denmark, Czech Republic, Norway . . . but my maternal great grandmother was from Kazakhstan. She was my great grandfather's mistress. He was a diplomat and he fell in love with her and brought her to Canada with him. She had red hair and green, almond shaped eyes."

"No wonder you three look as out of place as Jenny and me. I'm really glad you guys moved here," Willy mumbled.

Willy's dad gave them all kinds of old building supplies and came to help them put arched windows from an old church into the fort. They had five different colours of old asphalt shingle and the girls made a pattern like a patchwork quilt for the roof. The hardware store gave them seven gallons of light purple outdoor paint that had been incorrectly colour matched for a customer, and that they had been unable to sell and, much to Olivia's delight, they painted the little fairytale house in the woods purple. Miranda and Jenny scrounged quirky decorations from the strangest places. Miranda hung little chandelier crystals in the windows and scavenged a Victorian Persian rug for the floor, and Jenny painted a mural of mythological creatures on the walls. Violet drove them out to Charlotte's to look for blankets and curtains and helped them find a second hand sofa bed and a day bed. They repaired and painted old furniture from the garbage dump. By mid July they were done building the fort.

"We should camp out at the fort together some night and have a barbecue to celebrate finishing it," Olivia said. On the brink of thirteen, Olivia's brain had finally learned how to modulate her voice and she wasn't so loud anymore. She sounded older.

"I can get my mom to do teriyaki salmon and maki," Jenny said.

"My nanna would help," Miranda added.

"I'll ask my dad if we can do it at our house since it's closest to the fort," Andrew told them.

Once Jenny's mom, Janet, and Miranda's Nanna had been consulted and introduced it turned into a full on family barbecue and rolled into a double birthday party for Olivia and Miranda, who were turning thirteen and sixteen the same weekend. The five of them stacked scrap wood for a bonfire and helped Andrew clean their house. The day before, Lynne drove with the three girls to Victoria for Miranda and Olivia to get their ears pierced and Jenny went along as moral support. Andrew knew Miranda wanted her ears pierced, but he also knew that she was terrified. Andrew spent the day with Willy and they played video games at Willy's house for a couple hours. Andrew thought that maybe he'd been a bit too distant from video and computer games to *really* get them, but he still liked hanging out with Willy and gaming because it made him feel like he was having a normal male childhood, and Willy was cool. For all that Willy had virtually no social filter, he was deep and perceptive too, and really well read. Andrew could say anything to him and it would be fine. He didn't freak out when Andrew had disclosed his past. That afternoon Willy asked, "What did you get Miranda for her birthday?"

Andrew smiled. It had taken him a long time to figure out what to get her but he thought she'd like it, "I got her a vintage Kay Neilsen print in an original Art Deco frame. I found it on eBay. She collects Art Nouveau pottery, particularity Danish stuff and Kay Neilsen is from Copenhagen and painted during the same time as her favourite sculptor."

"You like Miranda, don't you?" Willy killed a grunt and then jumped his character into a truck like vehicle.

"She's my best friend," Andrew replied, desperately trying to avoid a promethean and jump into the truck, "of course I like her."

"Yeah, but you . . . you know, *like* her."

"I do. I like her . . . *that way*. I like her a lot." Andrew stopped talking for a moment because his character was about to die, "But romance, and all the shit that goes with it, it just seems so adult, and I lost years of my childhood, and this, what the five of us have right now, is amazing. We're gonna grow up some day. I'm not going to rush it."

"I get that."

"What about you? What did you get the girls?"

"I got Olivia an atlas that only has islands in it, and I got Miranda the New Order Temptation single on vinyl.

Charlotte had it in her basement and I was short cash so I mowed both her lawns for it."

"Those are good gifts. I wish I'd thought of the record," Andrew admitted, in admiration.

"I wish I'd thought of the art print. I'm concerned that you and I are setting a precedent. I'm already anxious about next year," Willy told him just as their truck exploded.

Treasure from the Sea

Miranda almost touched her ears again and then lowered her hands. She kept peeking in the little hand mirror in her purse. She looked over at Olivia who had nice little gold sleepers in her ear lobes now too, and smiled and then asked Jenny, "Do earrings make us look older?"

"I think they do," Jenny nodded, looking from Miranda to Olivia. Jenny's ears were already pierced and she had reassured Miranda that it wouldn't hurt. Olivia went first and said it didn't hurt, "It just feels like a bit of pressure. Honest," Olivia had looked at her, very serious, otherwise Miranda would have lost her nerve.

"They definitely make you look older," Lynne agreed, and then moved her water glass so the waiter could begin spreading the tea things. They were having tea at the Empress hotel.

Miranda watched the waiter but thought about how it hadn't really hurt at all. She still felt a bit queasy when she thought about the fact that her earlobes were impaled, but she knew she would recover. After the actual piercings were done Lynne had taken them to Birks and treated each girl to a nice pair of simple pearl earrings. Miranda and Jenny had chosen akoya pearls and Olivia had chosen Tahitian. Miranda knew that her dad, Jim, Janet and Daniel, had chipped in for the expense of the day. Her mother was on cloud nine. Miranda knew her mother had given up on the idea of ever taking her and a group of friends out like this for her sixteenth birthday. When they'd left Birks with their pearls, Lynne had said, "I know pearls seem boring, but when I want to look like a grownup the pearls that my mom gave me when I was sixteen are always the earrings I choose."

"They're not boring Mom. They're beautiful treasures from the sea. I can't wait for my ears to heal so I can wear them," Miranda said, and then hugged her mom again.

Jenny already had her pearls in, and she tucked her hair behind her ears so her black hair was a backdrop to the white pearls and declared, "They're like little full moons glowing in the dark. I think normal teenagers might think they're boring but we're not normal."

"No, you're not normal," Lynne agreed. "You guys are extraordinary."

* * *

Miranda's dad arrived the next morning and she wasn't sure what she thought about that. He gave her a birthday gift and told her that she could open it.

"I asked Nadine what to get you because your mother told me to figure it out for myself when I asked her," he admitted in a whisper so Lynne wouldn't hear him and he smiled sheepishly. "Go on open it," he urged.

Miranda could tell it was a big book and she tore off the paper. It was an art history text book.

"Dad! This is a really good book. I was going to ask for it. I've been researching . . ." She trailed off already placing the heavy volume on the table and diving into the introduction.

"Miranda! You're talking! It's been a *long time* since I've heard your voice."

"That might be all you get, but she might keep it up all day," her mom was smiling as she came back into the kitchen from the larder where she'd been looking for the tip to the frosting bag.

"Well, I was going to tell you that she looks feral, and ask you why none of the kids have shoes on, but if she's talking let them run wild. It actually seems very idyllic here right now," her dad said to her mom.

"We were quite civilized yesterday in the city at tea, although the impaling of earlobes had a barbaric vibe. But over here on the coast there isn't any reason to keep them hemmed in and they aren't trouble makers. They build forts, and invent complicated mythological worlds," Lynne told Jeremy.

Miranda kept her nose in her book but listened with half an ear to her parents.

"Aren't they a little old for that sort of thing?" her dad questioned.

"Andrew, on his own maybe . . . although I don't think so. You played that ridiculous fantasy geek game when you were seventeen."

"It was a card game," Jeremy defended.

"Well isn't it somehow more creative and ambitious to invent your own world?"

"I suppose it is," he agreed.

"And if you saw the fort . . ." Lynne paused, concentrating on piping the icing onto the cake, "We aren't talking about sticks and a tarp by the way. It's weather clad and insulated." Lynne put down the bag of frosting and picked up another colour and started piping out flowers.

"Miranda, get your phone and show your dad some pictures."

Miranda reluctantly left the book and got her phone. She plugged it into her mom's laptop and showed her dad.

"They did this by themselves?" her dad questioned her mother in incredulity.

"We needed help to install the windows, so Willy's dad helped," Miranda told him.

"Who's idea was it?"

"Olivia's. Andrew found plans and got it going, then I started helping, and then Willy and Jenny got back from Japan and they started helping. Willy's dad is a builder so it went fast after that because Willy already knew what to do, whereas Andrew had to go on the internet and learn how to do everything first, which made things slower. Also, Willy has better tools. Do you like it?"

"It looks like a mystical giant sized cuckoo clock, like a little farm house on a unicorn ranch, or maybe a griffon breeder lives there. What are the patterns painted on the front?"

"They're traditional Ainu patterns. Jenny and Willy's grandma is Ainu from Hokkaido. We got the purple paint for free but when the fort was just purple it looked very twee, so Jenny did the front with teal and lime green details, and it looked fantastical after that, which is better than twee, I think."

"Certainly better than twee," her father agreed.

"You can see it for yourself later. I'm going to take a bath."

Miranda picked up her book and went upstairs. The bathwater was relatively clean, probably owing to their day in the city. Miranda had come home so grubby lately that her mom and nanna had told her that cleaning the tub was now her job. She didn't mind. She loved their big old fashioned bathtub almost like it was a person. It made her feel like a very fine lady indeed when she sat in it scrubbing the dirt out of her skin with soap and water. She rubbed the washcloth over her knees looking for the faint scars, appearing as she scrubbed, that were the only evidence now of the run in with the hoodies. She thought about how carefully Andrew had cleaned the cuts and how they wouldn't have healed so nicely if he hadn't taken the time. She remembered that moment, sitting in her room with her torn up knees while Andrew cleaned away the blood. Suddenly her perspective shifted and her whole body flushed with a beautiful rush that made her hands shake.

Miranda went to her closet to choose a dress, feeling unsettled. None of her favourites seemed right so she slid her clothes to the end of the rod so that she could see the place where three of her grandmother's old dresses hung. They'd been too big, but maybe now . . . She took out the one that reminded her of Harlequin and Columbine. The colourful blue, pink, and yellow diamond print and full skirt were evocative of another time. It was feminine and innocent and just fanciful enough to be interesting. Miranda pulled on a slip and lifted the dress over her head then contorted her arms around behind herself to get the zipper done up, breathing out just a little as the zipper passed over the smallest part of her waist. She looked in the mirror and smoothed her hands over the voluminous cotton skirt. She couldn't tell if she was beautiful or plain, but the dress made her feel like she'd stepped out of a fairytale, and that was good.

Thirteen

Sometimes Olivia though that being the youngest sucked and sometimes she thought it was best. Most of the time she was equivocal about it though, and felt that being the youngest was simply just what it was. The youngest. It sometimes meant that she wasn't taken seriously, and it often meant that once she was, she got her way.

"Why not a dog?" her dad asked her.

"Are you saying that I can have a dog?" she asked brightly, full of hope.

"No, I'm saying that if you're going to have any success in talking me into getting an animal, that maybe a dog would be a better place to start. Maybe if a dog works out you can wear me down on a goat in a couple years."

"So you *are* saying that I can get a dog?"

"No. I'm saying you need to *talk me into* getting a dog. If you can talk me into getting a dog, *and* you join the 4H Club, we do have a small chapter here in town," he told her, "*then* maybe in a year or two I might consider a goat."

Olivia ran off looking for Andrew who was sitting in the golden field under the oak tree with Miranda. Andrew was wearing a nice button up shirt and khaki shorts and Miranda was wearing a beautiful dress that made her look like an illustration from a story book. Olivia stopped and looked at her brother and her friend and for just a moment she felt like she was looking in on something from the outside; for just a split second, and then they looked away from each other and up at her and the boundary dissolved so that she wasn't sure it had been there in the first place.

"I think dad's gonna let me have a dog! I have to research it and convince him," she announced breathlessly.

She had expected Andrew to tell her that she didn't need to yell but nobody had told her to be quiet lately and she thought maybe she just wasn't loud anymore. She hoped it was that, and not that they'd given up on her.

"Hey! You'll break him yet. If he's caving on a dog it's just a matter of time till you make it to goats," her brother encouraged her.

"We have a big book on dog breeds at home that you can borrow," Miranda told her.

And Olivia raced away to see if Lynne could find the book for her and Andrew yelled after her, "Go home after you get the book and have a bath. Put a dress on!"

Lynne was talking to Miranda's dad when Olivia barged into the kitchen. "Olivia close your eyes!" Lynne shouted. "Jeremy, get her out of here! Take her to the living room, see what she wants, then take her out through a different door!"

Olivia closed her eyes and was gently ushered, like if she were made of glass, to the living room. She hadn't seen whatever it was that Lynne was keeping hidden but she was grinning now because it meant there was some kind of surprise and Olivia liked surprises. Olivia also kind of liked Miranda's dad. She had only met him once and he had no idea how to deal with kids which made him kind of fun to mess with.

"Do you need something Olivia?" Jeremy asked.

"Miranda said there's a dog book here," she told him.

"It's in there Jeremy. On the bookshelf," Lynne yelled from the kitchen.

Jeremy looked blankly at the bookshelf and then dashed over to it like a spindly marionette. He examined the shelf, pounced on the book, thrust it at Olivia and then very gently, and yet somehow unceremoniously, ushered her out the french doors. Olivia giggled and then went home and had a bath. Once in her room, which was as pretty as Miranda's room now, only in a pink way, she opened her closet to discover that she only owned five dresses, and they were all too small. Had it really been that long since she'd worn a dress? Had she really grown that much!? Alarmed, she ran downstairs, "Dad! Dad!" she was on the brink of tears, "All my dresses are too small and I don't have anything pretty to wear and my nice pants from yesterday aren't nice enough!"

"Whoa, hold on Pumpkin. It's not an emergency. Let's talk to Violet. Miranda doesn't wear anything *but* pretty dresses, and she's growing too. I'll bet Violet will have something up her sleeve, even if it's just a hand-me-down."

Olivia nodded and hugged her dad tight because he'd known exactly what to do. He pulled out his phone and dialed Violet's cell, "We have a party dress crisis. Olivia's outgrown her nice dresses and I'm a neglectful dad. Can you help?"

Olivia waited with baited breath, wondering what the solution was going to be.

"You're at Janet's place?" there was a pause then, "Charlotte? She knows how to get there? Okay, will do. See you in an hour." He put the phone back in his pocket and looked at Olivia, "She says, 'Go see Charlotte,' and that you can get us there?"

"Yes!" Olivia ran to the car.

Charlotte gave a good-hearted laugh when they explained why they were there. "Come with me," she said leading them to the basement. "So, what do you like? Bright colours? Pastels? Are you demure wall flower or a passion flower?" Charlotte asked.

"Oh, she's a passion flower," her dad answered without hesitating, and when she glared at him he shrugged and smiled and said, "Sorry Pumpkin," and she smiled back.

They left fifteen minutes later with an armload of brightly coloured dresses from the eighties that were all made out of things like velvet, satin, and lame.

"I think this might be the start of a new era for you," her dad said to her loading the dresses into the car.

At home Olivia pulled on a purple velvet drop-waist dress with a silver lamé skirt and ruffled cap sleeves. She took a picture in the mirror and sent it to Isabella, then she smiled and ran downstairs to help her dad put up tables on the lawn. They had the tables up and dishes out just as Violet and Janet pulled up in Janet's Volvo with Willy in the back seat. "Jenny and Dad are coming through the woods with the salad and the sushi," Willy announced. "There's too much food for them to ride in the car."

They loaded the table as Andrew and Miranda appeared from the field carrying birthday gifts and bottles of Martinelli's then Lynne and Jeremy pulled up. Lynne opened the passenger side and lifted something out of Jeremy's lap and carried it over to the table. Olivia took one look and whooped for joy.

Andrew winced, "God, you've been so quiet lately I wasn't expecting that."

"It's a GOAT CAKE!" she yelled. Lynne plugged a stereo in on the porch and music started playing and Olivia thought she was going to explode she was so happy.

After dinner, after she ate so much that she was glad she'd been too excited to eat all day, after Lynne put twenty-nine candles in the goat cake and Olivia and

Miranda blew them all out, and after they ate the goat, they opened presents. The sun was only just disappearing behind the trees and Miranda told Olivia to go first since she was younger. Olivia laughed when she opened *The Atlas of Remote Islands* from Willy, and a book on goat husbandry from Andrew. Miranda gave her an iridescent blue butterfly wing pendant from the nineteen twenties that, against all odds, looked fabulous with the purple and silver dress, and Jenny made her a small but very beautiful hand embroidered pink square to hang on her wall.

Then Olivia watched as Miranda opened her gifts. Olivia had gotten Miranda a vintage copy of *A Girl of the Limberlost*—because Olivia had basically stolen Miranda's copy—, and Jenny had made Miranda an embroidered cloth to go on top of her dresser, like a doily only way cooler. Olivia could tell that the present from Willy was a record and when Miranda opened it she had smiled deeply and held it to her chest. Olivia always thought that when Miranda was happy it seemed like she was happy with her whole body. Miranda had looked at Willy and said, "I love this song. I hope you didn't shop lift it."

And Willy said, "I mowed lawns for it," and he looked pleased.

But then Miranda had opened Andrew's gift. Olivia knew what it was. Andrew had gotten their dad to order it on the internet over a month ago. Miranda opened it and looked down at the picture of the twelve dancing princesses in boats floating down the river through the woods, with the lanterns lighting their way, either to or from the castle. Olivia watched Andrew, who looked suddenly insecure, but Miranda's face had gone all soft and dreamy as he watched her, and then his face went all soft too.

"It's a Kay Neilsen," Miranda murmured and looked up at Andrew. Olivia knew that Miranda didn't really look at people's eyes, she faked it flicked them on and off, or she looked at your mouth, but Miranda was looking at Andrew's eyes and for just another brief moment Olivia felt like she was looking in at something from the outside, till Andrew smiled and looked away and said, "It's almost dark. We should light the fire."

And the world started to move again and Olivia remembered how happy she was.

Friends II

Willy had always known that he was where he was supposed to be, but he wondered when the others would arrive. He didn't know who they would be or how they would come, but he knew they had to. Someday he had to have friends, right? Until then he had his books to keep him company and feed his imagination. And he had Jenny. But he missed the days before the Seymour farm had gone bankrupt and Scott and Terry moved away, and before the Macintosh kids had gone Dark Side. He remembered how they used to run wild in the woods pretending they were battling Storm Troopers on Endor. Of course he was eleven back then, and he'd broken all his toy light sabres, and he'd rather play *Death Stranding* now, but that didn't matter, it was the feeling behind it that mattered. The feeling that he was supposed to be connected to other people, besides the people bringing him up, and the twin sister, three minutes younger than him, who he would be connected to for the rest of his life.

Willy loved their home. It was a masterpiece, and his mother was an artist who made it beautiful in so many ways. He never appreciated it as much as he did the day they came back from Japan, walking in the door and feeling the way the forest outside was almost inside with them, and the way his mother's carvings almost seemed alive in that setting. It was almost like seeing it with new eyes. Jenny said the house had a spirit. Willy didn't know about that, but he knew it was home.

Willy had always been the co-operative twin, and when his mother told him, "Willy I know it's the last day of school and there isn't much point in going, but help me get your sister out the door. If there's even half a chance of reconnecting with some of the other kids I want you guys to take it okay."

It had been a few years since he and Jenny had really had friends, and while visiting cousins in Japan and Haida Gwaii did provide a feeling of belonging in a sense, their home was on Vancouver Island, and Willy wanted people to belong with at home.

He knew he came on strong when he saw Miranda and Andrew that last day of school, but the moment he saw them he knew. And then a week later when Andrew finished reading *It,* and came over to return Willy's book and told him, "Okay, I get it now. I forgive you for calling me a loser," Willy had felt vindicated. And Miranda liked the same music that Willy did, which Jenny thought was really weird because Miranda was otherwise, kind of timeless. Willy thought it was weird when Jenny thought people were weird, because Jenny never wore anything but black and she was kind of morbid, but by the beginning of July, even Jenny had joined in the creative frenzy.

Willy posted pictures of their finished fort on his Tumblr blog—he held a healthy disdain for Instagram and refused to use it even though he kind of knew that Tumblr had been, as his sister liked to say, neutered—and he got thousands of comments. Mostly positive, although a significant portion were just confused after six months of travel posts about Japan. But Willy felt so damned proud of the fort, even if it did look like it belonged to a griffon breeder or a unicorn farmer, and it had been so much fun to do it with friends. And then came the barbecue. Willy couldn't believe he'd eaten a goat cake and danced around a bonfire.

After the bonfire burned down and they helped their parents clean up that night, they climbed into sleeping bags in the fort, Willy and Andrew sleeping in the loft because Miranda was still too nervous to climb the ladder. Olivia and Jenny didn't want her to feel left out, so the three girls took the hide-a-bed and daybed on the main floor.

"This is *not* what I thought I'd be doing this summer," Jenny's voice drifted up in the dark from where she was curled up on the daybed. "I thought I'd just listen to Placebo alone in my room all summer long and this is refreshingly different."

"This is better than I'd hoped for, and I knew we were going to make a fort," Olivia told them.

"I think the weird thing is that we didn't even know that other kids lived in your guy's house, let alone that you guys would be totally different from the other people in this town," Andrew was propped up on his elbows looking over the edge of the loft between the bars of the railing.

"There used to be more cool people here, and the people here used to be cooler," Willy told them, "but St Fina's kinda had it rough for a bit now."

"Why is it called St Fina? I've tried to find out but I can't." Miranda's voice came out of the dark and she almost sounded like she was talking in her sleep.

It had taken Willy a while to get used to the way Miranda communicated. She often sounded a little like she was faint when she talked, like she was struggling, but other times she could talk your ear off, like if she was interested in what she was saying or what she was talking about was based on facts. Sometimes she didn't talk at all and would just hold up her phone. Then Andrew had to say to Willy, "She's holding up her phone because she's trying to say something to you."

Willy wasn't surprised Miranda would ask why St Fina was called St Fina. That was exactly the kind of question she would ask.

"Do you want to tell them or should I," Jenny asked of Willy.

"Ooh, ooh! Can I!" Willy liked telling people the local legend.

"Knock yourself out," Jenny told him in her typical dry tone.

"Oh! I heard it Andrew!" Miranda crowed, uncharacteristically loud and excited.

"Heard what?" the others echoed.

"The nuance of, 'Knock yourself out,'" Andrew told them.

"Okaaayy," Willy drawled, "But I still want to tell you why St Fina is called St Fina."

"We're listening. We won't interrupt again, *right guys*?" Olivia told Willy.

"Okay," Willy took a deep breath. "So, Saint Fina was a young girl from a town in Tuscany like, nearly a thousand years ago, who was very devout. Apparently her family were well off once but had lost their wealth. She was still very giving even though she didn't have much. She became ill with a wasting disease and instead of lying on a bed she lay on a plank and never complained and never lost faith. They say her flesh fused to the wood eventually and that vermin nibbled on her. She had a vision of some other saint that predicted her death . . ."

"St Gregory the Great," Jenny interjected.

"Yeah, that guy," Willy continued, "Anyway, the thing is, that after she died and they took her off her plank, white violets started blooming out of it.

"So, the local legend goes," Willy paused for effect, "that early on in the colonization of Vancouver island there was a priest, a missionary, and he had a falling out with his faith and had begun to doubt that what they were doing was right, so he left and wandered out into the forest alone in protest. He came here and lived on the hill top like some crazy old hermit away from society, and when settlers eventually came they found his body on the hill. They made camp the first night they were here and there was a terrible storm and when they woke he was gone, but the hill top was covered in white violets. There were a few Italians in the group I guess, and they related it to the story of St Fina, and that's why they call this weird town St Fina."

A silence ensued.

"That's a . . . weird story," Olivia was the first to respond.

"I know right? And you want to know another weird thing?" Jenny asked.

"What?" Andrew asked, and Willy could hear the curiosity in his voice.

"There has never been a church that has stayed standing, or a residential school, here in St Fina. I don't mean to imply that colonization hasn't done its damage here, but not that kind of damage."

"Where did our windows come from then?" Miranda asked.

"An old chapel over in the Cowichan valley," Willy told her.

"Where did the Italians go?" Olivia asked.

"Oh, I think the island became a British colony just after that and they got sort of bred out or something," Willy said.

"So . . . It's a local *legend* right? I mean . . . That's a pretty strange story," Andrew mused.

"Yeah, very," Jenny agreed. "But white violets really do grow on the hillside in the spring."

*

The next morning they ate waffles at Miranda's house, then went to the beach and ended up watching movies at Willy and Jenny's house after that.

It was a funny thing, having three other kids in their house, because even though Willy's parents had wanted him and his sister to make friends, it was obviously a bit of an adjustment for there to actually be other kids in the house. Willy had to laugh at his mum who still seemed surprised when they came trooping in, tired from the beach, to play video games or watch Netflix, and even though it made him happy, every so often he had to pinch himself.

The Gentle Hands
of August

At the end of July the weather cooled just a little and there was a soft cloudy week that lead them into August. After the birthday party and the camp-out at the fort, the five of them had met up most days. Often not really doing anything together, just sitting in the same place together reading their own books or silently working on their own projects. Somebody would comment on what they were doing and a conversation would ensue. Deep, long, honest—and often hilarious—conversations that wouldn't have been quite the same without Jenny and Willy there, then they would drift back to their parallel activities. Andrew could tell that Olivia had made some kind of developmental leap over the last month, because she just seemed older. She'd grown too, but her conversational contributions were thoughtful and considered in a way that was new.

Since the party, things had been subtly different with Miranda as well. She had opened up and her sweet, dreamy, trusting, nature came to the surface more and more, making it harder and harder for Andrew to brush aside his feelings. It made him sad, nervous, and excited at the same time. He would look down and realize, only after he'd done it, that he'd taken her hand and that she was holding his in return. They often wandered the field like that, waiting for the others after dinner in the evening, just the two of them, watching the sun set, standing in the middle of what looked for all the world like a storybook universe. The golden field, the green oak tree, and the lavender sky, between the two houses at the edge of the world.

Miranda got violently sea sick, so when Willy's dad had offered to take them all out on his boat for the day Miranda had to stay home. Andrew told her, "I'll stay back with you so you aren't left out."

She had protested and told him that he should go, but he told her that he'd rather spend the day with her than on a boat. Olivia and Violet had gone on the boat trip and Lynne and Jim were at work.

Andrew and Miranda sat on the sofa in the fort reading quietly as a soft rain shower began to fall outside and the petrichor drifted in the open door. Andrew put his book down and looked out the door into the rain, breathing in the fresh cool air, then took his flip phone out of his pocket, as was his habit, just to check that he had it. Miranda was watching him, she had set her book aside as well. "That phone means something to you doesn't it? It's more than just a phone," she whispered.

Andrew opened the menu, pressed play on the saved message, and passed it to Miranda so she could hear it. Andrew knew it by heart. It went, "Hi my beautiful boy. I'll be home late tonight but I'm bringing pizza and we can watch a movie. Make sure Olivia does her homework when she gets home for me, and I forgot to start the dishwasher, can you turn it on so we have clean plates to eat off of? Dad says he'll be home just after six. See you tonight. Love you!"

Andrew watched Miranda listen to the message. She went still and tears rolled down her cheeks when she realized what it was. She passed the phone back and tried to talk. But she choked on her voice so she took Andrew's hand and pressed the back of it against her wet cheek.

"What happened to you to make it so hard for you to talk?" he asked her, not entirely meaning the words to come out.

Miranda looked at him, stricken, and she tried to talk again and then she hung her head as more tears fell into her lap.

"You said it was something like what Misty and Robin did, only worse."

Miranda nodded and then gasped in deep breaths that were panicked and shaky.

"It's okay, it's okay you don't have to tell. I shouldn't have asked," Andrew told her taking her shoulders in his hands to try to comfort her and feeling like an asshole for asking, because she was talking so much these days, and he should have left it alone.

But she shook her head and whispered, barely audibly, "But I want to, I want to tell you."

"Okay," Andrew nodded, very worried, getting scared by how hard Miranda was shaking, "What do you need?"

"Don't look at me."

"Okay," he told her, and took her hand, pressed it against his cheek, and looked away from her.

There was a long silence before she started to talk and when she did the sound of her voice made him feel like his heart would break. "They tricked me . . . I thought . . . I thought . . . I thought . . . they were being . . . nice to me . . ."

It wasn't even a voice that came out of her mouth, just a raw painful noise that could somehow convey meaning, and Andrew wasn't sure he could take it, but he was the one who had asked the question and, what was he going to do? Leave her? He couldn't take the question back, so all he could do was ride the wave with her and hope they were okay at the end.

"The girls, they wanted . . . to . . . to . . . show me something. I went . . . into the bathroom and the boys were there and . . . they held the door closed . . . and . . . they . . . laughed . . . at me . . . and . . . held . . . me . . . down . . ."

Andrew was scared of what she was going to say next, scared of what might have happened to her because being tricked and held down were bad enough but as much as he didn't want to hear the rest he wasn't going to stop Miranda telling him now, because he wanted to kill the kids who had hurt her and he wanted their names.

"One . . . One of the boys . . . he . . . he . . ." Miranda was shaking so hard her teeth were chattering, "He . . . he . . . opened his pants. He was going to . . . he was going to . . . he was going to . . ."

Miranda got stuck and she started to sob strangled sobs.

"He was going to what, Miranda?" Andrew didn't want to say it but he could tell Miranda had gone as far as she could and it was up to him now so he asked her, feeling truly horrified and quite sick to his stomach, "Was he going to . . . rape you?"

She shook her head so her hair swung and said, "No no no no . . . not that."

And Andrew realized, there were only a couple of things a guy would take his junk out in front of other guys for, and disgusted and enraged on Miranda's behalf he asked her, having trouble saying the words himself, "Was he going to . . . urinate . . . on . . . you?"

And he knew from her reaction that he was right. Miranda curled into a foetal position on the couch beside him and cried like something was being ripped out of her and she said, "Why, Andrew. Why . . .?" and cried and cried.

Andrew was so angry that *he* could barely talk, and he couldn't believe she had been holding this inside of her for a year. It was unimaginable to Andrew, doing that to another person, let alone to Miranda. He took her hand again and sat with her like he had the day they'd met and waited for the storm to end.

Eventually she whispered, "A teacher walked in, Mr Jonson, and the boy didn't really get me. Just my ankles mostly. The kids ran away, and Mr Jonson never did anything about what he saw. He just left." She was silent for a moment and then she asked, "Andrew? How is it that somebody wanted to do that to me? How is it that five different people wanted that to happen to me, and how is it that somebody caught them in the act and did nothing? I want to know! They shouldn't have done that to me!" She cried again but the sound of her cries had changed, and he could tell that the distress she felt was closer to grief over what had happened to her, rather than the shame and confusion that had kept her silent for the last year.

"Do you want me to take you home, and do you want me to tell Lynne?" Andrew asked stroking her hair once she was silent again.

"Yeah, I want to go home. And I can't tell my mom myself. I can't handle the way she'll look at me. *Will* you tell her for me?"

"Yeah. I can tell her. Can you tell me the names of the kids who hurt you before we go and I'll write them down?" he wasn't murderously angry anymore, but he was willing to bet that Lynne would be, and he still wanted those names.

"Eli Wright, Justin Cooper, Colin Montgomery, Jamie Cooper, and Chastity Anderson."

"And the teacher was Jonson?"

Miranda nodded weakly.

"Which one opened his pants?"

She pointed to the name Justin Cooper.

"Okay. Here we go." Andrew folded the piece of paper and put it in his pocket and then lifted Miranda up and carried her down to the path and up to the scrappy little Hyundai that he technically wasn't supposed to drive yet because it wasn't insured, it was his birthday present, and his birthday wasn't till October. He gently put Miranda in the passenger seat and drove the short distance to her house. He let himself in with his key and carried Miranda up to her room and sat her down on the foot of her bed. Andrew looked her over as she sat there limp and almost catatonic. Her feet were dirty and her face was smudged and he hated to let her lie down in her clean bed like that, so he went to the bathroom and found the clean face cloths and looked under the sink for a basin and found one. He went back to her and wiped her face and hands with a warm cloth and then washed and dried her feet. He pulled down her bedding and tucked her into bed like he had Olivia when she was little and their parents were out on a date, but this was different.

"I'll be back in a few minutes," he told her stroking her forehead. And then went downstairs to the kitchen. He turned on the kettle and dialled Lynne. "Lynne?"

"Andrew? What is it . . .?" he could hear that Lynne was distracted by whatever she was focusing on at work.

"You need to come home. It's Miranda."

"What happened?"

"Can you just come?"

"I'm coming. Be there in five."

The kettle boiled and Andrew scooped tea into the pot on the counter and filled it to steep while he called his dad. He got the same distracted, "Andrew, what is it . . .?"

"I need you to come, something happened and I don't know if Miranda's okay, but I kinda need you too."

"Is this an emergency?"

"Um, yeah," Andrew started to cry, "I think this is an emergency." It was the first time Andrew had thought, even if fleetingly, of needing a fix in a long time.

Toast and Tea

Andrew made himself a piece of toast and poured some tea because he'd realized he was hungry but he still felt sick from what Miranda had told him. He sat at the Hopkins kitchen table and waited for his dad and for Lynne to come home. Lynne arrived first, bursting in the door and looking around a little wild eyed, "What is it Andrew? What happened?"

Andrew felt like he was listening to himself from outside as he said to Lynne, "Miranda told me what happened in Kamloops." He pushed the piece of paper across the table to Lynne. "These kids held her down on the bathroom floor at school and this kid pissed on her," he stabbed the name on the paper with his finger. "This teacher caught them in the act, and the kids ran, but he didn't do anything about it. Just walked away."

Lynne did nothing at first, just asked, "Where's Miranda?"

"Upstairs in bed," Andrew told her.

Lynne nodded and then started to shake. She leapt from the table and went outside and started to beat the crap out of her car with her bare hands and that was what she was doing when his dad showed up. He listened to Lynne scream and cry as she explained to his dad what had happened and continued kicking her car. Soon the sound of her boot hitting the door panel slowed down and Andrew's dad came into the kitchen.

"Dad!" Andrew was up and realizing that he hadn't outgrown hugs before he'd even decided he needed one.

"Andrew? Are you okay?" Jim pushed Andrew's over-long hair off his face and looked at him closely.

"I'm really upset . . . and angry. I don't know if Miranda's okay but if I go up right now I'll start crying again if I look at her. I think she might be in shock." He wiped his nose with the back of his hand and wiped his cheeks again.

Jim sat down at the table, "I'll go check on her in a minute, I just want to make sure you're alright first."

"I think I am. I just don't understand why people . . . ? And I feel hurt for her. Don't people realize how much damage they can do? Don't they realize?" Andrew felt, for just a moment, like he had that day when he'd seen bleach being poured into Olivia's apple juice. But he wasn't on drugs this time, so he processed the feeling, knowing he'd done the right thing by telling Lynne. That tiny desire for a fix dissolved, and he felt suddenly drained instead, but also like he wanted to wake up and see the sun tomorrow, and he remembered that he wanted to take some toast and tea up to Miranda.

He looked at his dad and Jim told him, "Some people are cruel, and I've never been able to fathom that cruelty either. It doesn't get easier as you get older, to comprehend cruelty, but as adults we can sometimes avoid it more easily, and see how cruelty begets cruelty, and forgive the ones who learned it because someone else was cruel to them. But Miranda is going to be vulnerable her whole life, and that is unsettling, because she'd never hurt a fly."

Andrew nodded, "I'm going to make her a cup of tea and some toast. I told her I'd be back in a few minutes and it's been like twenty."

"I'll go make sure she's physiologically sound," Andrew's dad smiled sadly and went upstairs.

Andrew was up a couple of minutes later and Miranda was propped up on her pillows and looking very wan.

"She's alright," Jim told him as Andrew came in with the tea and toast. "She needs a rest, some quiet, and some gentle company, I think. Maybe read to her. I'm going downstairs to talk to Lynne."

Andrew let out a sigh and nodded, "I can read to her," he said navigating around his dad and putting the plate and mug down by Miranda's bedside.

She accepted the tea and ate the toast while Andrew read to her from *Little Women* for an hour. He paused at a chapter break and glanced up at Miranda who was looking at him from where she rested and she asked him, her voice scratchy from crying, "How is it that you're real? Where did you come from? How do you exist? How is it that you are so kind?" and she almost smiled, he could see the shadow of it resting on her face like moonlight as a single tear ran down her cheek.

Andrew put the book down and moved his chair closer to her bedside, and words started coming out of his mouth as he took her hand, "Being friends with you has always been based around an honesty, and an openness, that I haven't experienced with anyone else. I love you . . . I'm *In* love with you, and I *want* to be. I want to stay a kid a bit longer though, *with you.*"

She did smile then, the kind of soft happy smile she smiled sometimes, that seemed so unadulterated, "I *do* love you too. Very much," she told him, returning the hold on his hand with her own. "Shall we be sweethearts then, and hold each other's hand and kiss each other's cheek, until we want more?"

"I would like that, very much," Andrew smiled, remembering the day he'd met her and how it should have been a horrible day but somehow wasn't. "How are you feeling?" he asked her.

"I feel like there was a parasite attached to my heart that was slowly eating me alive, and now we've ripped it out, and it's *gone*, and I'm *glad*. It really hurts where it was attached though, and it's still bleeding, but when you say you love me, the blood slows a little."

Miranda fell asleep after another chapter of *Little Women* and Andrew went downstairs. It was nearly five o'clock and the day seemed to have passed so quickly. His dad was scrambling eggs and frying sausages and

Lynne was sitting at the table looking haggard and closer to forty-three than normal. She looked up at Andrew, "Can you tell me everything again? I'm leaving for Kamloops in an hour." Andrew repeated everything to Lynne, one more time, and then went back upstairs and watched Miranda sleep.

Rescuing Susan

For a while Jenny wasn't sure she liked boys. And then she'd gotten home from Japan, and she was *sure* she didn't like boys. When she and Willy came home, St Fina was full of gossip about the two new families who had come and bought the old McGinty houses that had stood empty for twenty years. The estate had paid her father to maintain the houses, to keep them from becoming derelict, and she'd grown up wandering the empty halls as he repaired the odd leak and repainted them every five years, and then just before they'd left for Japan, against all odds, one of the houses had sold, and when they got back the other had too. Jenny was burning with curiosity to see exactly what kind of crazy it took to buy hundred year old character houses in a ghost town like St Fina.

Jenny lived in St Fina because that's where her grandparents had landed. The Haida branch were loggers and her Japanese great grandfather had hidden out on the coast to avoid the internment camps and had worked with her Haida grandfather. Her Ainu grandmother had

188

come to Canada to escape marginalization in Japan and had heard that the west coast of Canada was friendly to Asian people, and then she'd married a Japanese Canadian man. Jenny saw the irony there. And then her parents had fallen in love and that was that. Jenny found life a bit surreal sometimes. She was glad to be home. She loved their house. It was a magnificent house. Most people didn't know that it was a real Frank Lloyd-Wright. Old McGinty had it commissioned back in St Fina's heyday, and then he'd been forced to start slowly selling off his empire. Jenny did get a kick out of the fact that they were living the good life in the old colonialist's dream home. She knew it was just bricks and wood, but Jenny believed the house had a spirit, and it was a spirit that loved her.

There were things she didn't like about St Fina, and the social isolation really was the biggest one, but she knew she wouldn't fit in anywhere, so alone in St Fina she was. Most of the time she could be equivocal about it, and she always had Willy.

She had fought her mother about going to school for that one day, "It's the last day? What, even, would be the point in going Mum? It's one half-day and a crappy hotdog!"

"I'll pay you twenty dollars if you'll look at the new kids and tell me what they're like,"

"Mother!"

"Oh for crying out loud Jennifer! Just go. Then you can spend the rest of the summer alone."

And so it was that Jenny found herself sitting at the table with her stupid hotdog, listening to stupid girls talk about stupid boys.

"I still think *that,* is super creepy," the stupid girl beside her said to some other stupid girl.

Jenny looked up and saw the two new kids standing in the lineup.

"He's, like, the hottest guy here, and he hangs out with the retard. There's something hinky about that."

"I still think he needs a haircut," stupid girl number two said.

Jenny watched the new kids. The boy was tallish with decent shoulders, golden hair and hazel eyes, and while she had to admit that his angelic countenance was a compelling counterpoint to his bad-boy aesthetic, it was the girl she was enjoying looking at. The girl didn't look like anyone else she'd seen really, ever. Except, she looked how Jenny imagined the heroine in a classic white people novel might look. It was the dress and the hair she realized. Most women with that hair colour started highlighting it the moment it started fading from child-hood blond into something different. This was virgin hair. They were probably invisible on their own, Jenny thought. She certainly hadn't paid much attention back in the fall when the girl had started school there, before they'd left for Japan. Other than to think it weird that they'd asked the whole school to respect that a student with 'communication difficulties' would be joining them, and to be patient if she didn't respond verbally. What, even, did *that* mean? But together the new kids looked pretty weird. Not that Jenny should talk. They looked as unimpressed with the hotdogs as she was, and just as she thought she might actually say something to them Willy shouted, "Hey losers!"

Jenny was mortified, but an hour later, stuffed with nachos, having been introduced to Andrew's little sister, and fully informed on just 'what kind of crazy' it was, that moved to a ghost town like St Fina, she'd decided that at least she'd had an interesting afternoon and would have something to tell her mother at dinner. Of course there were other things she thought once she was alone in her own room listening to music; like, did anybody else think it was ironic that a girl called 'Miranda' barely talked, or did Jenny just watch too much American TV? And if Jenny *didn't* think Andrew was hot, but loved looking at Olivia and Miranda, she was sure she was a lesbian. Jenny wasn't sure just how weird she thought the other kids were, but she and Willy had nothing to lose in befriending them, so she would try.

The moment of truth was the first time Jenny and Willy had them over to their house and Miranda had sighed and said, "Your house has a spirit too," and somehow the kids from the other houses had walked right into Jenny's own personal mythology.

"Yeah," Jenny had agreed, slightly gobsmacked.

And then Miranda had whispered, "This house loves you."

Late one night, lying under the stars, they had connected the dots between ravens and magical bears, of
lost boys and pirates, spiders and dragons, and mer-
maids and killer whales. They were connected by their
disconnectedness. Their ancestry wrapped the planet in
ribbons and saw the stars from every continent. They
had so little in common that they had *everything* in
common. They built something together that the kids at
school would sneer at them for, and it was so beautiful.

She hadn't expected the invitation to tea for Olivia
and Miranda's birthdays, and she'd come home feeling
incredibly close to the other two girls, and like she had
friends. She'd looked in the mirror in her bedroom that
night, loving the white pearls and the stark contrast to
her black hair and all black wardrobe. Unlike Andrew,
who she had discovered never wore black unless he was
at school—Jenny had gotten a good hard laugh out of
that, although she was still trying to articulate *why* she
thought it was funny—, Jenny wore black all the time,
and the glowing white pearls felt just a little magical.
Like everything did that summer. Like building the fort,
which Jenny had thought was silly until she got caught
up in the enthusiasm. And then they'd actually created
something impressive. A place in the world. A place with
a spirit.

* * *

Jenny knew that Miranda had a secret. Something that
sat inside her and hurt. Something that needed to

get out. Miranda's silence was like Jenny's sarcasm. Not that Miranda was always silent. As the weeks of summer passed she had become more and more talkative. Jenny was sitting in Miranda's bedroom looking around while they talked about art and history and traditions one afternoon, while the boys were playing video games, and Olivia was learning to knit with Violet. Jenny had been tempted by learning to knit. She quite liked textiles, but she also had really great intellectual conversations with Miranda when she could get her revved up, and in her own room, at her own house, where she felt safe, was the best place to do it. Jenny had noticed that the picture Andrew had got Miranda for her birthday held pride of place over her headboard and she commented on how perfect it was there. How it looked like it had always been there.

"Andrew knew it would be happy there," Miranda beamed and then pointed to where she had placed the embroidery that Jenny had done for her. It was an adaption of the traditional artwork from Jenny's own heritage, but she had done it with the colours and fairy-tale, ladylike, atmosphere of Miranda's bedroom in mind. Jenny looked to where Miranda pointed, at the very delicate French looking antique dressing table Miranda had placed the cloth on and arranged her treasures around, and Jenny couldn't help letting her eyes linger on the figurine that sat on the left hand side of the table, gently illuminated by a vintage lamp. It was of a beautiful, nude, very young woman, probably the same age as Jenny and

Miranda themselves, reclining in the lap of a fully, but fantastically, dressed young man who leaned over her, about to kiss her. "Is the figurine something special?" Jenny tried to ask as if her pulse didn't race and her skin didn't tingle every time she looked at it. The girl was so very beautiful.

"It's called Fairytale. It's the third in a series and the original design was done by a Danish sculptor called Gerhard Henning. He was particularly known for, and is celebrated for, his interpretation of the female form. But his Fairytale series is my favourite. This one is about to become an antique and celebrate its one hundredth birthday."

"What do you like about it?"

Miranda gazed at it softly for a moment and drew in a breath, "From an aesthetic perspective it's very beautiful and the girl's flesh almost seems real. The colours are lovely and gentle, and the figures are very finely worked. But it's the mood of the piece. She's so languorous and so trusting. The way the boy looks at her as if she were both the only, and the most precious, thing in the world are there in his expression. Right in the clay. When I first saw it two years ago it . . . awoke *things* in me. A desire, I suppose, that someday someone might hold me like that and see me as beautiful. It's profoundly innocent and starkly erotic at the same time. I love the contradiction of it. Dichotomy might be the word. I love when two seemingly opposing ideas exist in the same place. Do you like it?" she asked Jenny.

"When I'm in your room I can't take my eyes off it. I almost feel embarrassed for looking at it and then I remember that you look at it everyday and I feel silly for feeling embarrassed. I suppose we shouldn't feel embarrassed about finding something beautiful."

"There is so much in life to have difficult feelings about. We shouldn't feel embarrassed when we find beauty," Miranda agreed. "Do you want to see the other two in the series? They're just a bit more strange and erotic. Not quite as tender as number three. It's my favourite. I'll put one and two out where people can see them when I'm an adult, but for now I keep them here."

Miranda opened the door to a built in cupboard and the figurines sat together on the shelf in such a way that if Miranda were alone she could leave the door open and have them on display. Jenny agreed that number three was the most tender, but one and two were magnificent as well, and sent a queer shiver of arousal up her spine.

"My godmother found this one at a thrift store in Stockholm for a few dollars and she brought it home for me. Its retail value is in the thousands," Miranda indicated the figurine with the couple in elaborate dress. The boy was an androgynous elf-like creature, and the girl was almost entirely clothed in elaborate dress. 'Almost', being the key word.

"Do you like girls?" Jenny found herself asking as she gazed at the figurines.

"You mean sexually?" Jenny liked the way Miranda didn't shy away from clarifying questions, in order to give the best answer, no matter how awkward. "I guess I do," Jenny admitted, feeling silly again, because she already knew Miranda wouldn't take issue with the question or mind being asked.

"I'm autistic," Miranda responded. "There are heterosexual autistic people out there, but it's not so black and white for us. Gender is less important than other things for me. I find most forms of beauty arousing. But gender is secondary to the qualities that a person possesses. I don't have a label."

"I wouldn't have assumed you were autistic," Jenny said, suddenly more interested in that than in whether Miranda liked girls.

"Autistic girls are different. We don't tend to be such anoraks. But mean kids can still see us like we're glowing."

"Mean kids?" Jenny had questioned, and it was three days until she heard Miranda's voice again.

* * *

M iranda hadn't come on the boat trip and her grandmother explained that she would just huddle in a corner puking, so not to feel bad that she wasn't there, and Jenny had noticed that Andrew tended to stay pretty close to Miranda, so she wasn't surprised when he stayed back to keep her company. Jenny loved going out on the boat, being in the salt air, and seeing the wide horizons. It was a funny thing, being on the Pacific ocean. It was so wide and yet it was all that was separating the islands of her ancestors. When she touched the water she was touching water that was touching the whole world. She'd spent the day talking about sewing and dogs with Olivia and Willy, and coming up with an imaginary mystical purpose for their trip that day. "Like the Voyage of the Dawn Treader," Olivia had said.

"Yeah," Willy agreed, having been a fan of the Narnia chronicles too.

"I loved those books until I read the last one and they left Susan behind. It felt like a betrayal," Jenny told them.

"Maybe we're on a mission to rescue Susan?" Olivia suggested.

"Rescuing Susan. It sounds like a book title," Willy told Olivia.

"I was always upset that she didn't marry Caspian," Jenny admitted. "I liked the idea of the characters finding love, and the ending of the series was so . . . neutered."

"Then let's rescue Susan and bring her to our world, give her something better," Olivia said.

* * *

Mid-morning, the day after the boat trip, Andrew and Olivia showed up on Jenny and Willy's doorstep. "Where's Miranda?" Jenny asked as she let them in and they went to the family room where Willy was playing video games. Andrew looked exhausted and listless and Olivia looked confused. Miranda's absence felt palpable, as if there were a Miranda shaped emptiness sitting with them, taking up space.

Andrew looked at his feet then out the window and the four of them said nothing but eventually he sighed, "Do you guys know much about selective mutism or traumatic mutism?"

Willy asked, "Is that what Miranda has?"

"I thought she was autistic," Jenny said.

Andrew was quiet a bit longer before he told them, "She's both. She was diagnosed autistic last year. Lynne said that she never really talked much at school, that she was always a bit selectively mute, but last year something happened and she stopped talking altogether. Then they moved here and she gradually started talking again. Yesterday while you guys were out on the boat Miranda told me what happened to make her stop talking."

"Did it have something to do with 'Mean Kids'?" Jenny asked, "She told me, last week, that 'Mean Kids' could see her like she was glowing. Then she went really quiet for a couple days."

Andrew nodded and rubbed his face. Jenny could see him fighting back tears and for the first time she realized that Andrew was pretty fragile, not unlike Miranda.

"They ... didn't ... ?" Willy swallowed and looked pale.

Willy didn't need to say it. Jenny knew what he meant. Thankfully Andrew did too and shook his head and said, "No. Not that, but what they did wasn't that much better. They terrified her and demeaned her and made her feel helpless and worthless. They stole her voice and made her question her value as a human being. I'm not gonna say what they did, because it won't help anything. And saying it . . . ? I can't say it again. But I need your guys' help. We need . . ." Andrew wiped his eyes and Jenny looked around at the serious faces, "We need to get her back. To do something to get back what they took. I can love her, and read to her, and sit by her bed all day long, but I don't think it's enough. I don't know what to do."

Jenny thought deep and hard, with all kinds of thoughts stirring around inside her and then Olivia said, "Jenny! Jenny!" grabbing at Jenny's sleeve and shaking rather hard. "You know exactly what to do. Remember yesterday? You know exactly!"

With a certainty that swept over her like a Pacific wave Jenny realized Olivia was right, "We can save Miranda the same way we saved Susan! Willy go start building a wood pile on the beach! Andrew, do you know their names, the 'Mean Kids'?"

Andrew passed her the piece of paper.

"There's five of them?"

"Yeah," Andrew answered, slightly bewildered.

"That's perfect. Come on Olivia, I've got some black velvet we can use . . ." Jenny said leading Olivia away to the craft room. "Go sit with Miranda. Get her to the beach at sunset . . . However you can," Jenny called over her shoulder to Andrew.

The Magic Spell

A ndrew sat next to Miranda's bed and watched the sun move across the sky and Miranda lay there like a sleeping princess. She hadn't gotten out of bed that morning and she felt like she had been placed in stasis and she didn't know how to start moving again.

Willy collected all the wood he could find and built a pyre on the beach, filling the gaps with dry grass and twigs, thinking all the while that he wanted something to burn. Something to cauterize the wound.

Jenny and Olivia sewed. They stitched with intensity and intent, putting every ounce of desire they had into what they made with their hands.

The sun crept towards the horizon. Jenny put on an ankle length black linen dress and pulled a black corset on over top and cinched the laces. She threw a black fringed lace shawl over her shoulders, put in her pearl earrings, picked up her basket, and walked out the door to the beach path feeling the naked earth under her bare feet. Olivia waited on the beach path, in crimson crushed velvet, standing next to Willy. The three of them walked single file and silent down to the beach and sat waiting by the firewood.

Andrew looked out at the sky and looked at his watch. "I want to take you to the beach Miranda? Will you let me help you?"

Somebody had said something similar to her once, and it had been okay after that, so Miranda nodded and said, "Help me Andrew."

Andrew looked in her wardrobe and pulled out a long loose, floaty, pale pink dress. Miranda sat up and let him pull it on over her night gown and take her by the hand and lead her down the stairs.

"We're meeting the others on the beach to watch the sunset," Andrew told Violet, as they passed through the kitchen.

"You got her up!" Violet exclaimed.

Andrew nodded, not wanting to jinx it by saying yes.

"I'll throw on a bread pudding. Tell the other three they can come back here after, for a late night desert and some hot milk," Violet told him, and they headed out the back door and down the beach path.

The sun was resting on the sea like a flaming beach ball when Olivia saw Andrew leading Miranda through the tall grass, in the golden setting-sunlight, down the path towards them. She realized that somehow Miranda had become a part of her brother and the feeling she'd had of late, that maybe she was losing her brother, turned on its head and she realized she was gaining Miranda.

Willy watched Miranda's face as she followed Andrew down the path and he realized that she was there because Andrew had asked, and that she might not have come if somebody else had asked, and he was glad she had come.

Jenny stood and looked at Miranda. They were like two sides of the same coin as Miranda stood there in the pale pink dress. Like morning and night fall. But Miranda was asleep and Jenny was awake. Miranda was almost a ghost and Jenny was flesh and blood. Andrew was right, they needed to bring her back.

The sun was sinking below the waterline so Jenny looked at Willy, "Start lighting the fire?" Jenny knew the fire would light, because Willy had built it.

"Stand up guys. Make a circle," she told them and they did what she asked and she looked around at them and they looked back at her. Jenny took a deep breath, "I'm not going to be sarcastic about this because I use it to keep people at a distance and that would break the spell. I'm going to tell you a story, and the story is true and everything that happens tonight will be a part of that story so it will be true." Jenny looked at Miranda, at her eyes, and she didn't look away like she usually did when Miranda made too much eye contact, but instead started to tell the story.

"Once there was a mermaid who had lost her voice, but she didn't give it up, it was stolen, and once there was a 'lost boy' who was really a sleeping prince. He never dreamed but walked around all day like he was awake, and one day the speechless mermaid woke the sleeping prince. Once there was a girl who was from an island in the north, and an island in the south, and she had the power to turn the world around her from black and white, into a place filled with beautiful colours. When the prince saw the beautiful colours he had the magic to give the mermaid back her voice. Once there were two children from both sides of the sea. Twins. A boy who had the power to bind people together, and a girl who saw stories, and the boy saw the mermaid, the prince, and the island girl, and he bound them to himself and his sister, and his sister saw their stories."

The light was slipping away and the fire was getting brighter. Jenny picked up her basket and passed around the five bundles and the others looked down at the palm sized black velvet pouches, each embroidered with a brightly coloured bear and neatly blanket stitched closed in matching embroidery silk.

"But there was a story that the girl twin didn't know," Jenny continued, "a story about five cruel children who had stolen the mermaid's voice, and with it, five tiny pieces of her heart, and while her voice had been re-stored, her damaged heart stayed hidden, until one day the twins and the island girl went on a long voyage at sea and discovered a spell, and the mermaid used her voice to tell the lost boy prince about the five cruel children." Jenny looked down at the pouch in her hand and then up at the others, their serious faces lit up in the firelight.

"Every story is full of hardship and peril but we find friendship and love along the way, and it's only in the darkness, that we truly know what light is. There were five of them, and there are five of us, but the five of us are stronger. Each of these pouches has a name stitched in it, and we'll burn their names and use our combined will to send them up into the night sky so our spirit ravens can chase the five cruel children to the island of the Bear King's palace, in the centre of the sea, and he will see if the cruel children's hearts are truly black, and take back the pieces of the mermaid's heart." Jenny looked up at them and told Miranda, "In just a minute we'll place our pouches on the fire and while they burn you'll have chance to tell the other five anything it is you have to say to them. We'll give you a minute to think and when you're ready tell us, and we'll place our pouches in the fire together."

Miranda listened to the story, and dreamed it as Jenny's words sailed up into the night and out into the world. She looked around at her friends, at their faces, and in turn into each friend's eyes, and she told them, "We are here because of love. I love you. I want you guys in my story for the rest of my life."

She squeezed the pouch in her hand and looked down at it again and nodded to the others, "I'm ready." She thought about the beautiful pouch in her hand burning up, and she wanted the ravens to chase the five who had hurt her across the night sky, but Miranda was not a cruel person, and while she wanted them to face the

Bear King and truly feel fear, she couldn't truly wish them harm.

They placed the pouches in the fire and they burned with the scent of incense and evergreens and as they burned Miranda looked into the fire and said, "You tricked me. You held me down. You urinated on me. I'm reminding you because I don't want you to forget what you did. But I know things about love that you will never know, and you will *never* have what I have, and what you did to me will weigh on your hearts for the rest of your lives if you don't change." And as her words flew up into the night sky there was a sound of many wings overhead and she looked up into the darkness and laughed in amazement.

* * *

The fire had nearly burned down and they'd sat silently on the beach watching it when Jenny said, "Can I tell you guys something?"

"Of course," Olivia responded. "You can tell us anything."

"Yeah, anything," the others chorused.

"I like girls. I'm gay. I don't want other people to know yet, but I want you guys to know."

"I won't tell anyone. And I think it's good to know who you want to love. It's important to understand yourself," Miranda told her, and again there was a chorus of agreement.

"I feel better with you guys knowing," Jenny smiled.

"Okay then. If we're sharing. You guys know I used to do a lot of drugs, and I've been scared for the last two years that if life got hard again I'd run back to meth. I also did things when I was high like beating the crap out of the ex-stepmother, and I worried that it was *me* doing those things, and not the drugs. These past two days brought some of that stuff back, but I didn't run off to get high, and I kept it together enough to do the right thing and get help. I felt incredibly angry on Miranda's behalf, but I could process it. The things that I did when I was high were the drugs, not me."

"I could have told you that," Olivia leaned against him and put her arm around his shoulders.

Miranda took his hand and smiled at him, "But some things you have to discover for yourself, don't you?"

Andrew nodded looking into her eyes.

"Okay my turn," Olivia said. "I want to try to get my dad to buy the field across the street and I want to turn our property back into a working farm. I want to be a farmer. I know I'm thirteen and I don't always get taken seriously about things, but I want to tell dad. What do you guys think."

"I think you should tell him," Andrew told her.

"I think it would be a good idea to buy the field across the street even if you don't farm it because one day St Fina is going to come back to life, and it would be awful if someone built a hotel there," Willy told her, and then said, "Well . . . I guess it's my turn," he smiled. "I don't think I'm a complicated guy, but I still get really tired of feeling like I don't fit in, and I make myself stick out even more to compensate. You guys make me feel like I don't have to compensate. You take me as I am. So thanks, I love you guys too."

"When we moved to St Fina I had just been diagnosed with autism. It was just after I got attacked in the bathroom. I came here thinking that I would learn to be happy alone because other people were dangerous and incapable of understanding me. I never expected this. I never thought I would have friends who would do this for me."

"I would do this for any of you guys," Jenny said.

"Yeah, me too," Olivia joined in.

"Absolutely!" Willy spoke up.

"Anytime," Andrew agreed.

"Hey, is anyone else getting hungry?" Willy asked.

"Oh! I forgot. Miranda's nanna is making us bread pudding and hot milk," Andrew exclaimed.

And they climbed to their feet and back up the hill to Miranda's bright kitchen, and they ate the whole pudding, and drank the hot milk, chattering to each other all the while, and when they fell asleep, late that night, Miranda dreamed of Andrew, and of five white ravens carrying gold pieces in their beaks, and Andrew dreamed of Miranda, and of a great bear always watching their backs. Olivia dreamed that she stood on a hilltop and looked over the bright land like a queen, with a beautiful beast at her side, and Willy dreamt that he had built a kingdom. Jenny dreamt it all, and then wrote it all down.

Somewhere else, in a land far away, five other young people dreamt, and they dreamt of ravens and spiders, and dragons and a great bear, who devoured them whole and then spat them back out, and when they awoke they knew the had done wrong.

Grownups

Lynne didn't know what to do with herself so she kicked the crap out of her car. After, sitting at the kitchen table with Jim, he'd come up with a plan that didn't involve dismemberment. He'd gone back to his place and brought his bottle of tequila with him along with a few overnight things for himself and his kids. Lynne knew she couldn't face Miranda. Her combined anger and shame—shame at having been unable to keep her daughter safe—would just be triggering to Miranda. It was better if she let Andrew stay with her. Miranda responded well to the kids next door. Lynne had been surprised at the lengths Miranda would go to to make Olivia happy, and she was beginning to wonder about the exact nature of her daughter's relationship with Andrew, although she still trusted the kid. Obviously Miranda did too.

Lynne sipped the tequila and stared into the glass as she let Jim cook dinner. After he'd talked her out of racing off to Kamloops half cocked, he'd poured her a finger of booze and booked her a plane ticket. Then he told her to call Jeremy and have him meet her there with a good lawyer, which she did. Her blood pressure was coming down and she felt so, so old. Jim brought plates to the table and Andrew came back downstairs. Lynne asked Andrew to repeat what he'd told her earlier and she typed, in detail, everything that he had to tell her about the event. Lynne could see that it hurt Andrew to talk about what her daughter had shared with him and she felt horrible with herself for making him go through it again and she told him so. He said to her, "It hurts. But not as badly as they hurt Miranda, and not as badly as it hurt her when she told me, and not as much as hearing it from *her* lips hurt me today." He got up abruptly after that and put his plate in the dishwasher and then went back upstairs. A short time later Olivia and Violet came back from the boat trip. They came in, chattering about the day at sea and then saw the sombre faces and ground to a halt in the doorway.

Lynne whisked her mother into another room and explained as briefly as she could what had transpired and then told her, "Can you hold down the fort here? Jim is going to drive me to the airport."

"Of course I can. Have you eaten?"

Lynne nodded, "Jim fed Andrew and me. Miranda's sleeping but you might be able to get a meal replacement drink or a yogurt into her later. I don't think she'll eat much, she never does after a meltdown."

On the way to the airport Jim told her about the day he had come home to find ambulances and police cars on the lawn. Lynne listened and shook her head when he was done, feeling helpless. "God, did you just tell me that to give me perspective?" she asked.

"Nope." He smiled, "I told you so that you won't feel alone as a parent who, despite being competent and intelligent, has been unable to protect their child from the world we live in."

"How do you live with that every day?"

"I take it day by day. It gets better."

"I just want her to be safe. I want to know that people aren't going to hurt her. Is that too much to expect? Is it too much to expect that people not hurt our children?"

"When I'm feeling particularly morbid and self righteously indignant or hard done by I listen to old Portishead albums and tell myself that we could be in Syria, or that I could be an emperor penguin slogging across the Antarctic with an egg on my feet," Jim told her.

"And *that* makes you feel better?" Lynne asked, a caustic tone seeping into her voice.

"No, but I always try it on anyway. I'm not saying don't beat yourself up, we do that anyway and I think the guilt is part of the parental package, just try to remind yourself that you're doing your best. We're only human Lynne."

Lynne met Jeremy at the hotel in Kamloops. She gave him the rundown but after the late flight she was suddenly so very very tired. The next day in the principal's office the principal blithely looked at her and told her,

"Those children graduated this summer so there's nothing I can do at this point."

"What about the teacher?"

"He transferred to a different school."

Lynne was speechless, literally speechless, and then Jeremy took over, "I'm a data analyst. Usually I just crunch numbers but I like information, generally speaking, and I'm good at finding it. I had a look at the social media of the kids in question last night and I found out that the Cooper children are the offspring of the chair of the school board. Is that right? Additionally I found that their father is currently facing extortion charges. I also found photographs in their social media that implied that my daughter may not have been their only victim. I looked back a little further and searched the Kamloops Times online archive and found that he was accused of bribing the City to sign building permits. It was very interesting reading. I looked into the teacher in question and I even gave him a call last night. He's left the country, but like I said, I'm good at finding information. He had some interesting things to say about what happened to him when he came to you last year and told you what he saw in the bathroom. The kids had run, like Miranda told her friend, and while we keep saying 'kids' we are talking about a group of five adult sized people, two years older than Miranda. He was *one* teacher. He reported it to you, and he recorded his meeting with you and I have the sound file. His story matches exactly with what my daughter shared. You do understand that my daughter went through a year long episode of traumatic mutism don't you?"

The principal said nothing and Jeremy asked him again, "Do you understand what I'm saying to you sir? It seems that you knew what was happening at the school, that this group of kids was tormenting others and you were doing nothing. It seems you may even have been covering it up although that would be purely speculation on my part. I suppose the police would need to do an investigation to discover something like that, and if the chair of the school board is already being investigated perhaps we should simply go talk to them."

Jeremy was silent for a moment and then said, in the same conversational matter of fact tone that he'd maintained through his entire monologue, "Sir? I'm waiting for an answer?"

Lynne watched the school principal, and waited, as a wet patch bloomed in his pants.

* * *

Lynne had lunch with Jeremy after the meeting, after they'd called the police, and he told her the things that had gone unsaid during their divorce, "Lynne, I know I'm not a good father, and I wasn't a good husband. Work is so much easier. I really, deeply, and truthfully know that I'm not good at those things, but I love Miranda desperately. You will always be my one and only love. What we had back in university was the kind of relationship I can maintain. I don't regret trying to make a life with you though, and I'm not angry that you packed up and lawyered up like that. I had it coming, as they say."

Lynne just stared at Jeremy. He was the tall dark stranger type. Mysterious and charismatic with an intellect that never let up. She always felt like she was surrounded by village idiots after an hour with Jeremy. "That's why you agreed to all my terms in the divorce. That's why you lay down and gave up like that."

"Yes," he nodded.

Lynne almost burst into tears, "There was a part of me that was so relieved when you didn't fight, and another part of me that wanted you to fight for me. A part of me *wanted* you to fight for me. I still loved you Jeremy, and when you didn't fight . . ."

Lynne looked at him and he looked so sad. "I'm sorry Lynne."

He sipped his root beer. Lynne used to tease him about loving root beer, "What kind of grownup are you?" she'd say.

"What Miranda did, in telling her friend what happened to her, was incredibly brave, but I want her to be able to walk away from here on in. The company has me doing work for a firm in Chicago right now, but I can take some time. I will stay in Kamloops and deal with this. Why don't you go home to Miranda and in a week or two, when this has blown over, and she isn't so unstable, I'll come and visit."

"That would be great. Really, it would. If you want to impress Miranda bring her a couple more art history text books when you come."

Jeremy nodded and smiled, and then asked, "Would it be alright with you if I bought a small house in St Fina? I can stay there when I'm in town, work from there when I don't need to be in the office, and be close by without being a nuisance. I'd still only be around a few months per year, but . . ."

It cost Jeremy to ask, and Lynne saw that, but she appreciated it, "I think that's a good idea," she told him.

Wainwright

Jim got back from the airport at about midnight and he was exhausted as he pulled up to the blue and white farmhouse. He went in and Violet called out softly, "In here," and he followed her voice. She was in her dressing gown on a Victorian chaise longue in the parlour. "Olivia is asleep in the spare room and Andrew is on a camping mattress on Miranda's floor. I'm not really sure what happened and I didn't want to stir things up, so I kept Olivia busy with me, fed her some dinner, and got Andrew to convince Miranda to eat a yogurt. Would you care to update me?"

Jim sank into a plush velvet art deco arm chair and slid down till his head was resting on the backrest and his feet reached the ottoman, "Lynne has gone to Kamloops to talk to the school principal to at least report the incident," Jim told her. "She's meeting Jeremy there."

"And what Lynne told me before she left, I understood that correctly? That Miranda was physically assaulted in the washroom? That a boy . . . "

"You understood correctly," Jim confirmed.

Violet got up and came back a minute later with a crystal tumbler. "I've deduced that this is your tequila on the kitchen counter, and that after hours in a car with Lynne, in the state she was in, you probably need one?"

"Violet, you are a saint." He accepted the proffered drink, took a long sip, and then woke up with sunshine pouring in, his drink unfinished on the end table, and Olivia pulling a blanket off him and telling him gently that she and Violet had made an omelette and that he probably needed to get moving if he wanted to bathe and get to work on time.

He left for work, not looking forward to rescheduling the three appointments he'd had to walk out on the day before and wishing he could find good help. His last receptionist moved away two weeks ago. But he appreciated being able to drop things and run home to his kids when they needed him. When it was getting time to call it a day he called Violet. She told him, "Olivia is having dinner at the Araya house and I've fed Andrew so if you need to catch up after yesterday feel free to stay at the clinic," she told him.

"Thanks Violet, for keeping tabs on them. How's Miranda?"

"Not saying much, but she's talking a bit. She's frighteningly mild. Not herself. She's not eating much, just grape juice. I talked her into a meal replacement when Andrew went home to change this morning. She went three weeks last year on grape juice and yogurt. I'm a bit worried but . . . I hope she'll come out of it."

Jim called again just as he was leaving the clinic and the kids had talked Miranda into going to the beach to watch the sunset. Once he was home and nine-thirty had come and gone, just as he was feeling that he should check in on his children, the phone rang and Violet told him that watching the sunset with her friends seemed to have set Miranda to rights, and that she was feeding them bread pudding and hot milk and that if it was alright by him she'd keep them another night.

The next day, Saturday, he found out that Violet had had all five kids to contend with, but he forgot sometimes that she had raised three daughters and that she had probably had more than five kids around on many occasions.

He though he might have a quiet morning, but at eight o'clock Olivia came racing into the house and grabbed his arm dramatically, "Dad! I've found The Dog! Can we go meet him?"

Olivia had studied every aspect of dog ownership and shared every minute detail with him. He strongly suspected Miranda was helping her with the research when Olivia sited medical studies showing lower incidence of allergies in children who had dogs in early childhood, "Just because it's too late for me and Andrew doesn't mean we shouldn't still have a dog! They lower perceived stress levels too!"

"But where will it sleep?" Jim asked Olivia.

"On a dog bed, next to my bed. Unless it's an Italian greyhound. Then it will sleep with me in my bed. Did you know that they make excellent bed warmers?"

"Who's going to walk it?" he'd also asked her, because there was no way that he was going to walk a dog after work.

"I will," she'd said immediately, and then given him a long monologue on how there were other ways to exercise a dog too and that if they had a dog who likes to fetch they could get something called a 'chuck it' so that he could play with the dog from a lawn chair.

"Who's going to train it?" he'd asked her the next day.

"I will, and I'll need you and Andrew to be supportive and follow the rules. But I'm not going to get a puppy," she'd said confidently. "I'm looking for an adult dog who needs a home. I want the right dog and when a dog is fully grown you can judge their personality better. Besides, I want a dog who needs me." And she'd walked off completely confident that she was going to have a dog someday.

And then that Saturday morning she came tearing into the kitchen before he'd even had his coffee.

"I'll show you his profile!"

Olivia raced upstairs and grabbed Andrew's laptop computer and then with exaggerated care crept back down the stairs cradling the laptop. She opened a browser and pulled up the profile. It read:

Wainwright came to us after his owner became too ill to care for him. He is a sensitive, gentle soul, with an easy going nature. He loves to be near people and will happily sleep on your feet after a long walk. Wainwright is a very large dog, but he is aware of his size. Despite that we do not recommend him for very small children. At five years, Wainwright is in late middle age for an Irish wolfhound.

Jim looked at Olivia and thought hard. She looked back at him with an almost combustible intensity. He smiled and shook his head. "I'm going to call the rescue and make an appointment to meet him. Hopefully for this afternoon. After that you are going to leave this with me," he took the laptop, "and I will do a bit of reading and drink my coffee in peace and quiet. We will talk in the car on the way to Duncan. Alright?" he told her.

"Alright," she nodded serious and quiet. "I'll go take a bath and put on clean clothes."

They pulled out an hour and a half later and Jim asked Olivia if she had done much reading about Irish wolfhounds.

"They're the tallest breed, they're independent and individualistic," Olivia stumbled over the word, "and they don't live a terribly long time. That's part of why I think we should adopt Wainwright. He might only have a couple years left. His person got sick, otherwise he'd be living out his days with them. What if he gets stuck living at the shelter? We can give him a good couple years and we have the space for a dog that big. A lot of people don't want old dogs. I've been watching the rescue sites for the last while and the old dogs don't get adopted as fast. And they called him a gentle soul, but he looks like a dragon. Plus, I dreamt about him last night."

Jim had wondered if Olivia had done the math when she read Wainwright's profile, but he knew now that she understood what she was taking on, "You're an amazing kid Pumpkin."

At the shelter a staff member greeted them, "You must be Jim and Olivia. Hi, I'm Shelly. Give me just five minutes and I'll be back with Wainwright."

Jim had to school his features when Wainwright walked into the room and even then Shelly looked at him and smiled, "I know! He's big right?"

But Olivia wasn't phased. She walked up to the shaggy silver dog slowly and held out her hands for him to sniff and he snuffled them and, stretching his head up only slightly, he gave her cheek a perfunctory lick. "When Wainwright came to us he was very depressed so he lived in a foster home for a little while until he was confident enough to come to the shelter during the day, but he comes home with me at night right now, and he has very nice house manners," Shelly told them.

"He really needs a home that can provide him with some consistency, so he can feel safe and trust that he's going to be okay."

Olivia was now sitting on the floor with the dog, giving him a tummy rub and talking to him. She turned and looked their way, "He's really handsome isn't he Dad?"

"He's a striking dog," Jim agreed.

Wainwright rolled over and trotted over to Jim at the sound of his voice and butted his hand with his head so that Jim would scratch his ears. He didn't have much experience with dogs and wasn't sure what the dog liked, but Wainwright didn't seem to care. He took what you had to give and then gave it back two-fold. Jim rubbed the dog's head and tried to stay upright as Wainwright leaned into his leg.

"Normally we wouldn't recommend a dog as big as Wainwright to first time dog owners but with his temperament just being so gentle, and his mistress training him so well, he's very easy to live with. We can go out into the yard with him and I'll show you all the things he knows how to do. His leash manners are impeccable."

Olivia learned all Wainwright's commands and confidently lead him around the yard, giving him praise all along the way and stopping to give him big doggy hugs. Jim watched as she shut her eyes with her arms wrapped around the dog, and he knew the dog was going home with them.

"Sometimes you see that with children. They just step into a dog's life like they've always been together," Shelly commented, watching.

"Olivia was a foster child. Her mother had to give her up when she became 'too ill to care for her', and my wife and I adopted her, and then my wife died of cancer. It's not every day that Olivia meets someone who understands, and I don't think it matters to her that he's a dog."

Jim was used to their history and could hear it and say it now without feeling it sometimes. He

watched Olivia for a few more minutes and then turned to Shelly to suggest that they fill out the adoption papers and the woman was a dripping sniffling mess. She noticed Jim looking at her and she smiled, "Sorry, I'm sorry." She blew he nose and wiped her eyes. "I just feel pretty good about Wainwright going home with you. You obviously know how to bring a vulnerable creature into your home and help them flourish."

As they finished filling out the paperwork, Shelly asked them, "I promised Wainwright's mistress that I would keep her updated. Would you mind if I took a picture of you and Olivia with Wainwright to send to her, and told her a bit about your family? She hasn't got much time left and it would mean a lot to her to know that her best friend is going to be okay."

Jim nodded, being the one to choke up this time.

The Nature of Beauty

Miranda knew that she loved Andrew quite early on. She might even have known that she *could* love him the first time she saw him. Maybe partly because of the way he looked, but mostly because of the look in his eyes. She wasn't sure when she realized that she was *in* love with him. Perhaps the morning of her birthday, when she thought about her knees. Being in love was like a beauty that you felt, a kind of sweet, confusing agony that made you take a breath in wonder. She thought maybe she would die of it sometimes, and she wanted. She wanted. She looked, every morning when she awoke, at the picture that hung above her bed, and how it seemed that he must have paid very close attention, to have chosen that for her. Then she would look out her bedroom window, and if he wasn't already there, looking back at her from his own window, it would only be a matter of minutes before he was.

The day the others had gone on the boat trip, and she and Andrew stayed behind, she hadn't known what had come over her. She thought that what had happened to her was locked inside her forever, then when Andrew played the phone message from his mother, somehow it had come loose, and she knew that if she tried, she could drag it out of herself. That she could tell Andrew. And then he told her that he loved her. She had thought that what had happened to her would make her unlovable.

The paralysis, the terrible mildness, that seemed to come the next day had frightened Miranda. She thought she would wake up and be okay and then she'd woken up and felt muted and separate from everything. She could see that it frightened Andrew too and she didn't want to frighten him. And then he'd taken her to see the sunset and Jenny, Olivia, Willy, and Andrew had helped her come back out of that horrible mildness, and life started to move again, and it was still summer, and it was still beautiful.

Her mother came home from Kamloops and held her, and held her, and held her, until Miranda finally asked, "Are you okay Mom?"

"Yeah, I'm okay baby," her mom told her and Miranda was pretty sure her mom meant it and wasn't just saying it to make her feel safe. "How about you?" Lynne had asked.

"I'm pretty good. Jenny's coming over in a half an hour. We're going to watch a movie, and then we're going to help Andrew get ready for the dog."

"Dog? What dog?"

"Olivia's getting a dog!"

Wainwright loved everybody and everybody loved Wainwright. He went everywhere Olivia did and he was so big he felt like a guardian angel. Miranda would lie on the floor against him sometimes when he was sleeping, and she could feel her body chemistry change and her blood pressure sink so that she felt at peace with the world. Miranda loved looking out the window and seeing Olivia run with the dog. They would just run around in the field for no other reason than the joy of it and it was so beautiful to watch. Even Jim seemed much happier with Wainwright in his life.

During the last two weeks of the summer holiday Miranda and Andrew tried very hard not to spend too much time alone together. That was easy during the day with the others to keep them level, and it was easy the week her dad was there too. When her dad came to visit he explained to her what he'd discovered in Kamloops, "Those kids didn't only hurt you, and one of their fathers was blackmailing the principal to keep it quiet. The police arrested them. The teacher, Mr Jonson, and two of the other kids who were being bullied, and one of the bullies, came forward and told the police everything they knew. You can, er, how do people say it, 'wash your hands of this.' I think that's the metaphor people use, when you can walk away and not look back?" Miranda noticed that he used a metaphor that he understood to explain a metaphor that baffled him, "You telling Andrew was enough. You don't have to do more."

Miranda nodded. She still didn't like to think about what happened but it wasn't like before. It wasn't eating at her anymore, and she was so profoundly relieved that something had happened, that something had taken place to expose the people who had let her down, the people who were truly at fault, that it brought her some peace. She could imagine now that there was just a small pearlescent scar on her heart. She asked her dad, "Was it very awful? Being in Kamloops, and dealing with . . . that stuff?"

"It was awful, but the worst part was knowing that I wasn't there for you when it was happening last year. When I should have been there."

Miranda could only nod, look out over the ocean, and be grateful.

A couple days later Nadine arrived. "Nadine is the kind of weirdo who loves sleeping in attics with ghosts. Will you help me turn the attic into another spare bedroom?" Lynne asked Miranda. "Okay. Can I call Olivia though, because this is a three person job and Olivia's good at making wild colours work together, and Nadine likes wild colours."

When Nadine arrived she practically ran wild with Miranda and her friends. At first Jenny and Willy had been a bit dubious about this questionable and extremely flamboyant grown up, but then she grew on them. The weather was hot again and they were spending their days on the beach. They weren't allowed to swim without an adult there, so Nadine was tolerated for facilitating swimming when Lynne was at work. Miranda was lying in the sun on a towel trying to think of a way to articulate the sensation of the cold water drying on her skin, and the feeling of the towel, hot from the sun, under her body. How her limbs felt so heavy after leaving the salt water, and so firm from swimming in the cold, and yet she was melting in the warmth. They had their towels spread like a five petalled flower, in a circle, heads together talking. "The physical sensation of coming out of the water and lying down on the hot towel with the hot sand underneath is . . .?" she whispered.

"Divine, exquisite, pleasure?" Jenny offered.

"Like being a lizard, warming in the sun?" Willy suggested.

"Not the same when you have a wet dog sharing your towel," Olivia grunted, trying to reclaim a corner of towel.

"Purifying. The sensation pushes away everything but happiness and contentment. It's pure, happy, contentment," Andrew declared.

"Yeah, that," Willy said.

"Yes," Miranda sighed.

"Soon, hopefully." Olivia wriggled onto the edge of her towel.

"I can go with that," Jenny agreed.

Nadine was hiding under her umbrella with a book, "I don't mean to go all preachy grown up on you, but

I really hope you guys aren't taking this for granted. Even if it doesn't last forever, right now, you're living in paradise."

"We know," Olivia told her, very serious.

"I don't think many people have what we have. It was pretty lonely for me and Willy before these guys moved here. It's some kind of crazy, that we're all basically the same age, and that some dumb retired couples didn't buy the old McGinty houses," Jenny said.

"It's like Josephine road is our own world," Miranda told her. "We're safe here. And we all have *things* about us that are hard for normal people to understand, or empathize with. The odds of us being here together are astronomical."

"I take it your childhood wasn't ideal?" Andrew said to Nadine.

"My early childhood was good enough, but my parents were strict. They caught me making out with a girl when I was sixteen and kicked me out. I've been estranged from them ever since."

"Our parents would never do that," Willy said to Jenny.

Nadine picked up on the look the twins exchanged, and her gaze shifted to Jenny.

"I'm only *out* with these guys," Jenny said nervously. "I know my parents would be fine. They'd understand, we're all lucky with our parents, the five of us. It's the rest of the world we have to worry about. I'm not sure it would be safe to be out in St Fina. Miranda almost got beat up a few months back just for not talking at school. Being gay would be worse."

"I make the mistake sometimes, of thinking that the world is much better than it was when I was a kid. When my parents kicked me out my uncle took me in. I was couch surfing or on the streets for about three weeks before someone told him what happened. I didn't know him growing up and my family always acted like he didn't exist. He's gay too and he got it. He took care of me and put me through university. I was really lucky to have him," Nadine told them.

"I didn't know you got kicked out. I though you'd always lived with your uncle," Miranda said to her god-mother.

"No, but I sometimes feel as though my life only truly started when I went to live with him, and I'm sixteen years behind. That would make me twenty-six. Never mind, it doesn't make sense."

"No it makes sense. I feel like I'm picking back up from when I was fourteen. From just before the drugs and the rehab. I feel like I'm behind. Like everyone else got a head start and I'm lagging."

Miranda knew the feeling too. She knew she was six-teen. She knew that she was extremely intelligent. She knew she was going to graduate a year and a half early and in some ways she was ahead, but like Andrew, she also felt behind, which was why he was her sweetheart and not her boyfriend, and why they avoided being alone together. They held hands, they occasionally kissed the other's cheek or brow, but when the sun was up that was it, it stopped there. But at night that last week in August, with the moon high in the sky, after Miranda had brushed her teeth and hair, washed her face, and put on her nightgown, she would look out her north facing window and wait till she saw Andrew look out his window too. Then she would run downstairs, out the french doors and into the field to the oak tree with her heart beating and that fluttering in her chest. Andrew would already be there, breathless, waiting for her. It was an exposed place. Nothing could happen there. It was visible from both houses and the moonlight was so very bright. But they had just a little space, for a kiss, an embrace, close enough to feel the other's heartbeat, to say, "I love you," to one another, without being over-heard, under the one hundred year old oak tree, under the silver moon, in the golden field.

* * *

September came, and school started, and it wasn't as bad as Miranda had feared it would be. Olivia started at the secondary school that September, and with the Araya twins walking to school with them, and the five of them hanging out at lunch, there was, indeed—as Willy had yelled, on the last day of school in June—strength in numbers. Jenny had still taken Miranda and Andrew aside on Monday morning on the walk in and said to them though, "I know how you guys feel about each other, but maybe don't hold hands at school."

Andrew looked at her and asked, knowing, already understanding, "You've heard people talking?"

Jenny nodded, "Last year, the day we met. Some of the girls think you're . . . taking advantage of Miranda."

Miranda was upset and baffled, not understanding. But Andrew had already said to her, the night before, that if he was different at school, that it wasn't because of her.

"You knew people might think that?" she asked him.

"People always think the worst. I don't want to give them reasons to be shitty to us and I don't want . . . other guys at school getting ideas."

"People think I'm stupid and that you'd . . . do that?" she'd asked, feeling hurt, naive, and weepy.

Jenny hugged her, "Only some people. We just want to make sure we're safe at school that's all. We just want to be careful."

Miranda had nodded, bewildered, maybe a bit worried and self conscious, hugged Jenny back, and went to school that day looking around at the other students, wondering what terrible and unfathomable things they had in their minds.

History twelve was the only class that was being run by a teacher that Miranda and Andrew were in together that semester, and English Literature, which was the only other course Miranda was taking, and Physics, which was Andrew's other course, had to be done by correspondence, as the school didn't have a large enough student body for a teacher to run either course. There was a special room set up with teacher supervision and support for all the kids who were doing correspondence courses and Jenny and Willy were there in the afternoons too. They had a system down, a schedule, tracking apps on each other's phones, and codes they could text each other, so that none of them would be alone, and help would be there if they needed.

It worked like a charm. There had been moments when another student would make themselves vaguely offensive in a way that rang alarms, but a simple text and the others would show up in minutes, often breathless, but there in time. It was Jenny and Andrew who had to put up with the most aggravation because Jenny kept saying hi to Misty, the 'girl hoodie', in the hall—much to the exasperation of the others—and because Robin, 'the boy hoodie', had taken issue with being tackled last spring, but Willy had hit the six foot mark that summer, and Robin knew he couldn't take Willy and Andrew together. And after school they were free again, and the changing seasons were exhilarating.

Olivia and Violet entered Olivia's quilt in the fall fair and they got the blue ribbon for the needlecraft category and the Best in Fair award. Miranda was happy for them. For all that Miranda herself wasn't interested in the actual making of quilts, she loved them as an art form, and was so proud of her Nanna, and so happy that Olivia was taking on all the skills her grandmother had to pass on.

It seemed no time at all before the leaves were falling and Andrew's birthday had come. Andrew let them make a bit of a fuss but he didn't want to turn eighteen. Miranda knew that he was sad. She could feel it coming off of him in waves and it made her want to hold him. Miranda crept into his room the morning of his birthday and he hadn't gotten out of bed. She lay down next to him in the twin bed and stroked his hair and whispered, "It doesn't matter how old you are. You'll always be my lost boy."

He lay his head on her heart and sighed, "Am I being silly to feel this way?"

"No. One could say that it's just a number, but it's also a reminder of the passage of time, a reminder that things won't always be like this, that we won't always be the way we are. The only good thing I can think, is that your sadness at the idea of leaving this behind is also a reminder of how very wonderful this is, of how lucky we are."

All Miranda could do after that was hold him while he cried.

"But it's not over you know," she told him eventually. "And the things that come next might be just as good. The future might be just as beautiful. Can I give you your birthday present?"

Andrew had given a self deprecating laugh then, and sat up and looked at her, "You're right. The future might be *this* good. I have to stop thinking that everything's going to get worse. I'm going to jinx things."

"I don't see how it could be worse if we get to see each other every day." She gave him the wrapped package and he opened it and smiled. "*Peter Pan in Kensington Gardens* by J.M. Barrie." He smiled and carefully flipped through the pages, "Gosh, this is an old book. The illustrations are beautiful. Miranda . . . is this a first edition?"

"Make sure your dad lists it on your home insurance," Miranda told him. "I sold a Moorcroft vase on eBay so I could buy it."

Andrew laughed again but this time it was the laughter of delight.

Making it a
Big Deal

The days sped by. Halloween came. They stayed in, eating pizza and candied apples and watching horror movies at the Araya house. Miranda had never watched a horror movie before and almost couldn't bear it, but she got the distinct impression that Andrew enjoyed having her bury her face in his shoulder every five minutes, and Jenny said scary movies were better when you had a good screamer in the room with you. And then Christmas came and they had a big potluck dinner at the Warren house. Then it was January and she and Andrew were finishing school papers and studying for their provincial exams. They were just busy enough to avoid dwelling too much on the the actuality of graduating. She and Andrew had both told their parents that they refused to go to the grad ceremony that would be held for the whole school in June, and so Violet took over, as she knew Jim and Lynne wanted to make a big deal of their children making it through high school. Miranda

watched, that wet February day, as her grandmother prepared a dinner party that hearkened back to her early
life in high society as the ballerina granddaughter of a
wealthy and prominent international diplomat. A very
classy event indeed. Miranda observed, feeling distanced
from everything. School was done but it wasn't summer.
The next time she had to do something, it would be
something new. Andrew had his last provincial exam
that morning and then he was driving to Victoria for the
afternoon with his dad, and with the others in school
that day, Miranda could do nothing but haunt her own
house, listen to loud music, think too much, and watch
her grandmother make puff pastry by hand.

She rose the following day and helped clean the house.
She put out the silver candelabras, polishing them and
fitting candles into each space, ironed the table cloth,
arranged flowers in her best Royal Copenhagen art nouveau vase and placed it on the Arts and Crafts sideboard
as a centrepiece. She dusted, vacuumed the Persian
rugs, and fluffed all the throw cushions in the parlour,
and arranged more candles and flowers until their house
looked like something out of a magazine. Lynne came
home from work early to help Violet in the kitchen and
make sure Miranda hadn't missed anything when she'd
cleaned and decorated. Miranda went to her room and
opened her wardrobe. She pushed the dresses to the
side and looked to where the three old dresses from
her grandmother's youth hung. She knew which one she
was going to wear. Her nanna had dyed satin pumps to

match it when she was young and they fit Miranda now. She carefully donned a pair of pantyhose, and a silk slip, and then tucked her feet into the pumps. She'd been wearing them around her room for the last week to be sure she wouldn't fall. Miranda pulled the dress out of the wardrobe. Early 1960's pale blue silk dupioni with a nipped in waist, box pleated skirt, a beautifully tailored bodice with a slim bow detail. She put in her pearl earrings and then went to her door, "Mom I'm ready!" she called down the stairs. A few days earlier she'd told her mother, "I think the dress I'm wearing needs makeup. Can you do my makeup like this?" she held up a picture of Carey Mulligan in *An Education*. Jenny had made her watch it.

Lynne had, on many occasions, offered to do Miranda's makeup and Miranda had always said, "I don't want that stuff on my face," so Lynne had been surprised and delighted when asked.

Lynne came into the room in a little black dress, turquoise suede heels, and pearls. Miranda asked her, "Can you zip me up?"

Her mother zipped her and then placed the makeup box on Miranda's dressing table. Makeup was her mother's cherished incongruity. When people asked her mother what she was going to be when she was little, she'd always said, "A scientist or a makeup artist," and science won, but only by a very narrow margin. When Miranda was little she called her mother's makeup box her tackle box because it reminded her of her grandpa's fishing tackle box.

"You only need a little powder really. I won't put foundation all over you, I know you wouldn't like that," Lynne talked as she worked. "Close your eyes," then, "Open your mouth just a little," and, "This lipstick feels almost like lip balm and it doesn't have a funny taste. I'll leave it on your dressing table so you can freshen it up when you need. You saw how I put it on right?"

Miranda nodded.

"Look at your knees," Lynne told her, and then put mascara on her top lashes. "This mascara is very water-proof and very smudge proof so you'll need to use makeup-remover to get it off. You know which bottle that is in the bathroom and to use cotton rounds right?"

Miranda had to stop herself from nodding while her mother did her other eye, and mumbled, "Mm. Yes."

Then Lynne brushed out Miranda's hair and got the curling iron. "I'd give you an up-do but you don't ever wear you hair up and I don't want your head to start hurting. I'll just curl the ends and pin it off your face.

Miranda sat patiently again, feeling restless and grumpy, knowing that the dress wouldn't even look right if she didn't let her mom do her hair, but it was getting hard to sit still.

"I can feel you trying to fidget. I'm almost done," Lynne told her with a laugh. "There, now you can move. But don't look in the mirror quite yet. I have something for you." Miranda's mother took a little box out of her pocket. "This was my engagement ring. Your dad and I have been talking and, we'd like you to have it. It belonged to his great-grandmother. I've never really worn it and it's been in a safe deposit box for years. I think you'll like it a lot better than I ever did."

Miranda didn't really wear jewellery. She didn't like the feeling of it on her body and earrings had been her first foray into actually having it on her. She didn't know about a ring, but if it was a beautiful antique, that changed things, just a little. Miranda opened the box and took the ring out. "It's Belle Epoque," she told her mother. "It looks French but I don't know anything about jewellery."

Her mom laughed and said, "Nope, nothing at all. Only enough to tell me the era it comes from and its country of origin."

"It's really pretty," Miranda sighed.

"Put it on. It suits you better than it suited me and you're wearing a dress that just begs for diamonds."

Miranda looked at the diamonds set in a spiral around a platinum flower with a larger diamond set in the centre and she felt dizzy. She put it on her hand, trying her ring finger and then switching to her middle finger where it wouldn't slip off. The metal hugging her finger was unpleasant at first but as it warmed to her body temperature the feeling eased. She held out her hand to the back drop of icy blue silk on her lap and turned her hand this way and that, watching the colour-play in the stones, then she went to look in the mirror. She looked but turned away abruptly, looking out the window at the grey ocean instead.

"What is it Baby?" her mom asked.

Miranda looked at Lynne. She was taller than her mother now, and looking down at her still felt wrong and the heels made it worse. Miranda went over to her cupboard and hit play on her phone and New Order's *Ceremony* filled the room. "I can't breathe," she whispered and closed her eyes, hands out rigidly, and listened to the music trying to let it make sense of the way she felt but it wasn't putting her thoughts into a reasonable sequence. "Nothing makes sense," she gasped.

"Miranda," her mother said gently, "life is changing, and I'm going to tell you something and it is going to sound like an insensitive cliche." Miranda opened her eyes and Lynne looked into her face and her expression was serene. "Change is life's only constant," her mother told her. "You have changed, from a wild girl into a beautiful young lady, and I know that you don't like changes, especially when they sneak up on you like this, but this is a good change. You've got you're feet under you Baby. You do, and you have to trust me on that. Now go make sure you look how you want to, and then come downstairs because everyone will be arriving in about five minutes and Janet is already here helping your grandmother."

Miranda thought about what her mother said and it wasn't so different from what she herself had said to Andrew only a few months ago, but seeing herself

suddenly different, suddenly defined, suddenly . . . finished? brought everything rushing up fast. *Go make sure
you look how you want to,* Miranda thought over the
words Lynne had said.

She walked back to the mirror and the music blasted
out of the speakers as she looked at her reflection. She
thought about what she had said to Andrew on his birthday, and she decided that she looked how she wanted
to look.

"When the song ends turn off the music and come
downstairs, Okay?" Lynne looked at her.

"Okay," Miranda agreed, and her mother smiled and
left the room.

Miranda looked back into the mirror and decided she
was actually very happy with the way she looked and
stood there as the song finished playing, watching the
twinkle on her hand, and looking at her face with the
pearls and the makeup. She turned off the music and
tidied up her room before hurrying out and down the
stairs. There was a knock when she was halfway down
and she stopped so that she wouldn't take up space
by the door. Her grandmother was there in a lilac satin
dress being the perfect hostess and letting Jim, Willy,
and Daniel in and then Olivia came in with Wainwright,
but Olivia was preoccupied with taking him to his bed,
getting him settled, and making sure he understood to
stay in his place. Jenny and Andrew came in last. Jenny
was wearing a black velvet top with a navy chiffon skirt,
black nineteen-twenties style shoes, and engraved Haida

cuff bracelets on each wrist. She was talking to Andrew who was paying attention to what she was saying as they walked in the door. The others filed out of the way into the parlour. Miranda stared at Andrew. He'd gotten a haircut. It still wasn't short, the hair at the front was long enough to reach his cheekbones, and collar length at the back, but it was well cut and Miranda couldn't imagine any hairdresser in their right mind wanting to cut it all off. But it wasn't only that. He was wearing a suit. His dad was, and so was Jenny's dad, and her own dad, who was going to arrive a little late, always wore suits. Even Willy was wearing dress pants and a vest, but that wasn't the same at all. Andrew looked like . . . an adult, in the navy blue suit. Like a character in a book. It was as strange to see him in a suit as it was to see herself with makeup on and her hair done, in a dress that needed makeup and hair. Jenny looked up and stopped saying whatever she'd been saying and said, "Holy shit!"

"Jennifer! Language!" came out of the kitchen, and Jenny called, "Sorry Mum," softly down the hall without looking away from Miranda.

That's when Andrew looked up the stairs at her and all of a sudden Miranda felt weak in the knees and like maybe it would be better to be on level ground. She gripped the old carved banister and came down slowly looking at Andrew. When she got to the bottom he looked into her eyes. Miranda vaguely heard Jenny mumble that she'd see them in the parlour, but most of her focus was on Andrew.

Eventually he reached out and took her hand, smiled and kissed her cheek. "I want to kiss you but I'd smudge your lipstick," he told her, then he said, "When you look like this, it's easier to picture the future. I can believe that what comes next *will* be good. That it might even get better, especially if it's with you. You are so incredibly beautiful Miranda Hopkins."

A Suit, Really?

Andrew was in a mood when he finished his exam. He was sure he'd done fine, but that wasn't relevant to the mood. It wasn't how he felt about the exam, but the fact that he was *done* the exam. He was done. He'd just finished high school. What he actually really wanted to do at that moment was go see Miranda and just sit with her on the couch and do nothing, but his dad was insisting they go to Victoria, to buy a fucking suit.

"You've got two hours to make yourself fit for human consumption," his dad told him as they pulled onto the highway. "I know finishing school is a lot to process, but this is the day I was able to arrange to close the clinic for the afternoon, and I know you wouldn't have wanted to do this yesterday either."

"Mm," Andrew had growled, staring out the window at the wet forest and watching the world go by.

Andrew hadn't realized that his dad had also booked him a haircut and it put him in an even blacker mood when they arrived, but his dad left him at the hairdresser and told him he had a errand to run and would be back in an hour. Andrew glared at his father's disappearing back.

"If I had hair like yours I'd be mad if my father ambushed me with a haircut too," the hairdresser told him and Andrew couldn't help crack a smile.

"I just wrote my last provincial exam two hours ago. It's not that I mind that much, I'm just out of it, and making a decision feels like it takes way more brain power than I have."

"Okay, I'll make this easy then. How about we just trim it, give it a shape, and leave it long enough that in three months, you'll be back to looking like a devil-may-care surfer. It would be a crime to cut all of this off anyway."

"Yes, that," Andrew agreed emphatically, and then actually managed to have a conversation with the hair-dresser.

"Looks good," Jim said when he came back.

Andrew was still too annoyed to acknowledge the compliment even though he was starting to enjoy himself.

Buying a suit wasn't as painful as it could have been either, and Andrew appreciated the haircut as it made it easier to choose a suit looking somewhat tidy. They left with a practical but stylish navy blue suit that he could wear to any event or establishment at which he needed to look respectable, smart, and like he had his shit together.

By dinner time Andrew had decompressed enough to be glad of the outing. As he and his father sat down to a dinner of the best sushi in Victoria, he was able to see that getting out and doing something had stopped him from settling into a funk and instead he felt energized.

"So, what's next . . .? Are you going to go into farming with Olivia?" his dad asked delicately.

Andrew laughed quite hard because his father knew damn well that he didn't want to farm with Olivia, but Olivia farming seemed to be a certainty. She'd talked Willy and Andrew into building her a chicken coop in the barn over the Christmas break and she had a line on a local farmer with a small goat herd who might have a kid for her. She had even talked to their dad about the field across the street.

"You know she's right about the field, and Willy's made some good points too," Andrew reminded his father who was still reeling from Olivia's announcement.

"I know," Jim admitted. "I've talked to the Arayas about it, and to Violet. Don't tell Olivia because it's far from certain at this point, but we're looking into buying the field jointly. It was mostly Willy who convinced us because he is correct, that if St Fina were to turn around and become a tourist hot-spot like Tofino . . .?" Jim shuddered at the prospect of a hotel or some other such establishment spoiling their peace.

Jim turned back to the original topic though, "You've mentioned Uvic in passing a few times and even though you don't bring it up directly, I watched you pick your courses the last two semesters. You've got the provincial exams to get into any major you want. Are you planing for any contingency or for something specific?"

Andrew smiled and shook his head. His dad hadn't pressured him over school in any way. Because Andrew had turned eighteen in October he had actually already graduated according to the province's adult grad requirements, but he'd enrolled in physics and history anyway, knowing he would technically be done when he was halfway through the semester. He did have something of a plan, but declaring it out loud to his father made it a bit real. Being done high school made it real too though.

He decided it was time to discuss it with someone other than Miranda. "Ever since we moved I've wanted to do Historical Architecture. It's like how moving to an old farm woke Olivia's inner farmer? Moving into an old historically intact house made me feel, safe? Secure? We don't build like that anymore. I got more interested after we met the Hopkins and the Arayas and I got to go in their houses too. I'm not saying that the post nineteen-nineties townhouse we lived in in Toronto didn't feel like home, but that was because you and Mom made it a home. When we moved out, and it was empty it had no soul. Our house and Miranda's and the twin's houses have souls independent of the occupants, and I know that they are particularly nice examples of homes from their eras, but when I started really reading, and following some of the architecture blogs online, I started to understand why our house feels the way it does, and also why it actually matters. While the average family can't go back to living in homes quite as big and well appointed as ours, from a social and environmental perspective, there's a lot wrong with modern home design." Andrew stopped to take a breath, suddenly excited to brain dump all of the ideas he'd been having to his dad.

"So you want to do Historical Architecture at Uvic?" Jim asked.

"Well that's the problem. Uvic doesn't specifically offer it as a major, and I don't want to have to go far away from home to go to university, so I'd have to do an undergrad in something else and then apply to their master's program for architecture, but . . ." he stopped suddenly, and asked his dad, "Do you know about Miranda's antique collection?"

"I do, somewhat, from Violet and Lynne, but *you* tell me about it," Jim said, still listening intently.

"She's got an incredible eye for different artistic styles and she's good at finding things. She can glance at a painting or vase by an artist that she's familiar with and, even if she's never seen that individual piece before, she just knows who produced it. She's got this fascination with understanding why something is beautiful. When she was twelve she started collecting and her mom encouraged her. Her mom taught her how to use eBay so that if she found something she knew was valuable at a garage sale or a thrift store, but it wasn't something she wanted to keep herself, she could sell it for more, and use the money to collect things she really wanted.

Lynne helped her start a savings account so she could build some capital. She's made a nice little sum and has some beautiful Wedgwood Fairyland Lustre, Moorecroft, and Royal Copenhagen pieces in her collection. When Violet bought the house and decorated it, she decorated Miranda's room specifically with her personal collection in mind. Miranda's essentially been an amateur antique dealer since she was thirteen. She wants to do a degree in art history because it would make her more legitimate. There's lots of overlap between art history and historical architecture, and art history is one of the degrees *I* can do to get me into the architecture master's program. We figure we'll do the art history undergrad program at UVic together and then I'll do the master's of Architecture program, and she'll do a master's in Art History. That way we can stay close to home, maybe even come home every weekend."

Andrew's dad nodded thoughtfully as he chewed his seaweed salad then asked a question Andrew had expected for a while, "You and Miranda *are* a couple then?"

"Yeah, but the other students at the high school, some of them don't understand that Miranda doesn't have an intellectual disability, and they think that she has no agency over her life. We had to be pretty careful at school to look um . . . platonic . . .? I guess? We always made sure Willy, Jenny, or Olivia were there with us. We're not in the habit of showing romantic affection in public, we try not to spend too much time alone together."

Andrew watched his dad's face as he shared, wondering what he would say. "I wasn't sure," Jim admitted. "Jenny and Olivia are quite affectionate with Miranda as well. I couldn't always tell if there was more than deep friendship between you."

Andrew nodded. "It's more than friendship. We just wanted to take it slow. That's all. You don't . . . have a problem with it?" he asked hesitantly, because it was something he worried about.

"No. No, of course not," Andrew's father told him emphatically, then more thoughtfully, "I will admit that I do understand why other people might think there was something to be concerned about, but it's an erroneous way of thinking based on misconceptions about Miranda. As long as you are being . . ." Jim paused for a moment, "Responsible . . . if you catch my drift. I have no issues."

Andrew knew what his father meant by *responsible* so he told him, "We'll be responsible, when there's something to be responsible about."

* * *

The next day Andrew cleaned the house. He'd texted Miranda when he got up that morning and she'd told him that she wanted him to be surprised and not to come till the others did, that she was busy cleaning.

_I'll clean with you then, from my house though :)

And that's what he did. The whole house. Everything got dusted, polished, and scrubbed. Carpets got beaten, upholstery got vacuumed, sheets got washed, and then at three o'clock he grabbed a quick bath—before Olivia got home from school. He shaved, and put on the suit feeling pretty damn self conscious. It took him five tries to get the tie right but he was *not* going to ask for help. When Olivia got home she took one look at Andrew and said, "You look so old. Well, not *old* . . . but . . ." Then she disappeared into the bathroom for an hour. She came out of her room twenty minutes after that wearing a drapey, slightly clinging, sea green crushed velvet dress with magenta lace up granny boots and her Tahitian pearls. "I might look *old*, but you don't look like a little kid anymore either," he told her, and then their dad ran in the door, told them that they made him feel old looking the way they did, and then managed to bathe and dress in twenty minutes.

"Everybody ready? Okay? Into the car. It's too muddy to walk."

Andrew knew Janet had gone over mid-afternoon to help, but the rest of the Arayas were arriving just as the Warrens were, and he moved to the back of the small crowd and talked with Jenny on the porch as the others filed in ahead of them. "Hey, you look pretty," he told her.

She usually rocked a bit of a goth princess look and she'd managed to keep it up even in her formal wear.

"Thanks. You almost make me want to like boys in that suit," Jenny told him.

"I'm weirdly nervous and I don't quite know why," he confided in her.

"I'm nervous about going to school on Monday without you and Miranda. I think the other side of the coin must be just as nerve wracking. After twelve years, now what? You're just supposed to drift?" Jenny looked down as she stepped over the threshold into the Hopkins house and Andrew looked to see what had caught her attention and realized she was just paying attention to the floor because she was wearing heels. She said, "I'm comparatively steady in these shoes but I . . ." she broke off, looking up, "Holy shit!"

Andrew looked up to where Jenny's eyes were directed and his heart started to beat harder than he was accustomed and his feet felt like they might not be touching the floor. It was like he was seeing Miranda for the first time again, like the day they met on her driveway, and that feeling that she was taking him away to her own little world swept over him, and god did he want to go there with her. She came down the stairs to him, looking ethereal, sophisticated, and innocent . . . but desirable as hell. He would see her like this for the rest of his life he realized. His brain was trying to understand, and his body was making coherent thought nearly impossible. Jenny had somehow vanished and he was looking into Miranda's eyes. Despite everything, his mouth eventually worked and he told her what his heart wanted her to hear.

Miranda smiled softly and moved closer to him so that his arm unconsciously closed around her waist, and she leaned into him, so that her body was pressed against his, and his heart raced harder. "My mother told me that this lipstick is smudge resistant," she told him.

Andrew leaned down and kissed her softly, and then leaned his forehead against hers and whispered, still holding her and laughing just a little, "I don't know how I'm going to make it through dinner."

"Me either," she whispered, and they laughed under their breath and tried to slow their hearts enough to join the others.

"Miranda! Andrew! We're waiting!" Lynne yelled from the parlour.

"Be there soon," Andrew called back. He stepped away from Miranda, took a deep breath, and checked that he hadn't smudged her lipstick, "Are you ready?" he asked her.

She nodded smiling, "I think so."

He took her hand and they joined the others in the parlour.

The Glittering Night

They did make it through dinner but couldn't stop looking at each other all that glittering candlelit night. Miranda's grandmother had truly prepared the most unbelievable evening for them and Miranda was giddy. They had hors d'oeuvres and homemade fruit punch from her nanna's big antique punch bowl before dinner and everyone was talking and happy and laughing and congratulating her and Andrew on finishing high school. Everything felt shining and new, and their beautiful home seemed to glow with happiness. Violet had prepared a proper five course meal. There was a creamed soup, fennel and apple salad, a spinach and feta puff pastry tarte, and salmon, then a clementine-cream and almond cake for desert. Miranda's father arrived just in time to be seated before dinner and he said, "Oh my, Miranda? I almost didn't know it was you." There were napkins folded like birds on all the gold and green china plates and the best silver and crystal were on the table.

255

After dinner coffee and tea were served back in the parlour. Miranda was explaining to Andrew, Jenny, and Willy, after they'd eaten, how it was that her mother and grandmother could throw such a beautiful and sumptuous party, "My mom worked for an event planner all through university. She used to do makeup for weddings and work as a DJ. And my nanna might have married a farmer, but she was a high society ballet dancer before that. She grew up going to elegant dinner parties."

"Is that picture of the ballerina, up in your room, Violet?" Jenny asked a little incredulous.

"It is, just before she got polio and had to give it up," Miranda told her.

"I thought it was just a random vintage photo you liked," Jenny sighed, looking across the room at Miranda's grandmother.

Miranda listened to the song playing on the stereo. Her mother had spent two weeks making playlists and Miranda felt like she was in a fairytale world—like the Twelve Dancing Princesses picture that hung upstairs in her bedroom—with everybody dressed up and all the candles lit and flowers on the tables. It had her dizzy again. Olivia had helped Violet serve at dinner and now she was carefully carrying a tray of Turkish delight around the room for people to sample. "The pink is rose flavoured, the yellow is bergamot, and the white is mastic, which tastes fascinating. We made it yesterday," she told them proudly.

Miranda's favourite was the rose flavour and she chose a small square, reaching out and plucking the perfect dusty pink cube from the stack with her fingers and putting it in her mouth, delicately sucking the powdered sugar off her fingertips and savouring the subtle floral taste. Andrew took the same and she watched him as he tried it and their eyes met and the others seemed to disappear. Jenny followed Olivia away asking about the candy, and Daniel drew Willy into the conversation he was having with Jeremy about fixing roofs. Miranda and Andrew still stood there looking at each other. Breaking her gaze, she took Andrew's hand and lead him to the drawing room where it was quieter, but they could still hear the softly playing music. Mazzy Star's *Fade Into You* drifted over to them and Miranda whispered, "I just need some quiet. Everything gets to be too much."

Andrew nodded and put his arms around her waist and she rested her cheek against his jaw and her hands on his shoulders and they quietly swayed to the music, close like that.

"Tonight feels significant somehow," he whispered in her ear. "I guess maybe it's supposed to, but I feel like I need you right now. Like you're my . . . I don't know, my anchor, in all this."

"Don't go home tonight," Miranda whispered back. "Stay here with me, at least for a little while."

"I will, I'll stay," he whispered back.

When the song ended they went back to the others to talk, laugh, and be merry, but when the night eventually wound to a close and everyone else was filing out the door into the frosty night, Andrew told his father that he was going to stay behind for a little while, and then quietly, when no one else was watching, went up to Miranda's room. Miranda watched as he climbed the stairs on his own, looking back at her with a smile. She helped her mother and grandmother clean for a little while but then Violet told her, up you go, your mom and I have this, it was your party, so it's not your mess. Miranda climbed up the stairs, still so overstimulated, still feeling the difference in the way she walked in the blue satin pumps. She stopped in the bathroom and wiped the makeup off and washed her face. She rubbed some cream into her naked skin looking at herself in the mirror, still seeing the echoes of how she'd looked all done up. She slipped the shoes off and peeled off the pantyhose and stepped out into the hall barefoot, looking behind her to check no one was there, and went into her bedroom. Andrew was sitting on her bed, looking at the figurine on her dressing table. His jacket and tie hung on her desk chair. He turned to look at Miranda and she looked back at him and they stayed that way for a long time. Andrew looked so serious, but looking into his eyes still felt so right to Miranda and it made her want him to touch her. She wanted more than his hand in hers and more than his lips on her cheek. The months of school, of pushing all that aside and ignoring that she *wanted*, came rushing up to her and she asked him, "Can you undo my zipper?"

He walked around the bed to her and undid the zipper, his fingers brushing the skin of her back. She slipped the dress off, carefully hung it back in her wardrobe, and then took out her earrings and placed them in a small, but exquisite, Fairyland Lustre dish on her dressing table as he watched. She looked at the ring for a moment and then slid it off and she placed it in the dish next to her earrings.

"Is it Belle Epoque?" Andrew asked.

"Yes. It was my mother's engagement ring. My parents gave it to me as a graduation present."

"I can't imagine it on Lynne. It looks beautiful on you," Andrew told her, his voice low and careful.

Miranda nodded and looked down, away from his face, away from the ring, standing in her silk slip in front of him. He stepped closer and they let their fingers touch. She looked up, "I need you too," she whispered, and he kissed her and she felt it all through herself so her knees buckled just a little and Andrew had to hold her tightly to keep her from falling and, holding her against him, it became obvious to her that he *wanted* too.

They kissed that night, and held each other, lying in Miranda's bed, Miranda in her slip and Andrew in his underwear, no further that night, no further, but that far. That much further than they'd been before.

"It's past three in the morning," Andrew whispered eventually. "If I stay we'll do this all night. I can't stop touching you. Your hair and your skin and your lips are so soft."

"There's a part of me that wants you to kiss me all night, and if you stay I won't stop kissing you back, but another part of me is ready to fall asleep and dream."

"I'll go then, and let you dream. And I'll see you to-morrow. Will you watch out the window till I make it to my room, and blow me a kiss goodnight?"

"I will. Will you watch for me in the morning?"

He kissed her again, "I will. Check if the coast is clear?"

Miranda got out of her bed and peaked out the door, into the hall, and down the stairs as Andrew pulled his clothes on.

"It's clear," she whispered.

"Goodnight Miranda." He kissed her again so she sighed and leaned into him and put her arms around him not wanting him to go but knowing she wouldn't sleep if he stayed.

"That doesn't make it easier to go," he smiled, and kissed her longer and then gently untangled himself.

"Goodnight Andrew," she stepped away and he slipped out the door.

She watched him go lightly down the stairs in his socks, carrying his shoes, and then she closed her door and went to her window and watched him cross the field in the frosty moonlight. She watched as his bedroom light went on and he opened his window. She opened hers and blew him a kiss and then looked up at the stars, sparkling like diamonds.

And then Came Spring

Miranda was a problem solver. She was told that it was unusual for women to be problem solvers, that usually women were less concerned with fixing problems and more concerned with listening to them and being supportive, but Miranda wasn't like that. She couldn't see how trying to fix a problem was being unsupportive. She could recognize when the problem had no simple solution and how in those circumstances sometimes listening, and being compassionate, really were the closest one could come to fixing the problem, and she knew to ask people if they just wanted her to listen or if they were looking for solutions, but she couldn't help trying to come up with a solution on her own, while she pretended to just listen, and she knew that she and Andrew had a problem.

They had spent a lot of time alone together in the month after they'd graduated. A lot of time alone. It was obvious that the things that usually went with being in love were inevitable and they had come to want it all, with certainty, and conviction, but they also wanted the right moment to come. The moment almost had come once, and then Olivia had arrived home from school early with a nose bleed, and had barged in on them. That had been embarrassing. And then again in the middle of the night in Miranda's bed, it had seemed perfect, it was going to happen, and then Lynne had yelled through the door, asking if Miranda knew if there was more ibuprofen in the downstairs bathroom, and they couldn't quite get back the courage because Miranda was pretty sure her mother didn't really need ibuprofen. Then it happened again. They actually made plans that time, and no one was due home, and Andrew had put a lock on his bedroom door, and then Andrew's phone rang and Jim asked him if he could keep his ear open because the Fed Ex guy was due to come to the house that day and it was important someone take the delivery, so they put their clothes back on and watched Doctor Who and waited for the Fed Ex guy. The more it happened the more difficult it got. And then Andrew had begun working part time for his dad doing reception, and Willy's dad offered him part time work with his contracting company. Andrew couldn't turn down the money. He couldn't turn over revenue dealing antiques on the internet like Miranda could, and earning money made Andrew feel like he was accomplishing something, which Miranda knew he needed from a psychological perspective.

Miranda knew there was a problem and she was pretty sure she knew how to fix it. First of all she knew that Andrew had more to worry about than she did. He worried about hurting her, he worried that she might find it over-stimulating and have a meltdown. While he was perfectly able to roll with her meltdowns, even she could see how it would be a 'mood killer'—as Andrew put it—if she had a meltdown because they had sex, not to mention that he was the one who would end up feeling guilty. Also, sex was a thing that could be addictive. Andrew didn't even plan on ever drinking alcohol, so she could see how he might be apprehensive about that. It had also been confirmed to her over the last few months of school, that some people really did hold the attitude that she wasn't capable of and shouldn't be allowed to make her own decisions, and that there was something somehow wrong with the idea that Andrew could want her that way. Miranda found it infuriating and extremely hurtful. She knew Andrew tried not to let it bother him, but she could see all the ways *that* could weigh on him too. And, she had also come to realize that, Andrew was just randomly worried sometimes, and worrying wasn't conducive to arousal.

Miranda knew in her bones what they needed. She had to make it safe, with *no* interruptions. It had to be a place that was dreamy, a place where they could get away, psychologically, from all the things that could go wrong. Definitely not the fort, that would be too irreverent, and there was no guarantee of privacy because that's were

Jenny hid when she cut class. It had to be a place where Miranda could have a meltdown and Andrew wouldn't have to explain to anyone *why* she was having a melt-down. Because while Miranda didn't *think* she would have a meltdown, she couldn't make promises. And it needed to be lovely. After all the aborted attempts it had to be a big deal. She had to make it special.

Violet was going to Victoria on Thursday to have her knees looked at by a specialist and she was bringing Olivia because they were going on a fabric hunt. They wouldn't be back till Sunday. That eliminated two poten-tial complications. Miranda spent Thursday wandering outside. The weather was warm and the trees were blos-soming. The forecast for the next day was twenty-three degrees Celsius. She walked down the hill and into the woods that were between the beach and their house. No one walked there and access to their beach was blocked by a rocky point that extended out into the Pacific. They didn't ever have trespassers, and if you climbed down the little ridge there was a mossy alcove in the hillside almost like a little grotto with a large Arbutus shelter-ing it. Miranda stood and turned around, looking at the place from every direction.

The next morning she got to work. She texted Andrew the GPS coordinates and told him,

_Bathe when you come home from work, and then meet me here. I will have food, so don't eat.

Then she baked a cake. Miranda didn't cook all that much, but considering who her grandmother was, she was competent enough in the kitchen. She made chicken and brie sandwiches, and set aside some grapes. She made iced tea and looked in the larder to see if there was any Turkish delight left and boxed that up too. She went down into the cellar and looked on the utility shelf for a thing she was pretty sure her mother would never throw out, and then she gathered the thing up in her arms and lugged it to the grotto. She set the tent up in the grotto and smiled. Her nanna had made it for her mom when she was little and Miranda had also loved it as a child. She couldn't quite stand up in it now but the round tent, that looked like what trooping fairies might take camping, would provide a degree of privacy, and it was made out of velvet and brocade from old theatre props, with banners on it, like a castle. Miranda dragged a camping mattress down the hill and some old blankets and pillows, and made a bed in the tent, then she tied old chandelier crystals—her grandmother seemed to have an endless supply of them—and ribbons, into the Arbutus so that colours and sparkling lights were all around. She went home and had a bath and put on just a little perfume. Shalimar. She had asked her dad to bring it back from Victoria with him, curious as to what it would smell like after having read its history. She found she rather liked it in very small quantities.

Then Miranda looked in her wardrobe pushing all the dresses to the side, to her grandmother's old dresses.

She took out the last one, and pulled it on over her slip. It was ivory silk with dusty rose lilies printed on it and the condition was less than pristine. Her grandmother had worn it many, many times and there were stains and creases that would never come out, but the way the neck line plunged and the seams accentuated her body and the skirt was almost see through, was wanton and charming, like a vagabond princess. She left her hair a mess then put on just a little lipstick, blotting it thoroughly, looked at herself in the mirror, and started to giggle breathlessly and went to change her underwear yet again because she was so wound up it was already damp. She found the picnic basket in the larder and she carefully packed it. She texted her mother,

_Going out with Andrew. Be back late.

And then she started down the hill with her basket to wait in beautiful agony.

At four-thirty she heard his voice call her name, "Miranda? You there?"

"Here!" she called out as he climbed down the ridge and came to the place where she waited.

He looked around and smiled at the little encampment and she walked up to him. He still looked older, ever since their graduation dinner, and she could feel life pulling at them, could feel her body moving towards his, quite beyond her control. They'd done their applications to University together, and in September they'd go away together. This was a part of that story. "Do we have to eat first?" he asked, only half joking, and she could tell he felt it too.

She walked up to him and leaned into him, putting her arms around him, loving the feel of worn flannel over warm shoulders, and breathing in his smell, which she had begun to find quite intoxicating. "I brought food to sustain us. Eating isn't what I built this for."

"Thank god," he breathed, and scooped her up and carried her to the tent.

Paradise

Miranda had sent Andrew cryptic text messages all day, starting with the message to meet her. During the last semester of school he'd put his old flip phone in his desk at home so he wouldn't lose it, and gotten a smart phone, and today Miranda was using it for all it was worth. He had to laugh though. He found her charming when she asked him on a date by sending him GPS coordinates. She was one in a million. The next text came with a picture of a cake with icing sugar sprinkled on top, then a crystal in a tree, then Miranda's own bare feet in the bathtub. Andrew hadn't thought he was turned on by feet but he had to stop looking at the picture. Then a picture of the bottle of Shalimar on Miranda's dressing table had come through which shouldn't really have been particularly arousing either but Andrew knew it was sitting next to the Gerhard Henning figurine which always made him feel . . . . Then another picture of her feet in the forest somewhere, like a picture from a story book, but god he really didn't think that he was into feet

. . . and then a picnic spread on a lace cloth on a big rock, and he realized what she was doing and why it was getting him so hot and bothered.

"Do you still need me here?" he asked his dad, after the second to last patient left. "Miranda asked me if I could meet her," he told Jim, knowing that if his dad thought he might have someplace else, someplace *better*, to be, that he would let him go sooner, and needing, so badly, to escape the medical clinic.

"I'm just finishing notes. The last patient cancelled. I'll see you later?"

"Not sure. I might stay over at Miranda's."

Andrew drove home to bathe, his hands sticky with sweat on the steering wheel. Fresh out of the tub and shaved, he pulled on an old flannel shirt that felt soft. It was in rough shape but Miranda always touched this particular shirt a lot *because* it was soft. She could be very sensory seeking that way and he would wear that shirt into the ground if it meant Miranda would touch him more. He pulled on old jeans and tucked his phone, wallet, and a few necessities into his pocket and then walked out the door. Andrew looked down the hill and towards the Hopkins property and decided to see if he could find Miranda without pulling out his phone. She was easy to find and when he got to the magical little encampment and she was standing in front of him, breathing hard, in a dress that looked made for taking off, with rainbow lights twinkling in the trees all around her, they were in a world all their own.

It was its own kind of beautiful madness, being with her. Andrew was genuinely afraid of hurting her but wanted her so urgently, feeling conflicted about wanting her, all the while knowing that it was the outside world causing that conflict. But she reassured him, whispering to him, "It's just us here . . . I *know* you . . . I love you . . . This *isn't* wrong . . . Trust me," and then finally, "I need you so much. Please!" And she'd looked into his eyes so he got lost in her gaze, and she was so sure that he borrowed some of that surety from her and finally let go, sinking into her arms and kisses. When the awkward jarring moment of stopping to put on a condom passed and he finally made it inside her, he realized that it all might end much much sooner than he wanted, so he stopped and tried to hold back until the sensations were less overwhelming. Andrew just kissed her, lying in her arms, feeling like time had stopped until Miranda began to move underneath him, gently, her legs twined around his, and when he was moving too and she was holding onto him tightly he managed somehow to whisper, "Are you alright?" and she answered him with, "Don't stop. Don't stop!" holding on tighter, and then she made a sound like a sigh and gasp and a cry and her body felt like it was melting underneath him and it was all so much that he couldn't hold it back any longer.

An hour later—smiling, because it seemed to have become his default facial expression and he couldn't stop, and after they'd eaten cake first and sandwiches after, and then managed to do it all again without worrying—

feeding each other grapes and lying in the little tent with their feet sticking out the door, he asked her, "How did we wait so long? What was I so afraid of?" He could see the crystals twinkling in the tree outside and spreading little rainbows on the quilt they were under, and feel her skin against his.

"I don't know really. I made a list of reasons, but I can't remember much from before you got here. I don't know if I existed before that." Her voice came out dreamy and light, like her words would turn into butterflies.

"How long did this take you?" he asked picking a Turkish delight off the little gilded plate on which they were stacked and looking up at the blue velvet ceiling of the tent.

"All day. I remember that. I'm never going to be able to make a sandwich ever again without wanting you."

"As long as it doesn't go the other way too," he whispered in her ear, and she started giggling, which was new. He'd never heard her laugh like that before, and he loved it.

Not High Enough

J enny was a bit lonely, which was strange. She'd gotten so used to not having friends that it was strange to her now how much she could miss them. She was extremely glad that Olivia was still at school with her, as the younger girl was very dear to Jenny and always lifted her up but, ever since they'd graduated, Andrew and Miranda had been lost in their own little world. Not that Jenny could blame them, or felt any resentment towards either one. She'd known since the first time she'd seen them together that what was now happening was inevitable. She was also mature enough to recognize that she was jealous, not of either one in particular, Miranda was beautiful, but not Jenny's type, and Jenny didn't have those kinds of feelings toward her, and obviously she'd never feel that way about Andrew, but she was jealous of what they had. She wanted someone to look at *her* that way, like the figurine on Miranda's dressing table. Like she was the only, and the most precious, thing in the world. Jenny missed the depth and maturity that Miranda and Andrew had brought to their lunchtime conversations too, and she just missed spending almost the whole day, every day, with them. She realized that they were almost closer than friends to her, they were more like family, and she'd spent almost every day with them for months on end, from June till February. No wonder it was strange, and felt wrong, to only see them once or twice a week, but she gave them space, and she waited, and by May they had fully emerged from their bubble.

Not that things went back to the way they were, but the new normal, when it arrived, was good. Jenny could see, from the way they touched each other, that they must be lovers now, but they had spent long enough hiding their affection, that they were never excessively demonstrative. And Jenny thought that, as unlikely as Andrew and Miranda were—an autistic girl and a recovered addict—, they deserved to be happy. At the beginning of May Jenny got a really bad case of pink eye and her mother brought her to the medical clinic. Jenny thought it was weird to see Andrew at the front desk in a button up shirt answering the phone and booking appointments for his dad. "Holy conjunctivitis Batman," he said when she walked in, then he grinned and said, "Sorry, that was totally inappropriate."

"Ya think?" she said to him, slouching miserably into the chair in the waiting room and trying not to touch her eyes.

"How are things?" he asked.

"Between this and the Archduke Franz Ferdinand, just peachy," she snapped, then realizing she was being unfair she said, "I'm sorry Andrew. I'm having a shitty week."

"Jennifer, language!" her mother said beside her.

"How are you?" she asked, ignoring her mum.

"I'll be great, next week, when the new receptionist arrives and the nurse practitioner gets here. I hate . . ." he glanced at old Mrs Gallup who was almost asleep waiting for her appointment and lowered his voice to a whisper, "I hate working here."

"Mmm. I hate social studies."

"You said something about the Archduke?"

"I have to do a report," she whined.

"Just a second," Andrew said and then pulled out his phone and typed something, then he asked, "When is your project due?"

"In a week and a half," she told him.

"When this," he motioned to her eyes, "clears up, ask Miranda to help you with the report. If you tell her that I told you to mention the Archduke, she'll know what you mean."

Jenny had gone home with a tube of erythromycin for her eyes wondering what Andrew meant about the Archduke but Miranda had always got really good grades so maybe he just meant that she would help, or that Miranda knew lots about the subject which wouldn't surprise Jenny. A few days later, once the antibiotics had kicked in, she stopped by the Hopkins house with Olivia on their way home and asked Miranda for help, "Andrew said you would help me. He said mention Archduke Franz Ferdinand. That you'd get it."

Miranda started laughing and had a hard time stopping and it didn't seem funny to Jenny but obviously the Archduke Franz Ferdinand meant something to Andrew and Miranda. "Yes I can help you," she answered, still giddy. "Are you busy? Do you want to come work on it now?"

"I only have a couple days left to do it. I did some of the research then my eyes were infected and I got an extension but I'm only about halfway done. I have to get some of it done today or I'm gonna run out of time."

"Come on," Miranda ushered Jenny in and then looked around as if they were doing something covert.

Jenny could hear Olivia's voice coming out of the sewing room where she was talking to Violet and getting help with her knitted cables or something like that.

Miranda crept up the stairs like she was trying not to be heard and Jenny followed, absolutely perplexed. "Come on," she whispered and ushered Jenny into her room then shut the door behind them. She opened a cupboard door and reached in, "I couldn't make myself throw this out. I got rid of most of my school stuff, but I had to keep this." Miranda held out a report.

Jenny took it and looked it over. "Can I work on it here? I'll get in trouble If my mum finds out I'm using your report?" Miranda smiled and nodded and still looked like she was either going to burst out laughing again or explode . . . or something.

"Is this report significant in some way that I'm not getting?" Jenny finally asked.

Miranda answered like she'd been just dying to be asked, "Last year on the twenty-ninth of April I gave it to Andrew to use for his report. That's how I introduced myself to him. I still can't believe I did it. The day we *really* met was the day Misty and Robin attacked me. But I gave him my paper the week before that."

"Today is the twenty-ninth!" Jenny said, appreciating Miranda's excitement.

"I love synchronicity," Miranda admitted.

"There's more to it than just that," Jenny told her friend. "I heard yesterday that Robin got in a fight. He just turned nineteen, they think he'll have to do time. He's being held for assault."

Miranda blinked, "I can't understand violence. I just can't understand it. Doesn't he realize that he's hurting himself as much as the person he hits?"

"I don't understand what happened to him to be honest. When I was small Misty and I were best friends. When I think back I can't imagine Robin being the person he is now. I always thought he'd grow up to be gentle, like Willy and Andrew are. And I still can't believe Misty would smash your phone like that."

"I didn't know you were that close to them," Miranda said, incredulous.

"I forget that I was. I forget on purpose. When I think about it it I still feel . . ." Jenny shuddered as the hurt rippled through her like it was fresh. "God Miranda. When it happened I cried for weeks. One day when we were twelve Misty told me she didn't want to be my friend anymore. That I was a loser and she didn't want anything to do with me. That I should just go. It broke my heart. It was a real loss that I still feel in my body. I think that's why I can be so sarcastic now. It's as though I have to test whether people actually want me around." Jenny told Miranda what had happened and it felt like some invisible membrane between them dissolved. Miranda now knew Jenny's deepest hurt too.

"I want you around. You're my friend. You'll always be my friend. You rescued me. I'll never forget that." Miranda looked stricken and her lip quivered, "I've been preoccupied the last few weeks. I'm sorry."

Jenny waved the apology away, "You and Andrew spending extra time together is different. Hell, you and I still hang out once a week. We watched a movie together just before the attack of the pink eye monster. I guess there does come a point when people get older and don't spend all their time playing anymore." Jenny reassured Miranda.

"I'm sorry Misty did that to you. I won't do that. *Never*. I *wouldn't* do that," Miranda said very, very seriously.

Jenny gave the older girl a hug.

* * *

It was three days later, on Friday afternoon, when Jenny heard at school that old man McIntosh had died of an accidental drug interaction. After school that day she, Willy, and Olivia stopped at Miranda's house and they waited for Andrew to come home from work at her dad's current job site. "I know Misty was a bitch to me and to Miranda, but she's all alone now. Her grandma died over the summer and her cousin is fed up with her. I sorta want to do something for her but I don't know what. What do you do for someone who you've been estranged from, and who still apparently hates you?"

"I still wonder why she ended your friendship?" Willy asked of no one in particular.

"It didn't make any sense. It might have made sense if she'd done it after her mum took off but she did it a year before that. If she'd done it right after her mum left I'd have excused it and just brushed it off as her wanting to lash out because she was hurting."

"I don't know what to do. A casserole would be con-descending," Miranda said.

"What about a quilt?" Olivia piped up, patting Jenny's arm while she talked, "If you embroidered the squares and helped me with the cutting we could do it together. I've done two quilts now, I know what to do."

"A hand-made quilt makes a pretty big statement," Andrew reasoned. "Sewing together all those little pieces for someone . . . *I* would be moved. A quilt *literally* brings comfort. Symbolically that might mean something for someone in emotional turmoil."

Jenny and Olivia got to work. They even managed to get Miranda to help them organize the pattern, although she got bored and wandered off when the actual sewing started to happen.

* * *

Jenny heard sirens. Her teacher had just handed back her Social Studies report and she'd gotten a B+. Miranda had engineered the report so that it wouldn't look suspicious. Jenny was happy with the grade but she was distracted by the noise. The other students were getting up and looking out the windows as two ambulances rushed by. St Fina only had one ambulance. It must be a real emergency if the out of town emergency crew was here too. She packed up her bag and left school, walking towards Josephine road with Willy and Olivia.

"I wonder what happened," Willy mused, watching with concern as a Search and Rescue vehicle rushed past and then turned onto Josephine road. They passed the site where her dad was gutting and refinishing a house that had recently been bought by a couple from Nanaimo and Andrew was standing on the sidewalk, sawdust in his hair, with his phone in his hand.

"Do you guys know what's happening?" he asked. "I can't get hold of Miranda."

Jenny looked down at her own phone. She'd texted Miranda her grade and under normal circumstances, Miranda always texted back right away. Jenny started to feel uneasy.

"I don't suppose you've still got the tracking app we used last year on that thing?" she motioned to Andrew's phone.

"Oh, yeah. We use it for . . ." he swallowed and turned pink. "I hadn't thought of using it to *actually* track her."

He turned it on and it showed Miranda's phone next to the old railway bridge, on the edge of the ravine, on the other side of the field, across the road from his house. Jenny felt a little sick and Andrew turned white. Olivia started to cry, and Willy yelled, "Dad, somethings wrong! We gotta take Andrew with us."

A Search and Rescue helicopter battered the air and they could see that it was going to land in their field.

"Go, run, I'll be there as soon as I lock up the tools," Daniel told the kids, and Jenny felt worse because her dad was serious.

They ran as fast as they could to the scene of the emergency. The vehicles were congregated in the field that their parents had recently purchased and the emergency crew was working at the top of the hill near the edge of the ravine, by the old railway bridge. They raced across the field. Andrew pulled ahead of Jenny and then slowed as Jim appeared out of the crowd and jogged towards them, "It's not Miranda," Jim said taking Andrew's shoulders in his hands, "It's not Miranda. She's just bruised, scratched, and scared. Violet has her safe at home."

"What's going on then?" Jenny asked, adrenaline and fear pumping through her. "Why does Miranda's phone show her being here?"

Jim pulled Miranda's phone out of his pocket and gave it to Jenny, "Miranda called the ambulance and then dropped her phone. Look, you four need to clear out of here. Violet and Janet are at the Hopkins house, Miranda is safe. I want you to go there, and stay there."

They turned and walked quickly across the field but Andrew broke into a run and got to Miranda's front porch first. When Jenny and the others went in, Janet herded them to the kitchen and sat them down with hot chocolate which should have been wrong for the warm spring afternoon but somehow wasn't. She could hear Andrew's voice ever so slightly, drifting down the stairs from Miranda's room, but Janet had told them to stay in the kitchen. "Mum? What happened?" Jenny asked.

Jenny's mum's face went all soft and sad as she looked back at her daughter and Janet came and put her arms around Jenny and held her so tightly, whispering "My beautiful beautiful girl."

"Mum . . . What is it?" Jenny started tearing up.

Janet sat next to Jenny at the table and Jenny looked at her mother's proud beautiful face and wondered why tears were falling down her cheeks. Janet opened her mouth and then stopped and then started again, "Misty attempted suicide. She jumped off the train bridge." Jenny did cry then and Janet put her arms back around her daughter. That was when Jenny processed the word "attempted."

She pulled back and looked at her mother in horror, "But Mum, that bridge isn't high enough!"

"No, my love, it isn't high enough."

The Cruel Child

What a cruel child. That is what Janet thought that Autumn day when her Jennifer had come running home in tears and into her arms like a hurricane of grief. She had always though that Jennifer and Misty would be those friends who were maids of honour at each others weddings and brought their children up together. But no. Janet held onto a little seed of anger on her daughter's behalf and thanked her lucky stars that Jennifer had William. Her Sweet William. She was careful not to call him that anymore, but he still had such a big enthusiastic heart that he offered his sister a kind of shelter. Janet knew, before Jennifer did, that Jennifer didn't like boys, and she wondered, later, if that was perhaps the reason Misty had pushed her away, but she could never really know.

At first it had been a source of anxiety to Janet, when the old McGinty houses had sold and she'd heard that families with teenagers had moved in. But then at the grocery store, Marge in checkout, had said that the girl in the Queen Anne house was, "Touched," as she put it, and that the other two, in the Craftsman, were the children of the new GP. Marge called the daughter a, "Sweetheart," and said the son, looked like a, "Heart-breaker, you know? The kind you keep away from your daughter?" Marge had happily gossiped away to Janet, glad of having someone to relate the only events to have taken place in St Fina all year to. *Well maybe Jenny can make friends with the GP's daughter,* she thought to herself feeling slightly relieved that she didn't have to worry about the "heart-breaker".

And then somehow her gloomy, grumpy, surly, sarcastic, daughter had made friends with all three of the weird kids. Janet felt just a little ashamed thinking of them as 'the weird kids'. She had laughed though when Daniel had come home from work and looked at her and asked, "Where did those *weird* kids come from?" And it stuck.

Janet was glad in the end though, because they were probably the only kids in town who were weird enough to suit William and Jennifer. William in particular embraced the differences. Janet had to google autism because she was nervous at first, thinking she had a disabled child in her house and that she needed to know what to do. Googling it didn't make things easier because the girl didn't seem to match what she read, so she called the girl's mother one evening after dinner while her children were still out running wild with 'the weird kids'.

"You want to know about Miranda?" Lynne had been unsurprised at the call.

Janet had found out that the girl was intellectually gifted in some areas, and selectively mute, but that as long as you weren't angry around her she was quite stable.

"She's vulnerable though," Lynne had told her.

"How do you mean?" Janet asked.

"As smart as she is, Miranda can't tell if someone means her harm."

Janet wondered how Lynne got through the day without worrying herself to death and then Jennifer had come in, all wild hair and dirty feet, and Janet had felt a sudden kinship to the woman down the road. Janet worried about Jennifer all day too.

Having families in the McGinty houses again reminded Janet of when she was young, before St Fina had truly become a ghost town. When the other two families had suggested a barbecue, she'd been pleased to help and had discovered a kindred spirit in Violet. Violet was cultured but knew the value of hard work, much like Janet herself. Mid-morning coffee with the older woman became a daily ritual.

And so a thing that, at first, had caused her anxiety turned out to be a boon, a journey to the life she had imagined she'd have when she was young and had thought her own children would have friends and run wild and turn dark brown with each summer, just like she did, with big family dinners and movies on rainy afternoons.

One night, late in the evening at the end of August she stopped by Jennifer's bedroom door and watched her towel dry her hair and comb it out. "Mum. Tuck me in?" Jennifer asked.

Jennifer put a towel on her pillow and then scrambled into bed and lay down. Janet came and pulled the blankets up and then tucked in the edges smiling, because it had been so long since Jennifer had asked to be tucked in. "You had a good day?" Janet asked.

"I did . . ." she trailed. "Mum I'm . . . I like . . ." The silence stretched.

"Girls?" Janet finished gently.

Jennifer looked panicked for a brief moment and then nodded.

"I love you my beautiful girl," Janet smiled, glad Jennifer had felt ready to share.

"Does dad know too?" Jennifer asked.

"He does, and we want you to know that we will love whoever you love, and that we want you to be whoever it is that *You* want to be. We support you."

Janet left Jennifer's room and cried tears of joy, and worry, and overwhelmed mother tears, and then went to bed thankful that Jennifer knew who she was and that she wasn't in a hurry to grow up.

As the school year passed and holidays and special occasions marked the passage of time Janet watched as the five kids changed, her own two, and the other three. She talked with Lynne about worrying, and she watched as William became a little more thoughtful and Jennifer became a little less sarcastic, and then when spring came and Robin McIntosh went to prison, Janet started to get a bad feeling. She had never been able to find out why Misty had pushed Jennifer away, or why the family had imploded, but Misty had been a sweet girl once. Not a cruel child at all.

Watching her Fall

It took Miranda and Andrew about three weeks to get to a point where they could be in the same room, *and* keep their hands off of each other. Andrew had described it as a 'beautiful madness' and he was right, and the madness didn't so much pass, but perhaps they became accustomed to it. Perhaps they developed a tolerance. Miranda was still a little in awe. Sometimes Andrew would sleep over and she would watch him sleep and wonder how it was that he was hers. She knew they were living in their own little world and she knew that one day they would step out of it, but it was such a beautiful world. It was hard not to linger.

Then Jenny had stopped at her door and asked for help and the world had broadened again. She and Jenny were a part of the same narrative again, all thanks to the Archduke Franz Ferdinand.

They sat together finishing Jenny's report that afternoon, still talking on and off about Misty and Robin. Miranda felt quite badly for being unavailable to Jenny, especially after knowing about Misty, and she made a bigger effort to spend time with her other friends. Willy had grown several inches it seemed, and had developed a philosophical streak, and Olivia had trained Wainwright to pull a cart. Jenny had changed since February too. She was a little taller, and slender now, in a way that made her waist length black hair sensual instead of just long, and she was a little gentler somehow.

She and Jenny started spending an hour or two together after Jenny's school day almost every day, mostly just talking, and it was a relief to Miranda to have someone who she could share some of the new things in her life with. It had taken a little time to get back to the way they used to talk before, Miranda being unsure of where the line between sharing and oversharing was, and erring on the side of caution, making Jenny think she didn't want to talk about how things had changed between herself and Andrew. But eventually they'd figured it out.

"What's it like being in love, being *that* close to someone else?" Jenny had asked once she knew the topic wasn't off limits.

Miranda thought about it, "I didn't expect Andrew to exist. In some ways it's still very surprising to me. But that's not really what you're asking is it . . ." and she hesitated a moment, deciding whether it felt right to share exactly what she felt, *all* of it, and decided it was okay. "It's like an exquisite kind of beauty that you can feel. Like friendship, but with desire? There's a fluidity to it. A liquid exchange that has more to do with touch and taste and smell. Like you've become just a little tangled in someone else's existence. At first it felt like I had birds in my chest and then when I knew it was real, when Andrew said he loved me, and I said I loved him back, it was like the birds were free . . . but still with me, soaring. Some parts are like 'a beautiful madness', Andrew says, and it *does* feel like that. It also feels more innocent, and more spiritual, than I thought it would."

Jenny nodded and wandered over to the the Gerhard Henning figurine on the dressing table that Miranda knew she loved. "Is it like that?" Jenny asked.

"It is like that," Miranda admitted.

* * *

B ut with the others still in school and Andrew working, Miranda had quite a bit of spare time.

She did do some scrounging for antiques and struck gold at a joint moving sale. St Fina had a small population of old folks who were so old they had already been near retirement when the collapse had happened and had made their fortunes during the good times, but often all they had left was the value in their houses—which wasn't much even though home prices were slowly going up in the area—and the various items they had gathered throughout their lifetimes.

Two little old ladies of English and Scottish descent were moving into a retirement home together after the passing of their husbands. Miranda looked over the table of pottery and porcelain and set aside three rare Moorcroft vases, a wide and particularly nice selection of

Wedgwood, and a hideous Meissen figurine. She always had an ethical dilemma though. She couldn't rob the little old ladies, which was what she'd be doing if she bought the vases off of them for twenty-five cents each, which was seriously what they were asking. Not when she was going to turn around and sell most of them on eBay for hundreds and even thousands of dollars. But rather than argue with them, trying to give them more money on the spot, because they usually just looked at her and said, "Oh don't be silly dear. Just take it. My daughter said she doesn't want these old things and I won't have the space when I move," she told the little old ladies, "These vases are worth rather a lot," handing them the money for their asking price. "I'm going to re-sell them on eBay. Is there an address that you can give me, and I can send you a cheque for a portion of the proceeds?"

The little old ladies gaped at her, "Oh dear, I didn't realize. But I don't need much and the proceeds from the house will see me over. Really, I can't take them with me, and selling them properly myself in this day and age would just be . . . well. I'm ninety-five Dear!"

"Are we truly talking about that great a sum of money?" the younger little old lady asked in creeping dismay.

"A bowl very much like this one sold at auction last year for $4000 US dollars," she told them seriously, pointing to the Fairyland Lustre bowl. "And this figurine might be a fake, but if not . . . It's *Meissen*. I couldn't even hazard a guess as to how much it's worth."

"Well, you've bought them from us, and they *are* yours now, but," the younger lady turned to the older, "Martha? What if she sold them for enough that we could go to Tahiti? Remember how we always used to talk about that? When the kids were small and we were tired?"

"Give me your new address. I'll write you a cheque," Miranda told them. "I know a buyer, a collector down in the United States. I'll give you half of what I make. Would that be reasonable?"

Miranda carefully packed the pieces into boxes and called her mother for a ride, feeling pretty satisfied, and she spent the week processing her find and emailing out pictures. She packed and shipped half of what she had bought to the collector she knew, and added the Hazeldene Moorcroft vase to her own personal collection. It was one she'd been hoping to find someday, and the feeling of rightness she had, placing the graceful, serene, blue, cream, and green vase on her walnut dresser top, filled with dried hydrangeas, spread through her whole body right to her toes and her fingertips. She posted the rest on eBay. The next day she walked over to Martha and Enid's houses to see if they were still in town so that she could give them the cheque in person, and they were still there. She'd looked up air fare prices for Tahiti and the price of ten days at a resort. She estimated that she was giving them a cut closer to sixty-five percent, but she couldn't stop picturing them on the white sand beaches and she'd gotten a very good price on the Wedgwood bowl. It was a rare one. And the Meissen figurine . . . Miranda shuddered every time she thought about it. She disliked Meissen and couldn't *quite* wrap her head around it's value.

She looked at them and told them very earnestly, "You have to promise me you're going to go to Tahiti," and then passed them the cheque. "It's certified, be careful not to lose it."

"We're going to Tahiti!" The little old ladies clasped hands and and then kissed Miranda's cheek and called her a strange and wonderful girl.

Miranda started her walk back across town, slowly getting distracted by every brilliant and beautiful thing there was to see. The spring was exquisite, like love. There was a seal watching her as she walked by the waterfront and she stopped to look into its eyes before it sank below the waves. Sea birds flew overhead in the azure sky and the breeze tickled her skin. She untied her sweater and pulled it back on and wandered up to the main street. There was a row of empty storefronts and two of them had broken windows. Miranda imagined what it would look like if the shops were still there, a bakery, a deli, a gallery, a tea room, and imagined people on the sidewalks. She saw a flock of pigeons and she ran towards them and watched them fly up into the sky. And then she watched the rabbits on the old village green, pretended that there were families having picnics, and said hello to the imaginary people as she walked by, glorying at the way she could hear her voice come out of her throat without a hitch. She came to the intersection of Maple crescent and Josephine road and she climbed the elm tree there and imagined she was a bird and thought about where she would fly if she was one, and then she jumped down and ran as fast as she could into the field. It was *their* field. It would never have a hotel on it, or a surfing school, or any of the annoying things that could end up there, and it was full of spring flowers. Miranda picked wild sweet peas and yarrow, white violets and buttercups, and made a bouquet to give to Andrew, thinking about how much she looked forward to seeing him each night. She walked to the top of the hill and twirled until she fell down and laughed really hard all by herself looking up into the true blue sky. She heard the town clock in the far off distance chime two o'clock. The others would be done school in an hour. She could go help her nanna bake something for them. Miranda stood and brushed off her dress and turned around three-hundred and sixty degrees looking at the beauty all around her. The sunshine, the tall cedars, the glittering ocean, and the ravens flying above her—soaring, like her heart—and then she saw the girl standing on the train bridge in the distance.

Miranda's heart plummeted and she felt as if the wind had been knocked out of her, seeing the little figure teeter out there all by itself. She ran towards the edge of the ravine, close enough to see who it was out on the narrow trestles and her heart plunged further, "Misty!

What are you doing!" she yelled in a desperate panic, running back and forth by the edge of the bridge.

"Get the fuck away from me freak!" Misty, spat loudly.

"You have to get off the bridge it's not safe!" Miranda shouted back.

"You're an idiot! Do you think I don't know that! Why do you think I'm here!?"

Miranda realized that Misty was hysterical and it scared her because she didn't know the right thing to say. She was the last person who should talk Misty down, and she knew it, "Misty! Get off the bridge! Please!" she begged. "Get off the bridge! *Get off the bridge*!" She screamed it louder as if it might be somehow more convincing that way.

Misty went still, "That's what I'm trying to do! Just leave me alone!"

"Misty No! It's not high enough! NO!" Miranda screamed as Misty let herself fall and Miranda watched the girl's body plummet to the bottom of the ravine catching a branch an spinning like a rag doll.

Miranda grabbed madly for her phone and dialled emergency services and started yelling, as soon as the voice asked, "What's your emergency?"

"The train bridge off Josephine road! Misty jumped, she jumped she's in the ravine across the street from one hundred and one Josephine road she jumped you have to get someone!" Miranda ran to the edge and she could see Misty lying at the bottom. It was only about three stories. She might be dead but she might not be. That bridge didn't guarantee you a death. "She's at the bottom of the ravine!" Miranda screamed into her phone again.

There was an animal trail near the edge and the sides weren't as steep as they looked. Miranda dropped her phone and carefully edged along the animal trail, held onto the willow roots and eased herself down the ledge not thinking about anything but the broken girl at the bottom. She slid partway in the shale and then grabbed more tree roots and found another animal trail. She stumbled and took a spill but she was nearly at the bottom. She scrambled in the rocks, through more shale and then she was down. Misty had hit the ground feet first, next to the creek. Miranda could barely look. "Oh you stupid stupid girl! The bridge isn't high enough!" Miranda cried.

Misty was bleeding from the mangled leg where the bone had pierced her flesh. She was barely conscious but kept lifting her head to try and look around. Miranda tore the waist tie off her dress and tied it tightly around the bleeding leg, up near Misty's thigh, and then looked the other girl over as best she could, having no more than basic first aid. She took off her sweater and carefully put it under Misty's head and told her, "Lie still! Put your head down and lie still!"

Misty seemed to hear her and relaxed minutely. "Stay still. I'm going to climb back up and meet the ambulance. I can hear it coming." And Miranda scrambled in the shale grabbing tree roots and pulling herself back up the nearly sheer slope, along the narrow rocky animal trails.

She reached the top gasping as two paramedics jumped out of the ambulance and Jim's Toyota bumped along the dirt road. He got out and started up the hilly field. Miranda was so relieved to see him that she sat down in the grass and started to cry as the paramedics started towards her.

"It's not me! It's not me!" she told them waving them away, batting at them, and pushing them off. "Misty McIntosh jumped off the bridge! She's at the bottom."

Jim reached her just at that moment and Miranda was done. With profound relief to find herself in the hands of someone she trusted, she let go sobbing. She couldn't do anything more and she had done all she could. She could check out now. She didn't understand anything that happened or anything that anyone said to her after that until she was sitting in her bathroom at home in her underwear and her grandmother was running her a bath.

"Nanna? What happened?" she asked.

"Don't you worry. Just get in the water and let's see what's dirt and what's not."

Miranda undressed the rest of the way, looking at the dirty ruined dress on the floor, and sat in the warm water and watched it turn brownish pink while her nanna gently washed her arms, shoulders, back, and knees with soap and then rinsed her off, helped her stand up, and dried her off. She watched in confusion as the old towel came away from her skin streaked with red. She had scratches all over her body and she sat in a towel shivering while her nanna put polysporin on her elbows and

wrists and knees and shoulders, then bandaged everything she could. An old flannelette nightgown was pulled
over her head and she was bundled into bed. Miranda
lay down in her soft fragrant bed in her beautiful room
and the image in her mind was of a girl falling through
the air. "Nanna?" Miranda whispered again, as her grandmother sat down next to her, cut and filed her broken
fingernails and then rubbed ointment into her red sore
fingers, "What happened?"

The Aftermath

A ndrew kicked off his work boots and ran up the stairs of the Hopkins house to Miranda's room and looked in with his heart pounding. There was no describing what had gripped him when he'd seen Miranda's phone show up near the ravine by the derelict train bridge, just as the helicopter had flown overhead. Maybe like the world might be ending? Like something was slipping through his fingers that he desperately wanted to hold onto? And even after his father told him that Miranda was safe, the residual feeling of panic pushed him across the field and wouldn't let up until she was in front of him. He gripped the door frame of her bedroom. Miranda lay in her bed looking confused, tired, and battered. One of her cheekbones was scraped and there was a bump on her forehead. "Andrew?" she looked up at him.

Violet stood and told him, "I'll be right back," and then whispered as she passed, "I don't know how she was injured, but apparently she called emergency services because Misty MacIntosh jumped off the train bridge."

Even though their land ran close to that ravine, Andrew and the other four never went close to the bridge. It had a bad vibe and should have been blasted out years ago, but the age old argument of who would pay for it, and who owned the property it was on, and ultimately whose responsibility it was, had waged for generations. It wasn't on their property, Andrew knew. He'd seen the village surveyors map. He nodded, and Violet made her way down the stairs.

"Miranda?" he said her name gently, walking to her bedside and sitting next to her. "Are you alright?"

"She jumped, Andrew. It was such a perfect day. I picked flowers for you in the field, but she jumped, and . . . I forgot the flowers." Miranda dissolved into tears and he knelt by her bed and put his arms around her, relieved, oh so relieved, and he cried tears with her, although his were tears were mixed with the joy of relief and love.

"It's okay, we'll pick flowers together another day," he told her, stroking her hair carefully, just wanting to comfort Miranda.

"Are you hurt?" he asked once she was quiet.

"I'm scraped up. I hurt everywhere. I don't remember how that happened. I just remember begging her not to jump."

Violet came back in with three mugs on a tray and placed them on Miranda's night stand, "Hot chocolate," she announced. "I know it seems wrong on a day like today, but it always seems to level me out."

"We always do tea and toast for trauma, or the stomach flu, at my house," Andrew told her.

"That would do the trick too, probably even better for the flu," Violet settled into the green velvet parlour chair with her own hot chocolate.

Miranda picked up her mug. Andrew watched her blowing on the hot liquid and sipping slowly, relieved to see her do something so mundane and pedestrian. She wasn't too traumatized to want hot chocolate. All of a sudden he felt drained, wanting to just sit in the beautiful room and drink his own hot chocolate, and not think about whatever had happened, and just be glad that whatever it was, Miranda was there with him, safe and alive. But Miranda asked, "Where's Jenny?"

"She's downstairs," Andrew told her.

"Does she know that Misty jumped off the train bridge?"

"I don't know if anyone has told her yet," Andrew answered.

Miranda nodded solemnly, "I was so happy in the moments before I saw her, and she was right there, and she wanted to die."

The thought of it made Andrew's heart ache and he thought about Jenny, "Do you want me to go downstairs and check on Jenny?" he asked Miranda.

"Can you?"

"Yeah," he rose, kissed Miranda's unscathed cheek, and headed for the door.

He went downstairs feeling more relieved for Miranda as he went, because if she was worrying about Jenny she wasn't worrying about herself. As traumatic as witnessing an attempted suicide was, she wasn't trapped inside her own head. She was talking.

As he came downstairs Lynne burst in the door. "Is she upstairs?"

Andrew nodded and Lynne ran up the stairs just as his dad came in behind her.

"What happened?" Andrew asked.

Jim looked exhausted and instead of answering Andrew's question he asked, "Is Miranda still addled?"

"Yes and no. She knows that Misty jumped. She knows what she saw and that she begged her not to jump, but she doesn't know what happened after that. She seems aware of what's happening *now* though, and aware that there's a gap in her memory. She's worried about Jenny. She's upset but seems clearheaded." Andrew knew his dad was asking to get a sense of whether Miranda had a head injury.

Jim nodded, "I'm going to go up and take another look at her just to make sure I shouldn't be sending her to the hospital in the helicopter with Misty."

"Misty's alive?"

"As of right now. They're stabilizing her and working on getting her out of the ravine."

Andrew nodded and his dad went upstairs. Andrew went to the kitchen and sat down next to Jenny. She was pale and her lips quivered. She was sitting next to her brother and his arm was around her. "Miranda wanted me to check on you," he told her, then asked, "How are you?"

"I let Misty down," Jenny murmured.

"*You* didn't. Someone else *did*. We don't know what was going on in her life or what it's been like for her. And when you were twelve you were too young to fix whatever made her turn on you. Somebody let Misty down, but it wasn't you."

"I could have approached her sooner. I could have done something for her sooner. I could have pushed her to let me back in."

"She wouldn't have let you get near her. Last semester she told you to fuck off every time you so much as glanced at her in the hall. I was there, I noticed. You had to text us for backup that time you tried to ask her to hang out with us. Jenny, if she was as rock bottom as she must have been to jump off a bridge there wasn't much you could have done. She needed professional help. I've been there, *I know*," Andrew told her. "If Misty survives she'll need you. Don't waste energy on feeling like you should have done something, save it for when she has no choice but to accept your help."

A big tear rolled down Jenny's face and Willy said, "Hear, hear," and squeezed Jenny's shoulders.

"Is Miranda okay?" Jenny asked eventually.

"I think so. She wants to know about you though."

Jenny sighed, and didn't answer the question but asked instead, "Can I go see her?"

"We'll ask when my dad and Lynne come down. There's a lot of people up there right now."

Janet was at the kitchen counter and turned around with a big plate of sandwiches and put them down on the table. Olivia came out of the sewing room with Wainwright who spent his days with Violet. Jenny leaned over and wrapped her arms around the dog who seemed to know he was needed and stayed next to Jenny while she ate her sandwich.

Jim came into the kitchen then and gave them an update, "Miranda's well enough that she can stay home. I was worried about a head injury but I think her memory loss is dissociative. She is vehemently opposed to going to the hospital in any case. We'll have to watch her but she doesn't have any other signs of a head injury and the memory loss is very, very specific."

Jim continued, "When the rescue crew got down to Misty they found a part of Miranda's dress tied around Misty's leg as a tourniquet and Miranda's sweater under her head. The slope down into the ravine is very steep and Misty is in frightening shape. Miranda doesn't remember climbing down but it would have been a terrifying climb. Seeing a person's body damaged to that extent is hard for anyone not accustomed to it, but making that climb with bare legs, in a sun dress, would explain the state Miranda's in."

"Have you seen Misty yet?" Janet asked, extremely pensive.

"No, they've reported over radio about the nature of her injuries but I haven't seen her. I'm going to head back up the hill. They may have finished the rigging to lift her out."

"Can we go upstairs and see Miranda?" Jenny asked.

Lynne came down at that moment and they turned to look at her.

"They'd like to go upstairs and see Miranda?" Jim told her.

"She's asking for them," Lynne answered. "Just don't stress her out, use you're common sense guys. Kick the rest out if she seems agitated," Lynne told Andrew. "You've got some sort of sixth sense for her moods so I'm counting on you."

"I will," Andrew told her.

* * *

A ndrew spent the night because Miranda had asked him not to go and he hadn't wanted to leave her. They'd stopped with the pretense of the camping mattress on the floor when Andrew stayed over. Miranda had told Lynne what was going on and Lynne hadn't been unreasonable, as long as they were being—she'd used the same word as Andrew's dad—responsible.

He lay beside her in the semi-darkness as she slept, listening to the rain come down and looking up at the ghostly shapes in the canopy above the bed. The road would be washed out by morning, he knew, which meant Jenny wouldn't be able to go see Misty in the hospital for a while. Sleeping next to Miranda was still new enough that Andrew lay awake for a while, acutely aware of her. She startled in the dark, and he woke her, "Hey Miranda? Talk with me?"

"Oh, good. You're still here," she mumbled, and rolled toward him, gasped at the pain in her body, and stopped rolling.

"You okay?" he asked her.

"Sort of. Can you help me get comfortable? No matter how I lie, I'm lying on a scrape or a bruise. I'm glad I can't remember getting into this state, because sleeping like this is awful."

He shifted closer and she finished rolling very slowly, with help, and rested her unscathed cheek on his shoulder and draped a leg over him. "That's better," she sighed.

"Okay," Andrew smiled in the dark.

"Andrew?"

"Yeah?"

"I feel lucky right now, and slightly guilty for feeling lucky. I don't feel lucky about what happened, I feel horrible for Misty, and I'm so worried about how Jenny is taking this. And it was a horrible thing to see, but . . . I'm safe, and I have you and my mom and Nanna, and Olivia and the twins, and your dad, and the Arayas. I feel lucky. Even when I close my eyes and see Misty falling through the air on the backs of my eyelids, I feel lucky."

"I know exactly what you mean," Andrew sighed and wrapped his arms carefully around her, asking, "Does that hurt?"

"Go up an inch . . . okay, there. That's good."

He kissed her forehead and breathed in the scent of her hair, "I'm so glad, so relieved, you're alright. I don't know how I would be, if I'd seen what you saw, and I don't know what I'd have done if you were the one who had gotten hurt falling into the ravine, on purpose or otherwise . . . but you weren't, so I feel lucky too."

"I'm . . . surprised, that I'm alright. I'm trying not to think about it too much. Maybe in a week or two I'll have some kind of . . . *reaction*? Maybe I haven't processed what happened, except that I think that I have and I know, rationally, what happened, and I don't remember going into the ravine. Maybe that's not right somehow, but I think, in my head, and in my heart, that I really am alright. I think I am. I wouldn't have been alright before I had you."

* * *

News of Misty trickled in throughout the week. They were told that doctors would be unable to save her leg, but that it meant they could try to save her arm, once they dealt with the internal bleeding and the pelvic fracture. Each time a surgery was successful, each time a new specialist agreed to come from another country to put the broken girl back together, each time they received a piece of good news, they would exhale a little, but the five of them knew that saving Misty's body was only part of what needed to be done.

Daniel had halted work on the house for the remainder of the week so that he could be available for Jenny and give Andrew a few days to spend with Miranda while she recovered, but the five of them ended up spending those days in Violet's sewing room. Once Violet had discovered that Jenny and Olivia had been working on a quilt for Misty even before her suicide attempt, she told them to bring what they had done to her and that she would help them finish and the three of them put their heads together to make the quilt to beat all quilts. Andrew sat with Miranda who was sore, but would recover without any visible scars, and with Willy, who was tied up with worry for his sister, and they watched.

It was a strange and conflicted thing to watch, Andrew thought, from his position, because he had already been through the wringer and come out the other side. He'd already hit bottom and climbed back out. He had come so far and when he looked at his life he felt, like Miranda, incredibly lucky. All he knew of Misty was the gamine little bad ass who had done nothing but spit venom at him. He remembered grabbing Misty and pulling her away from Miranda that day by the portables. But if Jenny said that Misty had once been something different, that she had been full of sunshine, once upon a time, then Andrew would root for her and hope that Miranda had given her a chance to dig herself back out from the bottom. His father always said that bullies were often people who had been hurt themselves. But as he sat on the sofa with a blanket wrapped Miranda on one side, and a pensive Willy who was wiping his eyes every ten minutes on the other, he knew they had to do something more than watch and wait for the quilt to finish and for the road to reopen.

"We should do something more," he whispered.

"Like what?" Willy asked without a hint of sarcasm, obviously eager to be given something to do. Miranda always said that her favourite thing about Willy was that he was never facetious or sarcastic. She always knew she could count on him for uncomplicated wholesome honesty.

"Jenny would tell a story. She would pull Misty's narrative back into our own, like she did for me when I got lost in the mist," Miranda said.

"Can we build something?" Willy asked. "I built a fire for Miranda."

"Hey Miranda, how did you word it, that day last year when we had the run in with Misty and Robin, when you talked about seeing meaning in things?"

"Can you get me my laptop?" Miranda asked and Andrew ran up to her room for it.

Miranda opened her email, "I don't believe in god but sometimes you have to see meaning in things, and you and I are both here, and I choose to see meaning in that." She read it out loud to Andrew and Willy.

"She said that to you the day you met?" Willy asked Andrew.

"Yup, why?"

"Explains a few things about you two," Willy said, as if something had become clear to him.

"But if we choose to see meaning in the fact that almost exactly a year after Misty and Robin attacked Miranda, this happens? Maybe last year was a cry for help?"

"And we missed it," Miranda murmured, and then started to type. She looked up a few minutes later and asked. "Can you guys build a boat? It doesn't have to be big enough to carry a person, just big enough to carry a wish."

"I'm half Haida. I can build a boat!" Willy exclaimed and then hauled Andrew off to help.

The Moonlit Girl

A mermaid sat and remembered, and typed, while two island girls sat and made a quilt, and two young men made a boat. The sun moved through the sky and the trees reached their hands up to touch the light. The moon rose as the quilt was completed and the last threads were cut.

Miranda checked the tides and currents and she gave a letter to Olivia. "Tomorrow just before sunset, I need you to read this out loud for me down on the beach. And I need you to take Jenny out to pick wildflowers tomorrow on your way there. Tell her the flowers are wishes. Make sure you get some white violets."

Olivia nodded and took the letter and read it to herself over and over again so she would get it right.

Willy showed Andrew what to do and they chopped and carved and smoothed the wood until the small canoe revealed itself.

Jenny felt lost when the last thread of the quilt had been cut, like there was nothing left for her to do and she felt helpless. She went home that night and sat with her parents, doing nothing, letting them take care of her, and she went to bed and she slept, but woke and felt so dull in the morning, as if the sunlight couldn't reflect off of her to make her shine.

Miranda rose late that day and asked her grand-mother to brush her hair because her hands hurt, and then she pulled the long floaty pink dress on over her night gown, and pulled on soft hand-knit socks to cover the scratches on her ankles and a soft cardigan to cover her wrists. She slipped on her shoes and walked towards the beach path where she met Olivia and Jenny, and the three of them carried baskets full of flowers down to the water where Willy and Andrew stood waiting with the little canoe in the late day sun.

Miranda didn't have to say anything because they had done this before and the five of them knew what was happening and they made a circle around the small canoe. Miranda nodded to Olivia who had memorized the letter and Olivia spoke, "I'm going to tell you a story, and the story is true and everything that happens today will be a part of that story, so it will be true." She looked around at the others making eye contact with each one.

"Once there were five children, twins from both sides of the ocean, a lost boy, a girl from an island in the north and an island in the south, and a mermaid. But there was a story that came before and a story that wove through the story of the five; the story of the Moonlit Girl—who was also the twin girl from both sides of the sea—and the Sunlit Girl. Once upon a time the Moonlit girl and the Sunlit girl were beloved companions and all who saw them believed they would be so for all their time on the earth, but one day the light moved away from the Sunlit Girl and her heart turned dark. The Moonlit Girl grieved but could do nothing to help her friend as she was only a child, so she sheltered with her brother who had the power to bind people together, and he brought his twin sister into the light with him and they became two of the five. But the Sunlit girl seemed lost and cruel to all she met, especially the five, and she did all she could to keep her heart hidden. The Moonlit girl could never find out what had happened to her beloved friend, despite knowing all the stories, and the Sunlit Girl drifted further and further away until one day she fell to a place where no one could reach her.

Olivia stopped for a breath, "The five knew that the only way they could help was to find out what had happened to the Sunlit Girl, and hope that somewhere in her story there would be a clue to bring her back, so the mermaid asked the twin boy to build a boat that could carry wishes, and they knew it would float for he had built it, and the lost boy who had been a sleeping prince helped since he knew what it was to sleep without dreaming, and the girl who brought colour to the world picked flowers that were wishes, and the Moonlit girl wished for the Sunlit Girl's story to be revealed, so she could help her."

Miranda took a deep breath, because that's all that she had written for Olivia, and even though her voice didn't *really* want to work at that moment, she steadied herself, and told the others, "Every story is full of hardship and peril, but we find friendship and love along the way, and it's only in the darkness, that we truly know what light is. The tide is going to turn soon, and the full moon is going to rise, so before we lose the sun, we need to fill the boat with our wishes for Misty, so that they will be taken to the Bear King's Island, and he will send out his ravens to fulfill our wishes, and find out Misty's story, so we can help her."

Miranda placed an old oil lamp in the bottom of the boat and lit it, and the five of them began to carefully arrange the flowers in the beautiful boat, one at a time, making a wish with each blossom. "If there are any wishes you want us to share, you can tell us now, so that we can send them together," Miranda told Jenny.

Jenny nodded and looked out to sea. She could see the waves receding already and the red sun was just dipping its feet in the water. "I wish Misty knew I forgave her, that I love her, and that she doesn't have to be alone if she doesn't want to be." She looked at the others, at her brother, and her friends, "How is it that you guys live in my dreams? How is it that we have each other? How do you fit so neatly into my own personal mythology?"

"We were meant to be," Olivia told Jenny.

"We don't bother with pretense," Willy said.

"We know what it's like to be outsiders," Andrew admitted.

"We're a part of the same story," Miranda sighed.

They placed the last five flowers, white violets, in the canoe which was carved with bears and ravens and dragons, and Andrew and Willy carried it out into the sea and set it afloat. They watched as it sat atop the waves in the setting sun, at first going nowhere, and then the tide took it and it started to drift. They watched in silence as the little boat was caught in the current and pulled out by the sparkling waves and drifted further and further. The sun dipped below the waves and the tiny flame could be seen travelling out to sea and then, as the full moon shone down, out on the horizon, just past the threshold of what they were sure they could see, there seemed to be birds, and then the little light winked out.

They were silent for a long time before Willy announced, "Since we've done this before and I remembered how hungry it made us, I asked Mum if she would barbecue us a salmon and make us that rice thing she makes. I'm hungry, you guys hungry?"

"We're hungry!" they agreed, and they walked back up the hill over the grassy slope and through the trees, back to the Araya house where they ate a late dinner together and talked and laughed and hoped.

Late that night when they slept, Jenny dreamt that a single white raven brought her a golden heart, and that she was travelling. Miranda and Andrew dreamt of each other, standing by a statue in Copenhagen. Olivia dreamt of a lamb, and Willy dreamt of Olivia.

And in a city, not too far off, Misty dreamt that she wasn't alone, and when she woke Jenny sat by her bedside in the hospital.

The Broken Girl

Jenny woke early the next morning to her mother bustling around her room in the sunshine. "The road's open. Hop in the shower quick and we'll be on our way. Violet's packed us food. You can eat something in the car."

Jenny launched herself out of bed and into the shower. It felt like mere moments before she was in the car next to her mother and they were driving over the patched road and then turning onto the highway.

She tried to eat on the way to the hospital but her stomach felt like it was full of thorns. The drive to Victoria had never seemed so long, and yet when they pulled into the hospital parking it hadn't seemed long enough. Jenny had waited four years to mend her friendship with Misty, but standing outside the hospital room was agony. Luckily Misty was asleep when she went in, which gave Jenny some time to adjust. She looked at the broken girl. It was no wonder Miranda had repressed the memory of climbing down into the ravine. At first Jenny had to concentrate on Misty's face, the only thing that seemed to be alright. She looked at her wide set eyes, the lashes resting on her cheeks, the smooth skin, the perfect little pixie nose and the lips that always used to pull into an impish grin. Then she looked at the rest. Misty's right leg was gone from the mid thigh and there was a frame around her pelvis. There were all kinds of bolts and things sticking out of her right arm. Jenny was glad she hadn't eaten much. She sat and waited for Misty to wake up, holding the folded quilt in her arms, almost hugging it.

When Misty woke she looked up and for a split second Jenny thought she was going to smile, but Misty's face twisted and she said, "Get the fuck out of here."

"No. I came to see you. That's what I'm going to do."

Misty looked away and tried to pretend Jenny wasn't there.

"I made you a quilt," Jenny told Misty. "Olivia helped me. I know under the circumstances it probably just seems like a stupid blanket to you . . ."

"It *is* a stupid blanket. Leave and put it in the trash on your way out."

"No. I won't leave."

"Leave and take your perfect little life with you. Get Out!" Misty spat.

"No. I'm a lot stronger than I was when I was twelve. I can push back now."

Misty tried to look away again and Jenny took the quilt and spread it out in her eye-line so she could see it.

"I don't know if your favourite colour is still blue, but we made it every shade of blue we could."

"Get out," Misty whispered, and closed her eyes as tears started to leak around her lashes.

"Do you think I don't know that something happened to you to make you change. I'm not stupid Misty. I remember who you used to be, and you shut me out overnight. You were my friend and I loved you and you shut me out."

"Poor you, boo-hoo."

"Did it ever occur to you that maybe I'd understand whatever it is? You talk about my perfect life and yes, I admit that some parts of my life are good. I have parents and a brother and friends who love and accept me, but I'm a gay, Japanese, Indigenous, Canadian. I am a marginalized minority no matter what room I walk into. And my friends? They're an autistic girl, a half Jamaican foster kid, a recovered drug addict, and my twin brother—who has no choice but to love me."

Jenny had asked in advance if she could share their stories so she told Misty, "Miranda was held down in a public washroom and urinated on. Andrew got high and beat his stepmother so badly she needed surgery. Olivia's birth mother is Schizophrenic and had to give her up for adoption when she was four. Bad things happen Misty. Bad things happen all the time to people who don't deserve it. If you try to push me away again I'll just push back."

Jenny watched as Misty dissolved and begged her, "Go, I don't want you to see me like this." Jenny went around to Misty's better hand and took it in her own, and just sat as the other girl was wracked with sobs she was almost too weak to handle. In time Misty slept and Jenny stayed holding the tattered little hand until Misty woke again.

Misty looked at Jenny and Jenny thought about how much she'd missed those dove grey eyes.

"I'm tired of having a secret Jenny. I'm tired. That's why I jumped off the bridge. I just needed a break from it. Your friend called me a stupid stupid girl when she climbed down the ravine to me. The doctors say she saved my life and I kind of hate her for it."

"Miranda can't remember climbing down to you. She was pretty traumatized," Jenny told Misty and then a silence stretched. Eventually, sitting and stroking Misty's hand, Jenny asked her, "Do you understand that you can talk to me? That I won't judge you?"

"I do. I just need a minute. I've believed, for such a long time, that everything would fall apart if I told anyone what happened that I still believe it, even though I'm at the bottom looking up, and there isn't anything left to fall."

Jenny sat with Misty in the silence for about a half an hour before Misty spoke, "My mother figured out that I had a crush on you and she told me I was disgusting for feeling the way I did. She made me feel like I didn't deserve friendship . . . like me letting you be my friend was

. . . I don't know like, dirty or . . . perverted, or something. She got on my back until I couldn't stand it anymore and that's why I told you to get lost." Her voice came out in a childlike whisper. As if she were still that crushed twelve year old girl. "She was different towards me after that. Mean. I think she . . . couldn't love me anymore. Not like I am. It got worse all year until she started hitting me and then one day Robin couldn't stand it anymore and he got between us." Misty sniffed wetly and Jenny got her a tissue and watched as Misty awkwardly wiped her face with her non-dominant hand. "Robin pushed her away from me. He was just trying to protect me. He didn't mean to kill her." Misty broke down again and cried and the words shuddered out of her, "My mom fell and hit her head on that stupid scotty-dog door stop. My dad came home and he told us we'd end up in juvie if anyone found out and he got rid of her body. We've kept it a secret ever since, and Rob and me have been so scared."

"Oh Misty, I'm so sorry," Jenny said to her and made a monumental effort, that felt like a giant weight, not to break down in front of her friend. "Your mom should've never done that to you. Your dad should've been the one protecting you. That should have never been on Robin. He was only a kid. And your dad should *never* have covered it up."

"Really?" Misty looked up at Jenny and she realized, seeing the incredulous childlike look in Misty's eyes, how badly damaged Misty was.

"Really," Jenny nodded.

"Look Misty, I know someone, a grown-up who I can talk to, who knows about this stuff. Is it okay if I call her and ask her to arrange help for you? Her name is Nadine. She's like us."

Misty nodded and lay there like she was emptied out.

"I'll be back in just a little while," Jenny told her, and walked out of the hospital room and dry heaved over the garbage in the hall.

* * *

After explaining to her mother what had transpired, and discussing it with the social worker who had been placed in charge of Misty, they agreed to let Jenny call Nadine, who had the connections to get Misty exactly the kind of help that she needed. Jenny had passed her phone to the social worker after she explained Misty's situation to Nadine, and listened as the grownups took care of things. Jenny knew, now, how right Andrew had been when he told her that what happened to Misty was not on her, and that Misty needed more than just friendship. She spent another hour with Misty who was dazed and lightheaded. Her doctors asked Jenny if she could come back again the next day as they had taken Misty as far as they could with medicine and without something to live for her prognosis wasn't good.

Jenny stayed in a hotel with her mum that night. Her mum splurged on The Empress, "After this afternoon I just couldn't bear the idea of a roadside motel," Janet told Jenny as they had a room service dinner in the opulent room.

"Did you ever suspect anything like that Mum?" Jenny asked, snuggled up next to her mother on the hotel chesterfield after they ate.

"I feel as though I should have. I feel as though I let that girl down. I went over to the MacIntosh house once after she pushed you away to try to fix things for you. I thought surely it was some kind of misunderstanding that could be smoothed over. But Burt MacIntosh told me they just didn't want their daughter around 'our kind' and I put it all down to racism and kept you away from them." Her mother sighed, "Now that we know the whole story, I don't know what to think. *Somebody* let those kids down."

The Seasons Pass

After the year they'd had, a year of one unbelievable thing after another, Violet couldn't quite believe she was watching her granddaughter leave for University. She watched, standing on the front porch as Miranda climbed into the passenger seat of Andrew's scrappy little car, loaded with suitcases, and they pulled away, waving out the window.

"My daughter is going away to university with her boyfriend." Lynne had repeated those words to herself several times that week, usually followed by the question, "How is this real?"

Violet would tell her own daughter, "It's real because you did your job and raised a child who is resilient enough to keep moving forward and that's what she is doing." But despite what she'd said to Lynne, Violet understood how Lynne felt.

"I know they're coming back on the weekend," Lynne said standing on the porch next to Violet, "I know Jeremy is holding down the fort in Victoria, but . . . I just feel so friggin gobsmacked."

Lynne wandered into the house, but Violet sat down on the wicker love-seat and just stayed in the moment. In the two years since the move Miranda had become more and more resilient, bouncing back from trauma and making friends along the way. Even Violet was still a little stunned at how Miranda had recovered after witnessing Misty's attempted suicide.

She would never forget looking out the parlour window to see a paramedic carrying Miranda, filthy and bleeding in his arms, Jim walking along beside. Violet and Lynne had worried in the days following, wondering what it meant that Miranda had had a dissociative episode. But Jim reassured them, "What she did and saw were traumatic and it's her brain's way of protecting her. Her behaviour isn't ringing any alarm bells for me. She's more concerned about Jenny and very accepting of the fact that she doesn't remember. If I could choose to not remember some things I might go for it too. She's quite rational about it and understands that she has a gap. I don't think it's a sign of another disorder."

Violet knew that Andrew was a significant contributing factor to Miranda's steadiness. She worried that Andrew was taking care of Miranda, but Jim would come and sit at her kitchen table and worry that Miranda was taking care of Andrew. "She helped him with deadlines and keeping himself organized all year. She keeps him grounded," he'd said, and Violet had decided that if they were taking care of each other, that maybe it was meant to be. Lynne was, largely, able to take Miranda's relationship with the boy next door in stride, but one Saturday afternoon in April, when Miranda was off somewhere with Andrew, she'd come roaring down the stairs to Violet's sewing room and whispered loudly, "There are condoms in Miranda's nightstand!"

"What are you doing rooting around in Miranda's nightstand?" Violet asked Lynne.

"I was going to put a box of condoms in there and then talk to her tonight! But they're already there! I know she sneaks Andrew in here at night sometimes. I can hear her giggle through the door, which reminds me, since when does Miranda giggle? You know I've asked her if Andrew is her boyfriend but she told me that he's a sweetheart and then walked away. What does she mean?"

"Did she say 'a sweetheart' or did she say 'her sweetheart'?"

"Oh? Now you say it, she did say 'her sweetheart'."

"I bet if you asked now she'd say boyfriend," Violet told Lynne. "You've always been prepared for every contingency Lynne. You've always made sure she would be fine if a boyfriend came along. You never assumed that just because she isn't your average girl that she wouldn't have relationships. She knows to be responsible. This is no different from you and Roy Parker in the hay loft."

"You knew about that!"

"Of course I knew about it," Violet told Lynne.

A few days later Miranda had come to Lynne on her own and explained how things had changed between herself and the boy next door.

And then that fateful day in May had come.

After Violet had bathed and bandaged her grand-daughter and put her to bed, Jim had sat them down and explained to them that Miranda had climbed down into the ravine and put a tourniquet on Misty MacIntosh, saving her life, and then climbed back out again to meet the ambulance.

In the days following, the town had exploded in a buzz of gossip about the MacIntosh family. Jenny had gone down to Victoria to see Misty, and the next day the RCMP had come swarming in and removed a body from an old car at the back of the MacIntosh property. Violet felt awful for those poor children when it all came out. And as for her five—that's how she thought of them—they seemed to understand that life was about to change and they milked that last summer for all it was worth. They had a giant family barbecue at the end of June to cover all the kid's summer birthdays. Willy and Andrew worked part-time for Daniel. Violet watched them have picnics on the beach and lie in the field at night watch-ing the stars. Miranda stopped sneaking Andrew in after dark and simply walked him into her bedroom openly. At the end of August Misty was released from the hos-pital and for one week she came to stay with the Arayas before going to live with the foster family Nadine had found for her in Vancouver, where she would have better access to the services she would need to fully rehabilitate. Miranda stayed away from Misty though, and Violet had asked her granddaughter why.

"Misty needs to hate something for a while. I don't think she knows why it's me that she hates."

And when September came, suddenly it wasn't only Olivia and Wainwright spending the afternoon in Violet's sewing room and she had Jenny and Willy there too. Jenny, because without Miranda there she was available to follow her inclination to learn how to knit, and because Willy didn't want to be left out Violet passed him a pair of needles too. As September came to a close a letter came from Miranda. Violet put it in her pocket to read later and somehow didn't get to it till much later, sitting outside in her dressing gown, looking up at the stars late that night. There was enough light from the window behind her so she opened the envelope:

Dear Nanna,

It's been a busy week. I had my first paper due, and a group assignment that I didn't enjoy. I know I can tell you all this on the weekend but somehow I only remember all the things that I had wanted to tell you when I get back to school on Monday. So here are the things I forgot. I've gotten lots of compliments on the skirts you made me and they are just the right weight for the weather. I don't understand the girls I'm going to school with but I'm trying to be nice to them. Dad is a better roommate than he is a dad, but he's doing okay and we are following his rules. Victoria has some great estate sales. And I miss you.

Love Miranda,

P.S. Andrew and I know about you and Jim. Just say The Word and we will keep pretending we don't. I suggest: Antediluvian.

Violet laughed out loud as Jim joined her on the sleeping porch in his bath robe, settling onto the wicker bench beside her, and she passed him the letter.

Jim read the letter and then laughed, "Shall we tell them 'Antediluvian' then?"

"Yes. This is much more fun when we get to sneak around like teenagers. Don't you agree?"

"Absolutely."

The Ones Who
Stayed Behind

The day Jenny left for university was one of the hardest days of Willy's life. He'd never been away from her for more than a few days and now he wouldn't see her till Thanksgiving, that most detestable of holidays, because she was going to UBC on the mainland, so she could be close to Misty. Even though he'd secretly hoped that she would go to Uvic and come home every weekend like Andrew and Miranda, he understood that his sister's friendship with Misty was important to her. He also understood that Jenny wasn't as mentally fragile as Miranda and Andrew were, and didn't *need* to come home every weekend. He felt proud of her, and he knew that she wanted to go away to study, and that unlike Willy, she didn't have a built in career working for their dad. But he'd been near her since the beginning of time, and it felt wrong to have her so far off. Willy actually *wanted* to go into his father's business. He loved using his hands. He loved building. He was good at it too. It was one of the things he'd liked about being friends with Andrew and Olivia. Andrew liked building things too—although he was more of an ideas guy—and Olivia always wanted things built. Chicken coops. Fences. Dog houses.

Over the last two years, in addition to Wainwright, Olivia had acquired twelve chickens, two pygmy goats, two sheep, and a Great Pyrenees. Willy had been there for all of it and had watched with her as her first little flock of chicks had hatched from their eggs in their incubator, and sat up all night with her when her rescued pygmy goat had unexpectedly given birth to a kid, and then when Mr Stevenson from the farm over the hill had shown up with two lambs who had been rejected by their mothers and told her, "If they survive the night they're yours," he'd sat up all night with her again, feeding newborn lambs and hoping they didn't die. But farming wasn't so different from building—lots of hard work, dirt, and sweat—and Olivia had a soft spot for animals who needed her. Willy hadn't realized that he'd developed a soft spot for Olivia.

When he'd first met Olivia, Andrew, and Miranda, he had carried a torch for Miranda. It lasted for about two months, until he realized that she was never going to love anybody but Andrew that way. Willy could also recognize that while he had a schoolboy crush, Andrew actually *loved* Miranda in return. Willy wasn't going to get in the way of that. There were other problems too. She was a year older and two and half years ahead of Willy in school. Miranda would be going away to university while he still had two years of high school left. There would always be that moment when she opened the New Order record on her sixteenth birthday, and she'd looked at him and given him that innocent joyful smile. It was okay, he'd meet his Beverly someday. While he had decided not to do anything about how he felt for Miranda early on in their friendship, he couldn't adequately explain to himself why it took him so long to notice Olivia.

The day after Jenny left was a Sunday and the house felt empty. A beautiful wild summer of days on the beach and nights watching the stars had just passed and he felt as though everybody had left him. Andrew and Miranda had headed for Victoria the day before too, and he felt strangely bereft, but he hauled himself out of bed and told himself that he was being melodramatic. His parents had driven off together on a day long date and the house truly was empty, except for him. He went through to motions of pretending to be a grown-up, since it was the last day of summer vacation and for the first time he wouldn't be going to school tomorrow. He showered and shaved, scrambled some eggs—admiring the blue coloured shells of Olivia's araucana chicken eggs—and made toast, then went to the office to work on invoices for a job they'd just finished.

At eleven o'clock the doorbell rang and he opened the door. Olivia stood there, five foot ten inches of suntanned gloriousness, in jean shorts and a tie-dyed tank top. He'd never noticed the sea green colour of her eyes or her bee stung lips quite that way before. He'd never registered wanting to touch her hair before. The blood left his head so fast that he almost blacked out.

"Goats are milked, eggs gathered, garden weeded, dogs fed. Are you up for some Mortal Kombat?"

How had he not noticed that Olivia was his best friend? How had he not noticed how beautiful she was? How had he not realized that she was the reason he was not just content, but so happy, to stay behind?

Willy followed her to the family room in a daze. She looked at him funny as he stared at her, "Hey William, what's up?" she asked him.

William, that's what she had called him. His name from her lips did something to his insides.

He stared at her. "Olivia? Have you always been . . . beautiful?" he asked, hearing the words come out of his mouth and wondering what had possessed him to say that to her without tact or thought or anything.

She walked up to him and looked into his eyes and they gazed at each other for a moment. "I've been waiting for you to notice," she told him, uncharacteristically serious, and then she kissed him.

When Going
Forward is Going
Back

When Lynne met Jeremy there had never been any expectation of marriage. It was something that they kept in the moment and while Lynne had often seen other people she always went back to Jeremy and he never needed more than that. All he needed was for her to come back. Lynne knew that as long as she had Jeremy she would never be serious about anyone else because no one else could make her feel the way he could, but she also knew that he had limits. Limits to just how long he could spend outside of his own head. Limits to how much time he could devote to human interaction, but one day he told her that whenever he thought about losing her he felt scared. And so they tried to make a proper life together, and it hadn't worked out. But ever since Kamloops some of that closeness they'd had back in university had returned and Lynne wondered if every person on the face of the earth was really meant for constant togetherness. Jeremy couldn't divide his attention. It was either on her or it wasn't, but when it was on her, she had his undivided attention.

Miranda had finished high school nearly three years ago now and was due back for the summer in a month. Lynne found it a strange sensation, to have a twenty-year-old daughter who she rarely worried about anymore. She would, of course, never stop worrying altogether, but the intellectual freedom that no longer being constantly concerned for Miranda's safety afforded her had prompted her to start some new research initiatives at work. She felt young and excited each day when she woke, and the weather had been perfect for jogging to work. Lynne often stopped for breakfast at the new cafe that had gone in on the waterfront strip that was slowly being rehabilitated as new blood moved into St Fina. She took her coffee and breakfast sandwich and sat on a log by the beach breathing in the morning and watching the seal heads come up to look at her.

"You're Lynne Hopkins right? You run the research centre?"

Lynne looked around for the voice that had addressed her.

"Sorry. I didn't mean to surprise you," the voice came from a man in his forties in jeans and a black leather jacket, holding a motorcycle helmet.

"I'm Sebastian McGinty," he smiled and extended his hand.

Lynne looked up at him. His smile reminded her of a dog, or a wolf, and she couldn't decide if it made him look dangerous, slightly predatory—like he wanted to eat her—or friendly, like a labrador, although thankfully not face licking friendly. Lynne smiled and extended her hand, trying to keep her train of thought off of her face. "Yes I'm Lynne," she admitted cautiously.

"Interesting to finally meet you," he said.

"Are you a *McGinty* McGinty?" she asked, wondering if this was the mysterious heir to the McGinty empire.

He laughed, "I am, indeed. You live in my grandmother's house. I'd hoped to buy the property back someday. Ironically I had to wait till I inherited to have control of the estate, and the trust determined that selling was the best course, which was correct from a purely economic perspective. I've been checking up on the local gossip though and they all say that you, the Warrens, and the Arayas have bought up the rest of the Josephine road properties and that it'd be a cold day in hell before you could be convinced to sell."

"Pretty much. Our three families have become pretty deeply intertwined over the last five years. Our kids plan on living out their days here. They have a pretty serious agenda actually, especially for a bunch of teenagers and twenty-somethings." Lynne still had to shake her head when they started talking about the grand plan. "I've got everything I need here too. My dream job and a beautiful house and the ocean in my back yard. It still feels like a dream sometimes."

Sebastian looked thoughtful and sat next to Lynne on the log. He seemed to be weighing his words, "When I was a kid we spent summers here. Great uncle Rufus sold Forest House to Araya senior when his emphysema forced him into a home. He only held onto the other properties because my grandmother refused to move. I believed I was going to marry Janet Araya until I was sixteen, and Daniel was my best friend. My parents moved us to Germany that year and when we came back four years later for my grandmother's funeral everything was different. Janet had married Daniel and I was going to art school in Paris. The houses had dropped so much in value and the town had been abandoned. They stayed on the market sixteen years after my gran and her sister passed. My father died six months ago. There's not much left of the estate. A few million. Just enough to move back here and put the money back into St Fina. I was pleased to find the Josephine road houses had life in them again. I bought the old farm on the other side of town. I want to turn it into an artist's retreat."

Lynne smiled, "I see it now. You're a dreamer."

Sebastian blushed, "Is it that obvious?"

"I live with a couple of them. It gets easy for a scientist like me to spot you guys."

"A divorced scientist, from what I hear?"

"Divorced five years. You?"

"Two years. I have teen-aged boys but they're with their mother this summer."

"Was it rough on them?"

"I think it was a relief actually."

Lynne nodded.

"I know we've only just met, but would you consider having dinner with me?" he asked.

"You want to take me out to dinner?"

"I do."

"Okay, but I'm going to be upfront about something and damn the consequences."

"What's that?" Sebastian asked smiling.

"I still bang my ex and I'm not going to stop so you gotta be alright with that," Lynne declared.

"Where have you been all my life?" Sebastian asked her.

From "If" to "When"

Andrew wasn't sure when it was that he and Miranda
stopped saying, "If we get married," and, "If we have
kids," and started saying, "When." Their first year at university living at Jeremy's ultra modern Victoria condo
had been new and exciting. Jeremy had rules. The place
had to be immaculately clean all the time. No visitors
without prior consent. No loud music if he was there. If
his office door was closed they weren't to disturb him for
anything short of, "Blood, fire, or a zombie apocalypse."
Those were *his* words. Jeremy had made it clear that
in no uncertain terms, under any circumstances, were
Miranda and Andrew to share a bedroom until Miranda
was eighteen. "I don't care if it's a pretense, I don't care
if you're scurrying back to your own beds at four in the
morning, but until Miranda is eighteen the single beds
stay and you sleep in your own rooms." It wasn't that
big a deal because Lynne and Jim were chill about that
and they slept in the same bed at one house or another

whenever they were back in St Fina, but they didn't dare buy a double bed for Jeremy's condo till Miranda was *nineteen*.

University was much better than high school and, generally speaking, they enjoyed finally studying a course of material that they had chosen themselves and had some passion for. And being with people who were similarly inclined was refreshing. Academically, first and second year were easy and by third year they didn't have to put up with the posers who had chosen Art History because it sounded cool—they'd all dropped out. But socially, in some ways, the first two years were hard too. They tried going to the few parties they were invited to at first, but Miranda couldn't handle the crowds and Andrew didn't like being around the drugs. Andrew also had to appreciate how much smarter Willy, Jenny, and Olivia were than most first year students. It was hard to go into a social situation with such high standards. After the third party they tried attending he'd looked over at Miranda who was obviously miserable and asked her, "Why are we here?"

She'd answered, "I think that we are making sure that we aren't somehow missing out on something."

"I really don't want to be here," he told her.

"Then can we go? Because I think this might be a special kind of hell." And they walked out hand in hand and headed to the local second run theatre for a showing of *Orlando* starring Tilda Swinton. Andrew decided that he was definitely an introvert.

Going to university with his high school girlfriend was another thing that Andrew almost constantly had to defend—after convincing people that he couldn't stand parties—and he always felt conflicted because he could choose not to disclose his status as a recovered addict. It was harder for Miranda though, because she didn't have a choice, and her autism always came out in the end. Miranda made the other girls coming straight from high school seem like unformed lumps of superficial, trendy, opinions. Like they had no substance, conviction, or personality of their own, and they made Miranda look sophisticated, elegant, and incredibly intelligent. She seemed older even though she was younger. She looked like Grace Kelly or Lauren Bacall, compared to those other girls, which made it hard for her to make friends with them. And she had the opposite effect on the boys. She was fascinating to them. But she couldn't see flirting if it jumped out of the water and bit her nose. The first time she had a boy get mad at her for, "leading him on," as he put it when he'd tried it on with her and she reacted negatively, she had come home and had a meltdown, sobbing on the living room floor, afraid to go back to class and see the boy. She was rarely affected by her selective mutism anymore, and especially when she was confident in what she was talking about, she could actually be quite charismatic. Andrew could see how the average eighteen year old boy could mistake her enthusiasm for interest.

Lynne had told Andrew when they left, "If you feel even slightly in over your head with her, you call me immediately." And he'd called Lynne.

Lynne and Andrew tried to explain what flirting looked like, how to tell the difference between normal friendliness and a come-on, but it didn't work. The second time it happened Andrew was starting to worry that Miranda was going to end up being assaulted because she just couldn't tell what people's motives were, and what was she supposed to do? Just not talk to people? He made sure she knew never to go anywhere isolated with anybody, not back to a dorm room or anything. But Andrew still worried. It was Jeremy who came up with a strategy, in the end, that was more helpful than 'always stay in public'. "Where is your mother's engagement ring?" he asked. "Okay, take it to a good jeweller and have it sized down so that you can wear it on your left ring finger without worrying about it falling off, and then just keep wearing it."

"Why?" Miranda had asked.

Jeremy held up his own hand and his wedding ring was still there, despite the divorce. "It acts like a filter. A ring signifies commitment to another person in a way that most people respect. If they see a diamond or a gold band, they won't cross the line from friendliness to flirting, and if they do cross the line it gets easier to see. The kind of person who ignores a ring is easier to spot in my opinion. If someone seems like they might be flirting and you can't tell, you can *ask* them if they are flirting. It doesn't matter if you are engaged or not. If people ask you about the ring you can be blunt and say something like, 'It's a family heirloom. I wear it to stop people hitting on me.' The more of your classmates you say that to, the more they'll leave you alone." And the ring worked.

Andrew and Miranda didn't make many friends at university, only Ethan, who Andrew guessed was probably also autistic, although undiagnosed. Ethan was asexual and shared Miranda's love of the late Victorian and Edwardian artistic movements. They could have the exact same conversation about William Morris over and over again and not get bored. Andrew would shake his head and smile each time he heard it again. He realized that Miranda was more likely to form a bond with someone if she didn't have to mask her autism from them.

During the busy times, the mid semester grind with assignments coming out their ears, Miranda could see the things that Andrew couldn't. When he would freak out and think the world was ending, she would tell him, and bring him back down out of his anxiety spirals, "I know that you worry, but if you fail this course you'll just redo it. You won't die, or lose your foot, or be imprisoned. It will be inconvenient. That's all. Four syllables and some extra time. Just take a deep breath and do what you can today. What's the most important thing to do right now? Decide what that is and then do it." She had to say that to him at least once a semester. And then he would look around and realize she was right and somehow nothing was as bad as it seemed, and like that the semester would be over and they'd have passed everything.

Every summer they went back to St Fina full time and got lost in the beauty of it. Andrew usually worked for Daniel and William over the season but it didn't feel like work. Using his hands and being active, after an autumn, winter, and spring of study, brought him back to himself, and Miranda spent the summers stockpiling antiques from the garage sales that were popping up all over the village. Some years Ethan would come visit for a couple of weeks and he would look at Andrew and Miranda, Olivia and William, Jen and Misty and say, "Heavens me, it's no wonder you're all so otherworldly."

It was during the end of fourth year, Andrew thought, that the, "If," turned to a, "When." That's when they entered the home stretch, transitioning to graduate school. Miranda buckled down and worked like she was possessed. He thought it was partly because she was actually quite ready to be done and really just wanted to go home permanently. Andrew, on the other hand, had finally entered the architecture program and felt like he was just beginning in a sense. But they got through those two years. Although not without hiccups. For Miranda the higher she went educationally, the more people were like her, and her social quirks usually went unnoticed, but for Andrew, he had to work a little harder, and without Miranda in the same major, helping him, he really had to push himself. Socially speaking, like Miranda,

Andrew felt more at ease in grad school, but now he had a problem that wasn't so very different from Miranda's boy problem in first year. Girls liked him. It wasn't something he'd realized in high school, although some of Jenny's comments made sense now. He had to admit that it gave him some perspective on just how much aggravation women have to put up with because unlike Miranda, Andrew wasn't likely to be assaulted by an admirer. All he had to do if he caught even the slightest whiff of a flirt was work the fact that he had a girlfriend into the conversation and nine times out of ten the problem resolved itself. And he always preferred Miranda to the girl in question. There were a million ways in which he still preferred her to any other girl he had ever met.

Near the end of the program he was pulling an all-nighter, doing a group project, and the exhaustion was making him want to say, "Screw it all," and go home and crawl into bed with Miranda. But the rest of the group were still there working, and he'd been in the program with them for over a year and a half. Natalie, Logan, and Nathan. They were almost friends. He knew he wouldn't walk out on them so he pushed the feeling aside, kept working, and they had the project done by six that morning. Once it was in the professors in-box they walked away, grateful to be finished.

"Andrew!"

He heard his name as he walked through the rain to the bus stop and turned to see Natalie running after him with an umbrella and he sagged because he knew she had feelings for him and he was too tired to cope with it nicely that morning. Natalie was the exception. The one in ten that didn't get it when he tried to tell her nicely that he had no interest in a relationship with her. He'd even gotten Logan to drop hints too. Natalie had come to architecture from an engineering undergraduate program.

"Here, let me share my umbrella with you." She didn't ask if he wanted company but prattled away to him anyway, "I think we're going to get a good grade. I really enjoy working on projects with you."

"I'm just glad it's done," he muttered, trying to discourage her with his demeanour.

"You seem tired."

"I am tired. I'm tired and I miss my girlfriend. I haven't seen her in three days because of this project."

Natalie looked dejected, "I heard you've been with her since high school. Do you think you'll break up after you graduate?"

"That's a terrible question. Why would you even ask that?" Andrew just wanted the bus to come and rescue him and take him home to his bed.

"I . . . I just . . ." and then Natalie almost started to cry. "I'm sorry, this is stupid. I've known you for a year and a half and you've been taken this whole time. I just though that if there was any chance that maybe the thing you have with her was ending . . . If I had a heads up, I would be there, ready."

"Natalie, I'm too tired right now to say all the right things to you, but that thing you think you want with me, it doesn't exist. You don't even know me. I'm a recovered drug addict and I hate parties. I worry too much and if I had a choice I'd wear checked flannel shirts and torn jeans every day. I can't stand ice cream and I am madly in love with someone who likes and accepts all that weird shit about me. Someone who never plays mind games, always says what she means, and who is loyal and sweet and brave and incredibly smart. She's funny, and to top it all off, she's beautiful too. That's why I have an engagement ring in my backpack that I picked up at the post office three days ago, that I've been totally paranoid about losing. I haven't been able to get home and find a safe hiding place for it and do you know what? Even though I have a fancy dinner and a trip to the museum booked for tomorrow night, I'm going to propose to her as soon as I get home, even though I'm exhausted and my shirt has coffee stains and what looks like spaghetti sauce on it, because it took me a year to find this ring! That's how long I've been waiting!"

"I noticed you were always hugging your bag," Natalie sniffled. "How can you know she's the one though? If she's the only person you've been with since high school, how can you know?"

"I know because I still feel like a seventeen year old boy glorying in the beauty of the world when I'm with her. Imagine being with someone you love for long enough that you know them inside and out and they know you the same way. That they know you so well that they catch you, even before you fall, knowing how to touch someone so they shiver with pleasure every time, and getting that back? I know that's what I have. I don't need some stupid comparison experience."

Natalie looked crushed and humiliated. Andrew realized he may have overdone it. He took her arm and lead her away from the bus stop to a park bench and sat down, pulling her to a seated position.

"Give me your phone," he asked her. He knew that she drove to and from campus. "Unlock it for me. You live with your parents right?" he hit the icon next to 'Mom' and then passed her the phone. "I'll wait till she comes. Tell her that you're too tired to drive yourself home and that you need a hug."

Natalie sobbed into the phone to her mother, telling her exactly what Andrew had told her to, and then Andrew took his own phone out and showed Natalie pictures of Olivia's pygmy goats to pass the time.

"Can I see a picture of your girlfriend?" Natalie asked.

"You're a masochist," Andrew told her shaking his head, wondering what seeing a picture of Miranda could possibly do for her. He flipped through some more pictures of home, past a silly one of Miranda, Olivia, and Jenny on the beach posing with Wainwright in swimsuits, another of Willy with Olivia slung over his shoulder at the farmers market, hauling her away from the box of free kittens, to a picture, taken the night of their grad dinner, of Miranda looking like a nineteen-sixties high society debutante in blue silk, diamonds, and pearls.

"Your life looks really wholesome. At least I know she's pretty enough for you."

"Well, what you see from the outside is only a part of the picture. Miranda is autistic, and I think it makes her *more* lovable, not less, but we do have our challenges."

A car pulled up at that moment and Andrew told her, "Look, this never happened okay? Tomorrow in class you're just Natalie, a girl in my program. And I'm just some guy. Do we have a deal?"

"Yeah. A deal," she sighed, and then got into the car.

When Andrew finally got back to the condo Miranda was sitting at the table typing madly in her nightgown and bathrobe. She held up one finger without looking at him. Andrew sat next to her and waited until she finished her sentence and turned to him, "I was starting to worry," she said.

"God," he rubbed his face, "So was I."

"I'm glad you're home. Are you going to bed?"

"Yeah soon."

"I'll lie down with you till you fall asleep, then I need to get back to this," she told him.

Andrew sighed one of those exhalations you sigh when you can relax, when you let go because you are finally where you want to be, and he looked at Miranda and rummaged around in his bag. "Do you remember our first time?"

"Every time I make a sandwich," she smiled.

"I was going to make a big deal of this, like you did for me. I was going to take you somewhere nice and try to make you feel like you are as loved by me, as you are. No embarrassing public declarations or anything like that," he reassured her. "But after the morning I've had I know that the only safe place for this ring is on your finger, right now. Can we get married?"

Miranda was suddenly alert and looking at the ring box in his hand like a magpie, "Of course we can get married," she answered him and smiled and kissed his forehead.

"Good," he smiled and opened the ring box with the the art nouveau, eighteen carat gold, green tourmaline, Murrle Bennett, ring in it. She pulled the belle epoque diamond off, switching it to her right hand, and let him put the new ring on her finger while he told her, "I'd have asked a lot sooner but it took me almost a year to find this ring."

"That's okay. I knew you'd ask," Miranda held up her hand smiling. "It was worth the wait."

"I'm sorry I stink. I'm too tired to shower," he mumbled as they crawled into bed ten minutes later.

"That's okay, I stink too. We can be stinky and happy together."

* * *

Right at the end of it all, just as Andrew was finishing the architecture program and Miranda had handed in her thesis, and they were packing up to go back to St

Fina permanently, she approached him, looking pensive. "I have . . . Can we . . . I need to . . . There's something I have to . . ."

"Hey? Are you okay?" Andrew asked, putting his arms around her and holding her tight, because it had been years since Miranda had had difficulty talking.

"I did . . . something," she whispered, clinging to his shirt with her forehead buried in his neck.

"Whatever it is, I'm sure it's not a problem." He kissed her head and held her until she started to talk and the words spilled out of her mouth.

"I know you want to backpack Europe, and you know that I *don't* want to. You know I couldn't handle staying in hostels or carrying all my things around and the chaos of it, you know I couldn't do that, so you've just shelved the whole idea of doing it, because I can't. So . . . I applied for a paid internship at the Met and my application was accepted. It's ten weeks long. It starts in three weeks. I thought you could take the time to go backpack Europe without me."

"Miranda? Why didn't you tell me you applied for an internship in *New York*?" Andrew asked, taken aback.

"I thought they would say no!" she exclaimed into his neck. "I didn't want to feel scared, so I just did it and forgot about it so if I failed it would be like I hadn't tried! But it would look so good on my list of credentials if I interned at the Met, and I don't want to backpack Europe!" she was dissolving into tears.

"It's okay, I can let go of Europe. We can go to New York," he told her, totally bewildered now.

"But you don't want to go to New York! I asked you!" she sobbed. "You should do what *you* want to do and go to Europe!"

"But I want to go where you are!" he told her, feeling just a bit like she was pushing him away.

"We've been in each others' pockets for seven years. I don't want you to turn forty and realize what you've sacrificed for me, and then start hating me for it! You should do something *you* want!"

"Loving you has never been a sacrifice," he told her looking into her eyes now.

"Andrew! I'm trying to give you something! Don't you see that? Don't you want to know what it's like to not always look back to check if I've fallen? To not always watch the road ahead for the things that trip me up. I know that I'll always need you, I just want you to have a chance to not be needed!"

"Well what If I need you. You keep me steady! What if *I* need *you*!" he asked.

"Stay steady, *for me*. Stay steady, and then meet me and tell me all the stories from your travels and show me pictures. I'll book us a hotel, and I'll meet you in Copenhagen and we'll get married there, just the two of us, and then go home together."

It was the closest thing to a fight they'd ever had, and what followed was the closest thing to make-up sex they'd ever had, and lying there after, Andrew realized that she was right. "Promise me you'll meet me in Copenhagen," he whispered, kissing her.

"I promise. The idea of it is all that's going to get me through two months in New York without you."

City Nights

J enny loved the city, and she loved being on her own,
most of the time. Sometimes she wanted to go home
so badly, wanted her brother, her house, her friends, so
much that she sat and cried, but once she was over it
—and she remembered that Willy was currently so be-
sotted with Olivia that they were almost sickening to be
around, and that Miranda and Andrew were in Victoria
anyway—she would get dressed up to the nines go out
dancing and talk to people and just be alive. She loved
being on a campus surrounded by people. She didn't love
academics, she wasn't really wired that way, but some
of her professors were so good at what they did that it
wasn't just going through the, "University Machine," as
Andrew's dad called it, it was real intellectual develop-
ment. Jenny had too much common sense to buy into
the idea that her courses had any kind of real world
point for the most part, but she could sift through the
rocks for diamonds of wisdom. She settled into a Soci-
ology major by the end of first year and decided to do
a Writing minor even though she thought it was a pain

in the ass. She was there for the scene, for the chance to see what it was like to live outside St Fina, and to be around people her own age who were interested in the same things she was.

She was also there for Misty, but Misty had issues and needed a lot of space. For the first two years of University Jenny saw other people. There were no birds in her chest or beautiful madnesses—she would never forget Miranda's description of love—nothing that lasted, because they always sensed that Jenny was holding back just a little, and then eventually they'd meet Misty and understand. But Misty was rebuilding her identity along with her body, and she still had a tendency to lash out. Jenny knew she could wait for a while, and if the other relationships weren't enough to make her want to stop waiting for Misty, then she figured the relationships probably wouldn't have lasted anyway. But Misty was so angry. She was filled with an unfathomable, boundless, anger that scared Jenny. And then one day the anger seemed to sluice away, like water through Misty's skin.

"I'm not angry anymore, and I don't know what happened," Misty told her.

They were sitting on a log at Kits Beach in the dark looking at the bright city lights across the water. It was early September, a week after Jenny had come back to Vancouver from a summer at home. Misty didn't like going back to St Fina, and stayed mostly with her foster family in Vancouver. She had maintained a relationship with them, even though she'd aged out of the system, but she would go back to visit Jenny for a week or two over the summer. Jenny had noticed a difference in Misty of late, a softness, a vulnerability, like she had shed her spiky armour.

"What happened?" Jenny asked,

"I don't understand what happened. I just can't feel all the anger I was carrying and can't understand why I felt it in the first place. I hope I understand it some-day because right now I am infuriatingly confused, and feel like I'm in love with the universe, and like maybe I should come up with a name for my prosthetic leg because I love it almost like it's a person . . . instead of wanting to throw it off a bridge."

"Who are you and what have you done with Misty?" Jenny asked.

Misty elbowed Jenny in the ribs and they sat silently for a few minutes and then Misty told Jenny, "I want to kiss you, like so bad, but I don't know how to do that thing people do when they lean in and kiss someone at the perfect moment and make it natural and all that."

Jenny smiled and looked at Misty, "You do it like this," and she leaned in and kissed Misty's soft lips.

"Hmm. Okay," Misty said after a moment, sounding a little squeaky and breathless. " I think I got it."

New York

Miranda knew she was pregnant by the time she got to New York but she didn't tell anyone. She wanted to tell Andrew but she'd told him to go away and explore the world without her. If she told him he'd worry and come racing to her. If she couldn't tell Andrew, she couldn't tell anybody. She knew they'd been foolish and that it was as much her fault as it was his. They'd gotten progressively more careless ever since they'd gotten engaged, knowing that it didn't matter so much because they were planning on trying anyway, as soon as they moved back home. If it happened a little sooner, what was the harm? But that night—after the almost argument—had been so emotionally charged that they had lost their senses, even though it was bad timing. She'd held onto him and begged him not to stop.

"But I didn't put a condom on," he'd whispered.

"I know, I don't care," she whispered back, and they'd kept going.

Miranda knew she'd done it because if she got pregnant she'd chicken out and not go away and it would be a legitimate excuse to back out. All the terrifying things, getting on a plane alone, finding her way around New York, scary Americans, all those things, would disappear. An act of self sabotage. But then Andrew flew off before she was sure, and when push came to shove, she still wanted to go to New York. *Who gives up a chance like this?* She had to ask herself. It was once in a lifetime and even though she wanted to go home, to see Jenny, Olivia, and Willy everyday again, to be close to her nanna and her mom, and to live in her own house again and wake up there every day with Andrew, New York would be incredible, and she knew it. So she called the midwifery clinic in Victoria that provided service to rural communities and operated a satellite clinic out of Jim's Medical office, and once she was enrolled as their patient, they put her in touch with someone who could provide care for her in New York until she was back in Canada. It was all she could do, and after that she was determined to get all she could out of the internship, and New York.

Her dad had found her a place to stay with some clients of his. They were middle aged Wall street executives named Arthur and Milton. Milton was a university friend of her father's. They had a hairless cat named Amun, and an amazing collection of antiques that they loved showing off, especially to someone who understood. Miranda loved staying with them because being collectors themselves, they devoted every weekend to showing her every bit of New York and the surrounding area that they thought she could possibly be interested in, and they had such good food in their house that she could almost get past the constant nausea. And Arthur and Milton kept her safe. By the end of her stay she called them her Honorary Uncles. They didn't have kids of their own, but told her they loved being able to share their life with young people, especially young people interested in the arts. They knew her father quite well, better than most people knew Jeremy, and she had never realized that he talked about her to the people he knew. That there were people out there who had her picture on their fridge, who had heard about every milestone and event. Every trauma and triumph. Miranda saw her father in a new light after that.

And then there was Amun. Miranda sent Olivia a daily picture of Amun posing with antiques and on designer furniture. After a week of texting Amun pictures to Olivia, she received a text from Jim that said,

_If I end up with a hairless cat in my house I'll know exactly who put the idea into Olivia's head, and I am not above revenge ;)

So Miranda texted the Amun pictures to Jim too, so he wouldn't feel left out.

The internship was glorious. To see and touch all those old and beautiful things that so many people had touched before her made her feel at one with everything, connected to everything and everyone in the world. Miranda also spent part of her time there in a branch of the

Education Department that worked on Accessibility and Disability Awareness. Every night she emailed Andrew to tell him what she'd done with her day, and she'd wait for him to answer her. Sometimes it took a few days but an answer always came, along with pictures of Vienna, Prague, or Berlin.

And then, like that, it was over.

The last night in New York Milton asked her, "So what exciting things do you have planned for Copenhagen?"

Miranda couldn't lie. She still couldn't. She tried to not tell the whole truth but it was obvious that she wasn't going to Denmark just for the Royal Danish Ballet, Tivoli Gardens, and Edvard Ericson's Little Mermaid statue.

"That's not all is it?" Milton's eyes twinkled.

"Will you promise not to tell?"

"If you're running off to elope with your handsome fiance, my lips are sealed," he smiled.

"How did you know? Am I really that transparent?" Miranda asked, dismayed.

"It's a part of your charm darling. My silence has a condition though."

"What's that?" trepidation coursed through her.

"You let me upgrade your flights to first class, and give you a wedding present. I understand you by the way. I didn't want a proper wedding either. Too many people. Too much fuss," he admitted and then bustled off coming back with a velvet box.

"Now, I know you don't go all in much for jewellery, but every woman needs a good brooch and you wear such lovely coats. It belonged to my Grandmother. There," he placed the box in her hand. "In honour of your trip to Denmark."

Miranda opened the box. "It's Georg Jensen," she smiled, and went to get her coat so she could fasten the silver foliate wreath to her lapel.

"It does my heart good to see that on you," Milton said as she pulled on her coat and smiled.

* * *

After an internet deep dive, Miranda booked a cozy old hotel, and when she arrived in Copenhagen, she caught a taxi, checked in, undressed and pulled on her nightgown, and then opened her email. Her inbox showed one email from Andrew and he'd left it only moments before:

_Miranda, I've been on trains all day. Cologne was amazing. It's still strange to be in such old cities after spending my life in Canada. Can't wait to see you, touch you, kiss you. It's like the months have passed in a blink, but even that was too long.

Miranda hit reply:

_Andrew? Are you there?

_I'm on the train, I'll be in Copenhagen in forty-five minutes.

_I'm fourteen weeks pregnant.

she typed to him, the words on the screen so very real. She hadn't been able to hold it back any longer knowing he was so near. She needed him to know, and waiting for his reply brought back a feeling she'd had years ago, of telling him in an email that she was autistic and waiting for him to react. For him to draw back from her. For it to drive him away. If Andrew had died of a drug overdose all those years ago, Miranda would have been beaten to a pulp that day by the portables, because she was autistic. She didn't know what it was about the world that made her feel, sometimes, that because she was autistic she shouldn't have this; a relationship, a child, a life, like any other woman. Just because she was different in a way that was difficult for other people to see and understand. But she'd been wanted at the Met, if only as an intern, and Jenny, Olivia, and Willy had never treated her like she was less than. Her mother had raised her to believe that she could have it all, and she knew Andrew wanted a life with her. There were tears running down her face all the same.

The reply took a few minutes

_sorry ddropped laptopr. my hand are shakking too muc to typ. Im calling.

Miranda's phone rang, "Miranda?!" he said breathlessly.

"Hi," she said, her voice coming out small. "I was going to wait till you were here, but I couldn't wait. You'll take a taxi straight to the hotel, right away, right? You won't dawdle?"

"I sure as hell won't dawdle! Miranda, I love you, and you're crazy! Why didn't you tell me sooner!"

"I didn't want you to worry, but you can worry all you want now, just . . . get here!"

"I'll get there as fast as I possibly can," he reassured her and then hung up.

She arranged for a key to be waiting for him at the front desk and an hour later he burst into the hotel room looking around for her and he looked almost as overwrought as she felt. He dumped his backpack and she hurried to him and buried her face in his shoulder, breathing him in. "It's like a piece of me was missing, Andrew. Let's not be apart ever again. I love you," she mumbled into his neck as he put his arms around her and drew her into him tightly, breathing into her hair.

"I love you too. I love you so much. Thank you for making me go though. You were right, I needed to do that, but I don't want us to be apart ever again either," he mumbled into her hair.

Miranda felt dizzy with relief and just wanted to be as close to Andrew as she could so the cells in her body could realize that he was really there and he seemed to realize that and he pulled his jacket off and kicked off his shoes, picked her up, and lay down with her on the bed, "I'm sorry," he told her.

"Why are you sorry?" she asked.

"Because I didn't put on a condom the night you told me about New York."

"I knew you didn't. I was there too you know, and we are careless sometimes. I thought if I got pregnant I'd get too scared to go through with New York and have an excuse to call the whole thing off," she admitted to him. "But I didn't get too scared. I'm glad I didn't. Are you...?" Miranda was going to say the word 'happy', but she didn't. She wanted him to tell her that he was happy. She didn't want to ask. She wanted him to be happy, and *tell* her that he was.

"So this is *good* then?" he asked uncertainly, and she could feel his hand hovering around the curve of her belly as though he was nervous to touch her.

"What are you thinking Andrew?" she asked.

"I want you to tell me that this is good, so we can celebrate and be happy," he told her.

"You want to be happy?" she asked.

"*Of course* I want to be happy, especially if you're not angry with me for getting you pregnant."

"I'm not angry. It was my fault too," she told him honestly.

"Well then, this is what we've talked about, what we've wanted, and planned for. We're getting married to-morrow. Maybe this is perfect," he said softly, looking into her eyes.

"You're happy?" she asked, finally.

"I'm terrified, and I'm incredibly happy," he put his hand on her belly and it was the first time she really fully let herself register that she was having a baby, and tears of overwhelm rolled down her temples into her hair.

"Is this what *you* want. Are *you* happy?" he asked her.

"Oh god, this is what I want Andrew. This is what I want. I'm happy!"

"Then let's be happy," he smiled and laughed.

"Okay!" she laughed.

* * *

They got married the next day, under a big flowered umbrella standing in the rain, next to the water, by the statue of the Little Mermaid. Miranda had told Andrew that she wanted to wear the engagement ring he'd gotten her as her only wedding ring, but she'd bought Andrew a ring in New York. It was a plain, late Victorian, twenty-two carat gold, court fit, wedding band with English hallmarks. Miranda had it engraved with the letters A.F.F. for Archduke Franz Ferdinand. It was, quite unmistakably, a wedding band.

It rained for most of the week they spent in Copenhagen but that didn't make it any less magical. While it rained they went to Museums and the Ballet and as soon as it stopped they spent the day at Tivoli gardens, and then they flew home and they talked most of the way, about the things they'd seen and places they'd gone, the people they'd met, and how they were finally going home for good. Miranda's mind sometimes couldn't keep up with it all though, sometimes life rushed up at her so fast that she couldn't process it quickly enough to hold herself together and suddenly some part of herself was standing on her driveway in a green striped dress looking into Andrew's eyes for the first time, trying desperately to remember what she was doing and hand him the social studies report. She took Andrew's hand and pressed it against her cheek, waiting for life to stop rushing, "Sometimes it feels as though I just met you yesterday, that I'm still surprised that you exist, and that I'm just a fifteen year old girl who is so delighted with being understood that nothing else matters," Miranda spoke softly, "And then I realize that we're married and in our mid twenties and it's been years, and we're not just the two of us anymore."

"Just before I proposed, somebody asked me how I could be sure, and I told them that you make me feel like I'm still a seventeen year old boy glorying in the beauty of the world. When you talk about that feeling we had when we were kids, when we were finding each other for the first time, that feeling hasn't worn off for me either. I choose to see meaning in the fact that you and I are still together. It feels like we just met, and like we've been together forever. I want to be with you forever. Whatever the hell is going to happen tomorrow, I can deal with it if I've got you on my side."

Surprises

Jim Drove with Lynne to the airport that morning to get Andrew and Miranda. He was still bowled over each morning when he stepped out the door and saw Olivia's large flock of sheep, and that day was no different. There were five rescued pygmy goats, a lurcher named Merlin, and two Pyrenees as well, but it was sheep that Olivia had eventually hearkened to, having become quite the knitter and having developed a keen interest in textiles. Although edible flowers, honey, araucana chickens, and vegetables were also a huge part of her enterprise. After Jennifer and William graduated from high school Olivia had convinced Jim that it made sense for her to finish school via distance education because that was basically what their local school provided for senior secondary anyway, and if she was properly enrolled in the correspondence school, she had access to agriculture courses. Jim had agreed and hadn't regretted it because keeping busy with her animals and her gardens had held her focus when Andrew and most of her friends had gone away. Although Jim hadn't figured out what was going on with William until he'd started finding Olivia's bra in the barn. He'd asked her why it was there and she simply told him that she'd forgotten to put it back on. He'd asked Violet why Olivia would take off her bra in the barn and Violet had looked at him and said, "A man in possession of a hay loft has to ask me why his daughter would take her bra off in the barn?"

Merlin followed Jim to the car snuffling his pockets for a treat and Jim stopped to give the dog a good ear scratch that evolved into a tummy rub and he got into the car covered in dog hair, slobber, and mud. Wainwright had passed the previous spring and it had hit Jim harder than he'd expected it to, to the point where Jim cried every time he passed by Wainwright's empty bed. Olivia eventually told him, "The only way to fill the empty spot that a dog leaves in your heart, is with another dog," and she sat down next to him with the laptop computer and they found a new dog to rescue, one who needed them.

Lynne was waiting on the shoulder of the dirt road holding a thermos and a paper bag that he suspected contained some of Violet's famous cookies. "Is that coffee and cookies?" he asked.

"You bet. When would my mother ever *not* send us off with food?" Lynne chuckled, and poured them each a coffee and rolled down the edges of the bag placing it between the car seats.

"Have you heard from them over the last week?" Lynne asked.

"Just a text message with flight numbers and arrival times," he told her.

"I didn't expect them to go off separately like that."

"I didn't either," Jim admitted.

He had wondered what, exactly, had been going on the last three months when Miranda had announced that she was going to New York and Andrew had told him that he was backpacking Europe. He hadn't been surprised that they had gone travelling, having finally finished university and—although they hadn't announced anything and Jim was basing this on the new ring Miranda had been wearing—apparently gotten engaged, just that they'd gone separately. And the lines of communication hadn't been down per se, there had been many a hairless cat text from Miranda, and several travelogue type emails from Andrew, actual telling communication had been sparse. Jim didn't know what it meant, but in arrivals as Andrew and Miranda came to stand next to him and Lynne it was immediately clear, because Andrew was hovering.

Jim had long known that Andrew was a worrier. As a child he was always the one who asked, "What if"? What if the car goes off the road? What if the plane crashes? What if the house burns down? Had it been any worse Jim and Cheryl might have considered taking Andrew to a psychologist, but he could easily be talked down and it became apparent that it was his nature as versus a disorder. And Andrew had always hovered, just a little, around Miranda. Jim couldn't blame him though, because Miranda got into scrapes, but this was epic expectant father level hovering. Jim hadn't been prepared for that.

They got past the, "How was your flight, you must be jet lagged, how was the trip," part of picking up family at the airport, and they watched as Andrew loaded his own and then Miranda's luggage onto a cart, making sure she didn't do any lifting.

Lynne, like Jim, had been uncharacteristically quiet.

Andrew finally looked at them and said, "What's up with you two? You're looking at us like we're martians or something."

Lynne and Jim started talking at the same time and it was a jumble of exclamations about wedding rings, and expecting, and when were you going to tell us, and why didn't we get a heads up, and when are you due. Then, hearing the other Lynne and Jim turned to each other and more exclamations came out of their mouths, "You think she's pregnant?! What do you mean married?! Didn't you notice the wedding ring?! Didn't you notice the hovering and the bump!?"

"We can't understand you when you talk at the same time," Miranda told them, very serious.

"Where's the car parked? Do you mind if I drive?" Andrew asked and then headed for the exit before they could say anything.

* * *

"Does Olivia know?" Jim asked from the back seat of his own car.

"Know what?" Andrew asked being intentionally obtuse.

"Miranda, I still can't believe you didn't tell me!" Lynne exploded next to him, *again*.

"There's nothing to worry about. I'm taking good care of myself," Miranda responded calmly.

"When did you decide to do it?" Jim asked.

"Dad, 'It' is a pretty vague descriptor. You'll have to be more specific," Andrew replied.

* * *

At dinner that night it became apparent that Olivia *did* know. She had gotten up and started cooking at dawn that day and when Jim had asked her what was up, as he was heading out to the airport, she had told him, "Not much. I'm just getting a welcome home dinner together and I wanted to get a head start on it before I go out to milk the goats."

When they got back from the airport Violet was at his house and she and Olivia were cooking up a storm. The table was set, with with Jim's good wedding china and crystal. Andrew and Miranda had gone to the Hopkins house for a nap, and Janet had shown up an hour later and joined in the cooking frenzy. Lynne had gone off to vent to Sebastian and not long after Daniel and Jeremy had shown up on his doorstep, Daniel bringing beer.

"William tells me you you might need a beer," his neighbour passed him a can and they sat down on the porch.

Daniel Araya was a calm individual who, like Jim, had never banked on life being quite as interesting as it had turned out to be.

"Do you know what's going on?" Jeremy asked, accepting one himself.

"Only the vaguest notion," Jim told Miranda's father. "Just prepare yourself."

"William has been singing all week, and he only does that when he's too happy to feel self conscious. It's exceedingly unpleasant, so I know something's up," Daniel commented.

Jim had asked Violet and Janet what was happening and they told him essentially the same, that they had been enlisted to help, but they didn't know what, specifically, with, other than a welcome home dinner.

Jennifer and Misty pulled up an hour before dinner, having driven from Vancouver. Jim hadn't realized they'd be coming in from the city and they came and drank beer on the porch with Daniel, Jeremy, and himself. Jennifer had grown tall, although not as tall as Olivia, and Misty was one of those tiny people who seemed eternally childlike. She moved quite naturally on the prosthetic leg, "How's the Franken-arm?" Jim asked, as Misty had always been comfortable with Jim's medical curiosity and had always been forthright about her arm, "With chunks of leg in it," as she liked to put it.

"It's good. It's been *really* good lately. The last nerve graft took and I've almost been able to forget about it. I got a really awesome new leg too," she gestured to the shiny, turquoise sneaker clad, prosthetic.

"Come sit up," Olivia called out the door and they went in to the dinner table. Andrew and Miranda had obviously snuck in the back door and were already at the table. Lynne arrived by the skin of her teeth dragging her other lover behind her and scurrying to the stereo to plug in her phone for some relaxed dinner music. Soon they were all at the table and Willy stood up, and looked around, "So before we eat . . . the six of us have some announcements to make and I have been given the dubious honour of making said announcements, because apparently those four are too shy to make announcements," he gave his sister in particular, a look.

Willy continued, "Welcome back Miranda and Andrew, and welcome back Jenny and Misty. Jenny and Misty have finished their bachelor's degrees and gotten jobs here in St Fina. Misty will be starting her job at Family Services in two weeks and Jen has gotten a grant to develop a summer arts program for disadvantaged youth working in conjunction with Mr McGinty at his artist retreat."

Jim raised his glass of sparkling fruit juice and most of the table cheered and toasted the two young women. Miranda just held her hands together under her chin and smiled.

William cleared his throat and waited until the table was quiet again, "Andrew and Miranda would like me to tell you that they have recently tied the knot, are expecting, and due in December . . ." William paused and waited for the hubbub to die down. Jim watched Andrew turn red and Miranda bury her face in her hands until the noise died down. Then William continued with his announcements, "And last but certainly not least, Olivia and I have gotten engaged and are hoping, if the date works for all you folks, to get hitched on the first of October."

Jim wasn't sure he could handle all the surprises. And yet, he wasn't really surprised. He'd known that Andrew and Miranda would never follow a conventional path. A wedding of their own was probably a terrifying prospect. And Olivia, well, Olivia would have a wedding big enough for all five of them.

Later that night when everyone was starting to think about going home, Jim was back on the front porch, holding the letters Cheryl had written as she lay in the hospice knowing that she wouldn't be around for the nights like this one. Andrew looked out the door, "Hey Dad," he came out and sat in the rocking chair next to the porch swing.

Jim looked at Andrew and for a moment he looked like a kid again, then it passed. "Ironically, Olivia spaces life out. I give these to her one at a time, every two years or so, but with you I give them in handfuls," he passed Andrew four letters. The first handful had been around

Andrew's high school graduation, and the next handful six months after that, when he'd gone to university with Miranda. There had been a long stretch with no letters.

Andrew took the letters and looked down at them, holding them in his hands like he was touching more than just paper, "I'll read them tonight." He was silent for a moment and then told Jim, "Thank you for bringing me here. To this weird town, to Miranda. I don't think I'd have made it if we'd stayed in Toronto. I don't think I'd have made it without Miranda."

Jim nodded and took it in for a moment. He knew his kids wouldn't stop needing him and he didn't want them to, at least not until he started to need them, but it was something real to know he'd gotten them this far and brought them to a place where they had everything and everyone they needed to keep moving forward.

"Your mother would be very happy tonight. She would have wanted this for you. She'd have applauded you for going your own way and eloping, and she would have loved Miranda."

Jim didn't only mean that Cheryl would have loved Miranda, but that she would have loved Andrew more, for loving Miranda. That she would have been proud that Andrew was loyal, and brave enough to love out of bounds, to love where some others might have been blinded by a label. But even though Cheryl had been gone now, for over ten years, Jim couldn't always say all he wished he could on her behalf, and Jim wished Cheryl could know, that after all that had passed in the years immediately following her death, that after everything, Andrew had met someone who could look past what had happened to him in the throes of an addiction, to see through to the person he really was. Miranda would always mean the world to Jim, for loving his precious boy.

Andrew was quiet again for a long while and then he wiped his eyes and drew in a breath, "I'm going to move some more of my things over to the Hopkins house. It would be harder on Miranda to move here, and their house has more bedrooms. Violet and Lynne are alright with me moving in. I was hoping I could keep my room here as an office though. I'd be over every day, we can have coffee in the morning before work. I have a contract that I'm starting work on next week, and since my drafting table is set up here, things actually wouldn't change that much."

Miranda came out onto the porch at that moment, "I think I need to sleep?" she made the statement into a question.

Andrew laughed, "I think I need to sleep too."

"You should go get some rest," Jim told them. "And your room is yours until Olivia needs it as a nursery . . ." Jim shook his head. He had to watch what he said, "which, touch wood, I'm hoping is a ways off yet."

Andrew laughed, "I'll see you in the morning."

And Jim watched him walk away, to the house across the field, hand in hand with Miranda.

Sweet Forgiveness

Misty walked slowly along the waterfront, looking out to sea, in the hot summer sun. She'd been back in St Fina for two months now and she was finally getting over the surreal feeling that she had walked into an alternate reality, that somehow this was a different St Fina from the one she'd left. She supposed it actually was in a sense, and Misty recognized that she was the one who had checked out of reality. She'd done it to protect herself and coming back had been hard, oh so hard, but worth it in the end. Jenny had always intended on moving back home, and eventually Misty had let herself be convinced that it really was the right thing for her too.

She walked along the high street that Sebastian McGinty had rehabilitated and looked in the shop windows smiling at passers-by as she went. There was a deli with a line out the door, a busy tea room, a specialty soap shop that had a hopping internet trade as well as being a local favourite for gift shopping, and Miranda's art gallery. Misty watched through the gallery window as

Miranda dusted a piece of pottery and then adjusted the magnificent quilt that was hanging against one wall, delicately pinching an invisible piece of lint off of it. A tourist couple was standing and admiring it. The quilt was one of Jenny and Olivia's creations. Together they were *Island Girl Quilts*. It was their side gig and Miranda nearly always had one in her gallery. They usually sold in under a week. The dazzling blue quilt that they had made for Misty after her attempted suicide was one of the things that had gotten her through her recovery, all those hours of lying there, too weak and in too much pain to do anything at all, but gaze at that quilt. Misty scanned the window display for new and beautiful objects as a tourist joined her and then decided the window display was enough to entice them into the gallery. Years ago, when Miranda had first come to St Fina, the town had thought her "touched," or "simple." Misty remembered the things people had said about the strange girl and the inappropriate relationship with the doctor's son, but it was like the people of St Fina had gone back and edited their collective memories, and today they were all so proud to have something as culturally relevant as an art gallery, that it was like they'd never thought those things of Miranda.

Miranda greeted the visitors and then walked around to the other wall and straightened the paintings from the artists at the retreat that hung there, and then took a cloth and wiped the nonexistent dust off of one of Janet Araya's carvings and off the glass cases filled with antique treasures. She noticed Misty at that moment and waved. Three years ago Misty had finally gotten over her hatred of the other woman, and she waved back and smiled. That had been a hard thing to do, not hating Miranda, but it had been such a weight off, to let it go. One of the hardest things was that Miranda had been so understanding, and accepting, of Misty's enmity towards her. Misty had even hated Miranda for being able to carry that. Jennifer had been heartbroken, trying at first to make Misty be kind to her dearest friend, that week years ago, when Misty had finally been released from the hospital.

"What possible reason could you have to hate her. She never hurt *you*?" Jennifer had asked, in utter confusion.

"I don't know? Why don't you ask her why I hate her?" had been Misty's venomous retort.

And Miranda had actually replied. "Perhaps it's easier to have something to hate? Perhaps it's easier to lay all the pain at *my* feet? Perhaps you *want* to direct what you feel somewhere else, but that would be too much to carry?" Miranda had looked into Misty's eyes, making way too much eye contact, the way she did, and then she'd said, "It's okay, I can carry it." And she'd walked away and given Misty space, for three years.

Misty thought back to that day by the portables. She'd hated Miranda then for being so clean and glowing and pure. She'd hated her innocence. Misty still remembered the feeling of pushing Miranda down into the gravel and remembered taking her bag. She'd hated

Miranda for having what had been taken from her. And then one summer Misty had looked at Miranda, wandering outside like she did, being at one with the universe, and Misty couldn't do it anymore. Miranda was disabled like she was. Miranda had known cruelty like she had. Who was she to hate her, and in that uncanny way she had, Miranda had walked across the field to her, and asked, "It's lighter now, isn't it?"

"I'm sorry I hurt you," Misty told her.

"I know," Miranda told her, and then, "I'm sorry if I did the wrong thing the day you jumped."

"You don't remember do you?" Misty had asked.

"I remember you jumping, and then calling the emergency services. That's all."

"You risked your own safety climbing down to me."

"I don't remember," Miranda whispered.

"Thank you . . . for saving me," Misty had told Miranda, a whole three years after the fact.

Miranda had nodded, saying nothing, tears streaming down her face, and then walked away. Misty had found out through Jennifer, who had been told by Andrew, that Miranda had gone home and had a massive meltdown. Misty didn't realize for a couple more years how much the other girl had carried for her.

She wandered on, in the glorious sunshine, past the gallery to the cafe, to meet her brother for lunch.

The Walk Across
the Field

Olivia woke that morning at the Hopkins house, lying in what Miranda called her 'Nest'. Most people would call it a nursery, but Miranda wasn't most people. It was all done up in the softest possible greens and ivories with old pine furniture and Golden Age of Illustration art prints. A crib and change table, antique dresser, and rocking chair kept the big comfortable bed company. It had been the spare room, that Olivia had slept in so many times over the years, but it wouldn't be spare much longer which really made the imminent changes afoot feel so much more immediate. Olivia listened to the noises of the house waking up and tried to repress the urge to run to the barn and milk the goats. Ryan McGinty and Geoff Henry, her part time help, would be doing that right now. She didn't have to go running. She had other things to think about. She could hear Andrew through the door, which was funny because it made her feel like she was at home, except that she didn't hear Andrew through her bedroom door like this any-more. Olivia smiled and enjoyed the moment. There was a knock at the door, "Come in?" she said, sitting up, and the door swung open and Andrew came in wearing a new suit and carrying a tray.

"Hey! It's today already!" he smiled and put the tray down on the bed.

An egg fried over easy, ham, orange juice, toast made from homemade bread, and Violet's blackberry jam.

Olivia and William had picked the berries that August, rambling over the hills and through the woods together, knowing all the best berry patches, knowing the land where they lived as well as they knew each other. And then she and Violet had made jams and jellies, syrups and cordials. William had been game to try everything they'd made. Olivia remembered the day when she was fourteen and she'd noticed that William was the most like her, of anyone she'd met. He liked hard work and always saw the glass half full, always saw the best in people and things. He was always game for company, and his company was so easy. She was fifteen when she noticed that he had taken over Andrew's old position as the hottest guy at school. Unlike Andrew, who had been totally oblivious, William actually noticed and found it embarrassing. Olivia hadn't known what to do at that point, so she just acted like she couldn't tell what he looked like and got really into video games, and then she slowly realized that she was waiting for him to see her. To notice *her*. Notice her and do what? She hadn't been quite sure until that day in September, and then Boom. There was no explaining what had happened next. A chemical reaction she guessed. Andrew and Miranda had come home for the weekend the next Friday night and even though Olivia and William had tried to hide what had happened they'd been immediately sussed out.

Miranda had taken one look at them and then whispered in Andrew's ear. That was typical, Olivia thought, Miranda figured things out and then didn't know what to do about them.

Andrew had looked back at Miranda and gone, "Really?" And then looked more closely at Olivia, and then at Willy. "Oh. Oh! I see it now. Good for you guys."

Disconcerting was the word Olivia would have used if she hadn't been speechless, and she wasn't sure why she had thought she could hide from her brother. He'd never been able to hide things from her. And why should she hide the fact that she was madly in love with her best friend?

"Eat up! Quick! Dad's getting dressed. He'll be here in two hours to walk you to the garden." Andrew's voice cut through her reverie.

Olivia gulped. It *was* today.

"I'm heading over there now to help Jenny. I'll see you . . . when you arrive I guess." He smiled.

Olivia looked at Andrew and tried to see the nine year old boy who had held her world together when she was little, the person who had made the thing that should have been a huge trauma into a not such a huge a trauma, and maybe even an adventure. He was still there. Hell, he was bringing her breakfast in bed on her wedding day. And even though they were grown now, they lived next door to each other. Olivia almost started to blubber and she hugged Andrew, "Thank you for being my brother."

"Anytime," he hugged her back. "Thank you for being my sister."

She launched into her breakfast and was coming out of the bathroom as Lynne and Violet appeared with the dress and the tackle box.

Olivia mostly co-operated, fidgeting a bit and wondering why. She hadn't fidgeted in a long time.

"You're as bad as Miranda," Lynne muttered brandishing the mascara wand.

An hour later, all made up, feeling strange sitting there in her wedding dress, feeling much younger than twenty-one for some unfathomable reason, sitting on the edge of the bed waiting, Olivia sat looking at herself in the dresser mirror. Violet came in and sat next to her and took her hand, "Since you are an honorary Hopkins woman, and one of the dearest people in the world to me, I'd like you to have this." She placed an old leather jewellery case in Olivia's hand.

At that moment New Order's *Temptation* blasted out of Miranda's and, Olivia supposed, Andrew's bedroom. Violet tried to keep a straight face and turned to call out to Miranda to turn it down but Olivia stopped her, "It's okay. It's William's favourite song too. Let her play it loud. She's probably just stressed out."

Violet smiled, "Alright, but go on and open the box."

Olivia opened the latch and pulled the lid up to find a little flower pendant made from stones of different colours. It was delicate, sweet and beautiful, without being ostentatious or affected. It was the kind of piece Olivia would actually wear.

"Miranda told me that the stones spell out the word 'Regard' and that the pansy shaped flower means, 'Thinking of you'. Something to do with the French word for 'thought'. All the times I saw my grandmother wear this and I never knew that," Violet told Olivia.

Olivia's own family hadn't provided any cherished heirlooms for a moment like this. Neither her biological or adoptive mothers had anything of that kind. She turned and hugged Violet. "Would you do up the clasp?" Olivia lifted the chain and held the ends over her shoulders so that Violet could clasp it for her and looked back into the mirror. She'd put on the Tahitian pearls from her thirteenth birthday, and the engraved ruby Haida engagement ring—which William had given her in Iceland when he'd proposed—was on her hand. The tiny precious things that marked the significant moments in her life. She knew her father would give her a letter from her mother in just a short while which reminded her, "Hey Miranda!" Olivia yelled over the music.

The volume came down and Miranda walked in wearing a lacy green and pink vintage dress with an empire waist, "Do you need something?" she asked.

"Here, take a picture please?" Olivia passed Miranda her phone and Miranda took a picture of Olivia and Violet sitting together. Olivia typed the words,

_Me with my Fairy Godmother.

And then sent the picture to Isabella.

Olivia had hoped her birth mother would make it but she was in the middle of a rough patch. At least Olivia could give her a sneak peak of the dress. She had asked one day, sitting with Miranda and Jenny, "What did they call those old fashioned ladies with the big hair and frilly dresses?"

And Miranda had answered, "A Gibson Girl."

"That's what I want," Olivia declared. "Big hair and a romantic old fashioned dress to go with our romantic old fashioned house."

"It's almost the right era for your house," Miranda had told her, and then started searching the internet and emailing Museum contacts for old dress patterns and antique lace and buttons.

Jennifer embroidered the silk, ivory on ivory, with dragons and ravens and bears and violets, and Olivia and Violet sewed all the pieces together, carefully hand stitching the antique lace onto the silk. Olivia couldn't believe it was her dress. It almost felt magical.

"I'm going over to your house now," Miranda told Olivia. "Is there anything you need before I go?"

"I have no idea. I'm in a state Miranda," Olivia admitted.

Miranda hugged her and said, "A state that can be found on no map. The strange place in-between one thing and the next. You have left, but are not yet arrived. A nascent glimmer. You'll feel better when you see William." And then Miranda turned and left, turning off the music and heading down the stairs.

"We'd better go downstairs now and wait for Jim," Violet sighed.

Violet locked the door and then left Olivia on the front porch and Olivia watched as Violet passed her father on her way across the field and their hands touched as they passed each other in a way that Olivia hadn't noticed before. Jim smiled as he reached the Hopkins house. "You sure look beautiful Pumpkin," he told her.

"Thanks Dad," she smiled, and laughed as Merlin appeared out from behind her father.

"Hope you don't mind a wedding-crasher?" Olivia gave the dog's head a rub. "Come on Merlin, heel."

Merlin fell in beside Olivia and Jim offered his arm and Olivia took it as the three of them started across the field, towards the back garden.

"Hey Dad?"

"Yes Pumpkin?"

"Is this how you thought life would be when you brought us here?" Olivia asked as she strolled through the field in her beautiful dress with her dog and her dad.

Jim laughed, "I don't know what I expected. I wasn't expecting miracles, but I feel like we got them."

"I know what you mean," Olivia agreed, and then they rounded the corner of the house and all the people she knew were there and her sweet William was standing there waiting for her and she had a feeling that *life* was just waiting for her.

The Mythology of Childhood

Andrew stood with Miranda, under the oak tree, in the golden field, under the harvest moon, looking out on the ocean. They leaned against the thick trunk, keeping warm in each other's embrace. He still had the image of his little sister—little being a misnomer at this juncture in life, as Olivia was as tall as he was and larger than life in character—in the dress that had taken six months and the combined effort of four women to make, clear in his mind.

Andrew and William built a pergola at the back of the Warren house, going off a set of Edwardian landscape plans, and Olivia planted late blooming plants all around it and grew climbing nasturtiums all over it, as if she were certain they would have an Indian summer, which they did. When the day came it was almost as warm as July, and the sky was blue, but the autumn leaves were all around them. Andrew would never forget standing next to Willy holding the wedding rings in his sweaty hand, not sure how it was that Olivia wasn't little and loud anymore, but regal, and confident, like a queen. Willy whispered, "Andrew, I think I might faint," as they stood waiting for Olivia who was walking down the garden path on Jim's arm with what felt like half the town looking on.

"No man, trust me you've got this. I don't know anyone else who's got what it takes to marry Olivia," Andrew whispered.

And William had nodded, straightened, and watched as Olivia made her way to him. He'd always known he'd meet his Beverly. Always known he'd have his people, and Olivia was beside him now.

Miranda leaned deeper into Andrew and looked over to the Warren house, to where she could see the glow of the wedding reception still in progress through the window. It was worth all the flower arranging and cooking and all the cleaning and hauling all her Nanna's Limoges across the field. It was a beautiful day full of more beauty than one day should have been able to contain. She understood now why people cried at weddings. But Miranda was tired, and needed some quiet, and to be away from all the people, so she had taken Andrew's hand and pulled him outside with her, to the oak tree.

"Do you remember how we used to say goodnight here?" he murmured.

"I do. I always felt like a princess running out into the night, to some magical world."

"I used to feel like we lived on the borders of a magical world, but I'm not sure which side of the border we live on anymore. Sometimes I feel like *this* might be the magical world. I used to think that when we grew up the magic would die," Andrew mused.

"I think that's the mythology of childhood," Miranda replied. "That somehow all this, the things that make us feel wonder and gladness and magic, are going to disappear when we grow up, but they don't. Not unless we let them."

They were quiet for a space, and then Jenny came out onto the porch and yelled, "Are you guys ready?"

"We'll meet you on the path," Andrew called, watching as wedding guests began to wander to their cars, or to either the Hopkins house or the Araya house, to the spare beds waiting for them.

But Andrew and Miranda walked to the head of the beach path and waited there until they saw William and Olivia, in jeans now, and then Jennifer, who came carrying a lawn chair and a blanket, and then the five of them made their way down to the water in the moonlight.

William had built a wood pile the day before and he went about lighting it as Jenny set up the lawn chair, "You're feet must be killing you Miranda. For my sake, please sit."

Miranda hugged Jenny then lowered herself into the lawn chair with a sigh as Jenny put the blanket around her shoulders.

"No Misty?" Andrew asked.

"Robin is leaving for Montreal in the morning and she wants the extra time with him," Jenny explained. "Besides, this is our thing."

They made a circle and waited as the fire got bright.

Jenny stood holding a sheaf of papers and once the fire was warm she spoke, "I wrote a book. A book for us. I'll give you each a copy to read tomorrow. It's a fantasy for kids, but it's also *our* story. I want to publish it but I want to send it out on the wind too. I want it to fly up into the sky so that the ravens can hear it and tell it to the Bear King on his island. I want it to be in the world. I want to offer it up with you guys. Can I read you the first page?"

"Yes, read it to us!" Olivia piped up.

"Of course, we want to hear it," William told his sister.

"Go for it," Andrew encouraged.

"I love stories," Miranda sighed.

And Jenny began to read, "I'm going to tell you a story, and the story is true and everything that happens tonight will be a part of that story, so it will be true. Once there were two children from both sides of the sea. Twins. A boy who had the power to bind people together, and a girl who saw stories. Once there was a mermaid who had lost her voice, but she didn't give it up, it was stolen, and once there was a 'lost boy' who was really a sleeping prince. He never dreamed but walked around all day like he was awake, and one day the speechless mermaid woke the sleeping prince. Once there was a girl who was from an island in the north, and an island in the south, and she had the power to turn the world around her from black and white, into a place filled with beautiful colours . . .

When Jenny finished reading she divvied the manuscript into five and they fed their story to the flames and when it had burned away they heard wings above them.

"We're all family now, you know," Willy told them. "As of today, when I married Olivia it became official."

"There's something about that that's pretty profound, really," Andrew admitted.

"We were meant to be," Jenny said. "You guys will love the end of my book."

"Is it happy?" Olivia asked, taking William's hand and resting her head on his shoulder.

"Is it real?" Miranda asked, rubbing her belly.

"I'm not telling," Jenny laughed. "You have to read it for yourselves."

And they waited for the fire to die down and then made their way up the hill to their own beds and when they slept, Miranda dreamt of a golden child and Andrew did too, and Olivia dreamt of two. Willy also dreamt of twins, and of all the things that he would build for them, and Jenny dreamt it all, and then wrote it all down.

Epilogue

Under the Oak Tree

Miranda set aside her knitting. There had been something about being pregnant that had finally made her want to learn. Perhaps the fact that her Nanna was starting to look old had something to do with it too. That, and the passage of time having become so much more pronounced in those months leading up to Emmeline's arrival. Miranda hadn't wanted to wait until it was too late. And it turned out she liked knitting. It was a socially sanctioned repetitive behaviour which, unlike rocking, didn't get any strange looks.

She still tended to hold her sweet Emmeline in her arms for her afternoon nap, sitting in the rocking chair in the parlour, looking out the window. Miranda would settle the baby into the nursing cushion in her lap and eventually pick up her knitting. She didn't knit fast. At this rate the toque she was knitting for Andrew would take months, but that was alright. It was spring and he wouldn't need it till November. Miranda looked out the window, at the blossoming trees and the daffodils, at the wildflowers and sheep in the field across the street where she could just see the sweet little house that stood there now. Andrew and Willy were restoring a small storybook bungalow, moved from the other side of town onto a foundation in their field, that her mother was going to move into. Andrew had been busy doing full historical restorations on several buildings in St Fina including the town hall. He usually worked in conjunction with Daniel and William. He would be home from work in another hour.

She watched the sleepy baby in her lap start to squirm and slowly wake. "Hello my darling," she whispered, and then gathered Emmeline into her arms and breathed in the sweet baby smell and kissed the velvety head, still only half able to process the fact that this little miracle was hers without losing her voice. Miranda fed Emmeline and then took her upstairs for a fresh diaper. There was a bag of sleepers that Emmeline had outgrown sitting in the corner and Miranda had been trying to remember to take them down to the kitchen. She mentally patted herself on the back when she grabbed them and headed downstairs with a now bright, happy, and alert baby on her hip. Emmeline wasn't always happy, but Miranda wasn't usually phased by the crying baby moments. Not like the moms she had encountered at the Mother and Baby drop in. If Emmeline cried Miranda went through her checklist of reasons why, maybe, baby could be unhappy, and once she'd checked them all off, if Emmeline was still crying, Miranda took her to the parlour and put some music on. Emmeline preferred the Cowboy Junkies, which Miranda had decided she wasn't going to try to understand, but a half an hour of swaying to the music was usually enough to set them both to rights. Even though Miranda knew that she had, perhaps, a stronger support network than some, it was hard for her to see the perspectives of those other mothers. She had disliked being pregnant, feeling anxious and incredibly vulnerable especially after she started to show, and instead of getting better the nausea had gotten progressively worse. Socially speaking, pregnancy had been difficult to deal with, as she never knew what the correct answers were when people asked her about it. Towards the end Andrew and Jenny were the only people she could tolerate touching her, but labour had been a snap, and after Emmeline arrived it had been so natural. Miranda took it in stride and nothing about taking care of her baby felt like work. Her Nanna told her she was like a mamma cat. She didn't feel that getting her child through the day was anything to be complained about. Miranda hadn't gone back to the Mother and Baby drop in, but she'd felt like that was a failure of sorts, that it was a normal thing that she should be doing, even though she'd felt alienated.

She'd told Andrew how she felt and he'd said to her, "Miranda, Emmeline is four months old. She's not missing out on anything, and she gets plenty of socialization from family. If going to those things makes you unhappy don't go. You being happy is far more important. When Emmeline is old enough to want to play with other kids I'll take her out. With any luck she'll have cousins soon and then she'll have built in playmates. You don't have to go to those things. They don't matter. You have a right to be an introvert. You're a good mother as you are."

So Miranda enjoyed her time at home since Ethan had come to St Fina to run her gallery, which was paying for itself and providing Ethan a paycheck. She looked at the clock again. She took the chopped veggies and the casserole ingredients out of the fridge so all Andrew had to do was saute the onions, throw everything together, and put it in the oven. They had gone back to their old arrangement from university, where if Miranda decided what was for dinner and did the prep, Andrew would cook it, indecisiveness being his problem, and attention span for things she wasn't interested in being hers. Miranda was good at sandwiches, and could manage deserts if she wasn't too preoccupied, but tended to burn dinner. Emmeline held her attention all day though.

Lynne had gone on a sabbatical to the Maldives. "Just because I'm happy to be a grandmother doesn't mean I want to live in a house with an infant," she'd told them, and then flown off to have an adventure while her house was being finished, and Miranda's Nanna had had her left knee replacement done two weeks ago and was still pretty much bedridden. Miranda was enjoying the quiet. Jenny came every morning and made tea and cuddled Emmeline while Miranda had a quick bath, and then they had a half-hour to visit. Just that morning Jenny had come running in with news of a publication deal for her book and they'd celebrated over tea in Violet's bedroom. Olivia was usually there by lunch to help Violet for an hour. Miranda had been trying to remember to give the bag of sleepers to Olivia for over a week. Understanding how hard the pregnancy had been on Miranda, Andrew had asked her if she though she could tolerate another, and she'd said no. He didn't want to take risks so without hesitation he had booked an appointment for himself with the specialist in Victoria. Emmeline would be their one and only, so Miranda had been giving all the baby things she outgrew to Olivia.

Miranda wandered back to the parlour, "What do you think, hmm? Will your dad be home soon? Shall we watch the road?" She sat in the window seat and settled Emmeline in her lap. The little birds, chickadees and juncos, outside the window caught the baby's attention and Miranda watched Emmeline watch the birds, glancing up periodically to see if Andrew was on his way home. Soon she could see him walking along the dirt road with Willy. ."There he is! Let's go wait on the driveway," Miranda got up and slipped on some shoes and, realizing she could give the bag of sleepers to Willy, she grabbed the sleepers and headed out the door and down the driveway in the springtime sunshine and waited under the cherry blossoms at the end of the driveway, relishing the feel of plump warm baby in her arms and knowing that, in a moment, she'd be expected to share. She kissed Emmeline's cheek and murmured nonsense to the baby for a moment and then Willy broke into a run and Emmeline wiggled and squealed in excitement.

"Quick, quick, let me have a baby hug," Willy begged when he got there. Miranda passed the baby over and

Willy held her for a moment and, mostly just to himself, sighed, "Oh dear, I need one of these." And then he passed Emmeline to Andrew who was just catching up, grinning.

"Here, we're done with these," Miranda gave the bag of sleepers to Willy.

"Oh man, more baby clothes. Hopefully soon . . . I didn't know dudes got broody like this. See you guys tomorrow," Willy said and then strode away to the yellow house down the road.

Miranda looked at Andrew and smiled.

Andrew smiled back, and looked into her eyes and they stood there like that for a long moment. It had almost become a tradition, standing on the driveway like that looking into each other's eyes, anytime the weather was good, anytime Andrew hadn't driven to work. He knew she couldn't process anything much in those moments. He'd asked her when they were younger, sitting under the oak tree one afternoon that August, long ago, what it felt like for her when their eyes met, and she'd told him, "It's like falling, and like we're occupying the same space, and like time stops. It's like . . . It's like it's the only thing in the world. Like everything else stops existing."

"Should I . . . stop looking at your eyes? Is it wrong of me to do that to you?" he'd asked, considerate of her differences in a way that didn't occur to most people.

Miranda remembered the moment like it was yesterday. She'd always been surprised by Andrew. She hadn't expected the question. He related to her differently from other people. He didn't take things for granted. "It's not wrong when *you* do it," she had told him softly. "It never has been. I look at your eyes and I know it's going to be weird, but you've never minded. Somebody hit me once when I looked too long. I don't mean to do it. But with you it's always been, well . . . what is it like for you?" She'd looked at him, up at his eyes and then down again so she would be able to hear what he said.

"It's almost the same for me, but it only happens with you. It's only like that with you," he told her.

Miranda nodded and moved closer to him and rested her head on his shoulder. "I could stay here forever with you. Just sit here under the tree and sink into the earth next to you," she sighed.

"When we're old we should tell our kids that we want to be buried here next to each other."

"Our kids . . .?" Miranda questioned, bemused.

"Yeah, I mean . . . I guess. Do you want kids someday?"

"I never really . . . I never let myself consider it. People make me feel like I shouldn't."

"I think you'd be a good mom. There's things about you that would make you good at being a mother."

Miranda had never truly considered it up till that moment, but when she tried to imagine herself holding a baby in her arms that was hers, she felt good inside. "I'm used to people focusing on what I can't do, or what I'll have trouble with. Either that or the things I'm so good at that it's weird. You don't focus on that stuff as much. You ask me about normal things."

Andrew laughed, "I don't know if asking my teen-aged sweetheart if she wants kids so that we can plan our burial is normal but, what do you say?"

Miranda laughed, "If we have kids I totally want to be buried in the field with you."

"For sure?" Andrew asked her, smiling.

"For sure," she responded.

Miranda couldn't help smiling at the beautiful absurdity of the memory, but two weeks after Emmeline was born they'd done their wills together and stipulated that their ashes be spread under the oak tree, having decided burial was a bit over the top, but still.

Andrew smiled back at her and then turned to Emmeline, "So, how are my smart, interesting girls? Hmm? Did you do anything exciting today?" Emmeline patted his forehead then tried to pull the buttons off his shirt in response, and the three of them went in for dinner.